IN THE SHADOW OF THE DRAGON'S SPINE

Marvin D Bare

ISBN-13:9798569809080

Cover design by: Hailey Foster
Library of Congress Control Number: 2018675309
Printed in the United States of America

CONTENTS

CHAPTER 1

From Ingrid Eplidot's "Stories of Creation"

Long ago the gods played on Ymir. They hunted, battled. It was a golden age, an age of legends. They built Bifrost. Their bridge to the stars. They created the folk, the yetann, the etunazi, and the pyris. Midgard was their canvas. Then the great tree, Yggdrasil in his vanity challenged the gods. He woke the lorki, something the gods feared. The gods commanded that Bifrost be destroyed. So, Thor's hammer, Mjolnir fell on Bifrost. Midgard was abandoned by the gods and the folk left to suffer.

The nineteenth day of Einmanudur. The twentieth year of King Awrick of Alfheim.

*

Slowly he awoke, the warmth and energy from the sun brought an end to his slumber. He began to withdraw from the earth, exploring his body, sensing growth and strength. Not all his time this past winter was spent in darkness. And now it was spring. To his north was the highest pass over the dragon's spine to Niflheim, the plains of ice, hymriursar (the frost giants), great white bears, and death. Where he had been.

Opening his eyes, he gazed up at the great blue expanse. He had someplace to go. Where or to what he was headed he did not remember. When he awoke in the far north, south, just south was the demand. Now he needed to journey farther. He had no idea how far. He spotted Asgard fading in the morning light. Fair Asgard had been his guide when it was visible in the sky.

Sitting up he looked out and down. Below he saw a wide mountain valley with a small stream passing through the dryad. The dryad? Definitely, a dryad no mistaking the shimmer of the leaves. Her grove filled the valley. She was heart-shaped with (from his perspective) a scar in her right lobe. What a lovely sight. Downhill and to the left was a camp, with smoke ascending from several fires. Uphill on the right was a smaller cold camp. An eagle flew over the valley hunting his breakfast.

Closing his eyes, he reached out. Ah, contact. And a request, "May I share your sight?"

Below opened the wide expanse of the valley. Near the center of the larger camp were a wizen old man and a girl. She was a captive, tied with her arms behind her. The old man appeared to be feeding her. Three large warriors, almost feline in appearance, were armor-clad. Each carried several blades. They looked like professional warriors and stood around the old man. There was also a group of eight or so ugly warriors, almost bear-like in appearance. They had a patchwork of armor, some on and much of it scattered about them. They sat around one of the other fires watching the larger warriors. Some were casting furtive glances at the girl. A third group was scattered about several small fires looked fearful. Their prominent tusks and dark mahogany skin marked them as pyris. Poorly dressed and carrying no weapons, possibly they were porters. They watched the dryad grove and the others of the party as if they didn't know which to fear more.

The girl looked absolutely miserable. The mornings were cold this high on the dragon's spine. Even in mid-summer, this northern reach would be chilly every morning. The girl's skirt was torn and muddy. The blouse was stained with old food. What kind of creature would so mistreat another person? It must have been weeks since she had been allowed to comb her hair. It was so matted and tangled.

The dryad's scar was old. Very old. Mostly healed but still very noticeable. Not much to be learned by looking.

The cold camp was made up of a Vanir, a dzwerc, two daonna.

No match for those guarding the other camp, no wonder a cold camp.

Oh, another vanir just coming out of the dryad grove near a pile of stones. Young, tall, over 6 feet at least. He wore his hair long in a braid down his back. What beard he had was also braided. There was tension in the way he walked, things were not going as planned. He was armed with a bow and a sword. No armor, he was dressed to be quiet and quick.

The dzwerc was short, as was his kind's nature. Rounder than some he remembered. He had a bow and carried a battle ax. The light leather armor he wore had chain mail sewn across the shoulders. He might have trouble if he planned a surprise attack.

The other vanir was about the same age as the first, and similarly clad. The whole group had the look of a scouting party. Maybe even a training party. Only the two daonna looked to be over twenty. The larger one, with short cropped brown hair, that might even have some gray in it, was sewing a patch on a shirt. A pair of walking boots sat beside him. His bare feet were being given an airing out.

The other daonna appeared to be the leader. The young vanir from the grove went straight to him. Explaining something with gestures that got more violent as they continued.

Hmm. Can't leave the child with those beasts much longer. Moving his thoughts to the larger camp. He gave study to the three large warriors who dominated the camp. They stood on two legs and had large feline heads. One opened his mouth in a yawn revealing his fangs and a mouth full of sharp teeth. Their boots were open at the toes, claws extending and contracting as they walked. Large paws instead of hands. How they used the weapons they carried were answered as he watched them pick up food and other objects. They used their claws like fingers extending one, two, or all five depending on their use. The largest towered over everyone else in the camp. He looked perhaps to be 10-foot-tall. His dark gray, almost black pelt might have darker spots. The grey striped one was almost as large. His torn ear and scarred face attested to many battles, but very few if any defeats. The smallest was still huge. He was only a couple of feet shorter than the others. They all appeared to be close to 500 pounds or more. It would take more than strength and luck for him to defeat them by himself. Now, what were they called? What were these creatures? Yetann perhaps? The largest he could remember seeing. Each wore armor. The large one had a fine set. He had the breastplate off, and he looked to be burnishing it. Steam rose from it as he used a wire brush and some liquid to sweep away whatever had obscured the design. The breastplate had an intricate design on it. Curves and swirls surrounding a great cat ripping a tree from the ground. Could that be Fenrir killing the great tree? The other yetann's armor was more concerned with functionality than beauty.

With the few moments he had before the eagle reclaimed control of his sight, he studied the smaller guards. Except for the tusks protruding from their lower jaws, their heads were bear-like. Like the yetann, they walked upright. They had five fingers and wore regular boots. That could only be etunazi. Their armor was a mixture of materials and designs. Nothing special, they appeared to be an inexpensive band of mercenaries. If it were only them, he could kill a couple and the others would run. But, with the yetann present, he would have all of them to battle. Could the other camp be persuaded to be allies in what he had determined to do? A plan wiggled to life in his brain. Perhaps a talk with the dryad would help. It looked to be a long walk, two maybe three days. Best get started.

*

Frustration poured through Jae. He had been sure that this time he would find a trail through the grove. But for the fifth time, he failed. Impossible! He followed the stream this time. He knew that the raiders might be near it on the other side of the grove, but he was getting desperate. He knew the downhill flowing stream would not betray him. And now here he stood on the exact spot he had arrived at the other four tries. The pile of stones he had marked the spot with after the third try, seemed to laugh at his dilemma. Nothing to do now but report back to Crispin, that once more he had failed. Drew would tease mercilessly, years from now that dzwerc would be relentless.

Crispin watched as Jae drew near. He figured this would be the result, something haunted that aspen grove or some other magic was at work. They needed through or around, but the grove stretched across the whole valley. How they had arrived at the wrong side of it while following the raiders was another mystery. Mystery upon mystery, starting with the raid that resulted in only one death and the kidnapping of one young woman. The raiders had no reason to move through so quickly. The village was defenseless, full of food and drink, men to kill and women to rape. But no, the raiders hit fast, grabbed the woman, and killed the unfortunate cattle herder that had picked the wrong time to milk his cows. Why did they want that woman? The sign around the village had indicated that they had watched that village only a short time before the raid. And the band was made up of yetann and etunazi! They never traveled together. How they had made it through so much of the king's lands without attracting attention was incredible. It was only blind luck that Crispin's group of scouts happened that way right after the raid. Maybe the seior (magician) that had been spotted with them had some spell that lessened the tensions between them?

Now the band was stalled. They hadn't moved for days. "Maybe they were having the same trouble we are?" mumbled Crispin as a very unhappy Jae approached.

Drew watched as Jae left the grove at the same spot, he had exited it five times now. He knew that he had one more thing that would turn Jae's ears red. He let a small smile cross his lips. He could wait. Later in the day or even a month from now, just a mention of an aspen grove would bring a bright hue to Jae's ears. Drew wouldn't let Jae know that last evening when he had left the camp that he wasn't scouting the slope to the northeast for a trail around the grove. No, he had tried his hand at getting through it. Only to find himself at the very spot Jae had just exited. Whatever was keeping them from the raiders had a sense of humor.

Drew stood in sharp contrast to his friend. Where Jae was tall, lean, and blond. Drew, well, Drew was short, stout, and dark. Jae's fair skin got golden in the sun and never darkened enough to hide when he was embarrassed. His ears always betrayed him. He stood over six and a half feet tall. An accomplished woodsman he walked through the woods almost silently. His blue eyes could spot a fox hidden in the grass. On the other hand, the sun gave Drew a ruddy complexion as it did almost all dzwerc. Five feet two inches and around two hundred pounds. His brown eyes were better at catching things he could tease his friend about than finding foxes. All muscle, of that Drew, was sure. And he could move. Move faster than most would credit him. He was a woodsman, too. Not as skilled as Jae but still he had the skill.

Drew flexed his shoulders and tried to listen in on Crispin and Jae's conversation. The jingle of the chain mail that covered his shirt reminded him of home. The shirt was a gift from his step-father. Given with pride to a boy he had raised as his own. Drew took comfort in the weight of it. He knew that when it was time to stalk game or an enemy that this gift would be left behind, for more silent garb. But in camp that didn't matter.

*

The Dryad was furious. There he was, looking as handsome as ever. The scar she remembered on his face was gone while her scar remained. She watched him through her thousands of eyes. She strained to hear his voice, but he was silent. How dare he saunter as if he was returning from a morning stroll. In her wounds, she had been abandoned. She had no idea how long. How many years was she lost, before she remembered herself? He had been above her all last summer. She had seen his figure stumble over that accursed pass late the fall before that. She knew that the winter had caught him above the snow line, but still last year had an early spring. She knew when he had moved below the ice and snow and then he stopped and didn't move till now, the end of another year's spring. And it was him. His walk so much him, no one moved as he did. She yearned to be with him, to feel his presence. Even if he had been away more than a thousand summers. At the rate he was walking it would be two or more days before he reached her.

*

"Why, papa, why?" "Oh, my little one this is for the best. You'll learn so much from widow Sturlasda and she needs your help." "But, papa, you need my help. You've told me how much help I am mixing the potions, finding the jars of herbs." Papa looked grim and worry creased his face. "My dear, you will go and learn. Here with me, well, here with me your experience with people will be very limited. No patient here wants a child in the room while being treated. Where you are going the villagers will be so happy to have you around, because of your gift." So late that evening bundled away in the back of a covered cart, without a good-bye, away she went. "I'll stay awake the whole trip" her 8-year-old self, promised. But she was fast asleep hardly out the back gate. Catherine shivered as she woke from the familiar dream.

Miserable, that's how she felt. Horrible, her head and body ached. Her auburn hair once neatly braided down her back was now a tangled matted mess and so dirty it appeared mouse brown. That thought struck her. She was no mouse! Her green eyes flashed at the thought. Here she was laying on the ground with barely a ground cloth and a cover, cold. Her arms, almost numb from being tied behind her. She had spent most of the journey tied like this. An attempt to keep her from casting spells? She didn't need hands to cast her spells if you called what she did spells. But what did she know that would help? Slowly she raised her head. She shook off the light blanket and fought to sit up. The aches and cold were welcome, really. Her mind and body were finally conquering the strange drug the seioknar was using on her. She knew it and now, with the help of her lorki, could change it, break it down to something harmless. Knowing it, she now could think of several medicinal uses for it and its varying components.

What did that stupid seioknar want with her? For weeks now, they had been stumbling about the countryside. The poor fool of a guide lay dead little more than a day's journey down this mountain. Her captors were lost. It appeared they too were captive, but to what she could not say. Four days now they had stayed at this camp. The longest time since her kidnapping.

The yetann were getting restless. "Curse that stream and curse the fresh meat," Prysivolar grumbled under his breath. "Curse that damn guide, to get us lost on this mountain." The Huldra would have his head if he didn't lose it to one of this misbegotten band. The potions to control the various races under his command were very effective if he could get them to take theirs. Losing control over their food and water would cost him.

"Here, girl. Eat." She glared at him and slowly opened her mouth to take a spoonful of stew. He watched her slowly chew the gristle and then swallow. Was she growing more aware? Maybe he should increase her dosage.

*

Singa sat scrubbing at the coating that had been placed over his breastplate to disguise his origins. No one here would recognize the significance of his herald. Things were going horribly wrong. Death had always been the possibility; he knew that when he joined this hunting party. Now he wanted to get a message back to his liege lord. His breastplate might be the only thing left. His head buzzed, and his emotions were barely checked.

An etunz moved up behind the girl grabbing her left breast and licking her cheek. "Let's share her and head home" he growled. Singa slapped the etunz across the camp. He landed in a fire and exited cursing, only slightly burned.

"If we do anything with this ney snack, we'll eat her." Roared the yetann. "and that may not be long from now unless this seer heads us back to the huldra." Lowering his voice to what passed for a whisper for him. "Seioknar Prysivolar, I know you've drugged us. It would not be wise to do that to me again." Baring his teeth, he turned and stalked to the stream looking for game. Which had gone missing for some unknown reason. The raucous band behind him couldn't be why.

*

Cu lain sat under a tree far from the others. He was miserable, cold, and hungry. The grasblett (herbalist) had food true but, his head was much clearer when he ate something else. There had been no chance to hunt further from the camp. Besides the seior's demands, when he had tried to leave the immediate area, the trees had seemed to close off the pathways. He had caught a few rabbits and field rodents were plentiful. Enough to share with the girl anyway. "I would flee the area if I could," he thought.

"Cu lain" He shook his head, now he was hearing things. "Cu lain are you just a cur? Or something better?" The raspy voice sounded like twigs rubbing together. It couldn't be, could it?

"Real or a dream" it came again "you must choose very soon. Will you run, like the pyris? Die with the yetann, or be Cuhulain, the guard dog?" The wind blew, the smell of the maiden drifted to him. "Choose you must. Be hultia (guardian)."

It was a few hours later that the old man ordered him to bring him some freshwater, so here Cu lain stood bucket in hand. He kneeled to fill it with water from the cold mountain stream. He remembered the first time he had been sent to fetch water from this stream. Somehow, he had tripped and fallen in. He could have sworn that he had been pushed but only a few saplings were around. Now knowing there was something magical about, he very well could have been pushed. Pushed or not he was thankful for that dunking. The cold chill of the water had taken his breath away. While trying to regain his footing he swallowed almost a bucket of water. Then when he had finally regained his footing, the water wasn't even knee high. It was then he noticed the watercress. Watercress had been his mother's favorite herb. She cooked with it when she could get hold of it. The market in Tawnia seldom had any, but on one of their walks to gather herbs they stumbled upon a stream full of it. While his father was still with them the family had taken meals at the stream. He remembered the smile on his father's face as he watched his child and wife gather watercress.

"I wonder," He thought. "would the maiden like the peppery herb?" Cu lain reached into the cold water and pulled out two or three large handfuls. He hid some inside his shirt, to save for later. Maybe he would have the opportunity later today to share it with the maiden. The rest of it he would eat on the journey back to his master.

As he stood and picked up the heavy bucket of water. He asked, "Who are you? What are you?"

The babbling stream replied. "I am the dryad. This is my valley and you are one of my champions."

The thought of himself, Cu lain, being a champion brought a brief smile to his lips. Then he started trudging back to his master. How he longed to be free of the old man. He had developed a hunger for freedom. It seemed to him that he had been in a drugged daze for most of his life. Now that he had tasted food without the master's spice, he never wanted to taste that spice again. He cherished his clear thoughts. And he yearned for the chance to experience life without the haze. If he did what the dryad wanted, he could be dead in a short time. Yet maybe death would be more desirable than living in the fog of that hated drug.

CHAPTER 2

From the lecture "Myth and History" by the learned Ljot Jartasen
The oldest myths of Fenrir call him a wolf. Today he is recognized as a great cat. The yetann worship him as Fenrir Cathpalug (clawing cat) destroyer of the great tree Yggdrasil. Thus, freeing them from slavery. In yetann legend, Fenrir brings freedom to all Ymir by slaying Yggdrasil. While in a discussion with Karl Greenman I discovered that he agrees that the death of Yggdrasil freed Ymir from his tyranny, which for most amounted to slavery. He believes that Yggdrasil had become dormant because of the fall of Bifrost. And while he was dormant that the yetann Fenrir burned him to the ground. The death of Yggdrasil marked the beginning of the great migrations and the resulting chaos over two millennia ago.

*

The path down the mountain was difficult. It was mid-morning the third day as he approached the grove. The green man opened his mind, questing out for the spirit that enlivened the aspen.

"Where have you been?" There was no mistaking the iciness of that raspy voice. "I'll take you to task later. There's a maiden in distress, and you're almost too late to help. Those felagi whelps would have been foolish enough to battle the yetann alone if I hadn't stopped them. You've been above me all spring, dawdling and now you finally come down! Did you have a nice nap?"

"Do I know you, dryad?" he asked.

Two stones grated together, "You don't remember me?" "My dreams tell me, that it was almost forever that we've known each other." She replied. "When I awoke. Hmm, when I awoke, you were first in my thoughts. That's been, oh a thousand summers ago. You've been gone over a thousand summers. I had thought you had abandoned me. And now you don't even remember me!"

"A thousand summers?" he responded. "I only remember twenty since I started my journey south across the ice. I had traveled and died; I don't know how long. I remember a body far to the north. I have a charm from it, but I don't remember why I killed him."

"Oh. I believe I am why." She murmured. "It all seems like dreams from before I awoke. Vague visions of dancing with you, before we were what we are now. Nightmares of change and pain. It's very hard to tell truth from those."

"I'm sorry, my lady. But I barely remember stumbling over the pass, before winter struck and I was buried in ice and snow." The green man was confused. She seemed familiar in some way. But how? who?

"It doesn't, matter. The yetann and etunazi are disturbed. I won't be able to hold them much longer." She responded. "If we are to help that young woman, we best come up with a plan. And I do think we should include that felag (fellowship) of scouts in it. They have traveled a long way tracking that wicked band. They deserve to be a part of this."

I'm sorry, but I can barely understand what you just said." He replied

"Doubtlessly that's true." She said. "you've been away a thousand years. The world has changed in that space of time. In the beginning, Ymir had the three tongues, given at the whim of the great tree, Samia Vestan, Norreni, and Cymraeg-Austri. Your Norreni is excellent as I'm sure the others are. But now I am aware of over 100 languages. As we plan, we can concentrate on the languages that the scouts and yetann use. When we meet with each. I'll whisper in your ear to help to translate." As the green man walked through the dryad toward the felag, a plan began to become more developed. The more they talked, the clearer their course of action became. In her company time became, a refreshing breeze. Her intelligence and humor became more apparent the longer they talked. She seemed so familiar. He remembered loneliness, somehow, he had forgotten that feeling (or suppressed it) during his long solitary trek south.

"You know my darling" she began again. "It's been a wonderful morning,

"There you go changing dialects again." Shaking his head and smiling at her, he continued. "Do you really believe I can catch up on all the changes of the past thousand years in just this morning?" I didn't understand a word you said."

"Of course not." Her voice grew serious. "But it will help at least to hear what little I know. You're not dressed for meeting strangers. You can get by with a kilt. See that old birch? He won't mind you borrowing enough of his outer bark to make one. We can find something more permanent later. If you are to rescue the maiden tomorrow morning, as you said you would, you need to meet the felagi and win their trust. Appearing naked would make them believe you were some wild man."

She had called him darling again. At least eight times in eight different languages. She called him darling. It made his brain ache.

*

About noon the murmurings of the yetann drew her attention. They were growing more and more restless. The pyris would have bolted days ago if they could leave her trap. But while they still ate the grasblett's food and drank his drink, they would be too fearful and docile to run through her gauntlet. The yetann were another matter. They had hunted till the game fled the area. They drank from her stream. They were no longer in the old fool of a grasblett's (herbalist) sway. Though he appeared almost unaware of the danger he and the young lady were in. The etunazi were growing bolder. Some of their number pawed the maiden when the yetann were not close by. They had become so bold that one of the yetann was always standing guard over her. Was the larger spreading his scent on her? Claiming her as his?

Singa ordered Hiisi and Treisa to guard the maiden as he stalked over to where the etunazi were gathered. He bared his fangs and let his low rumbling growl notify them of his presence. The growl was enough to bring all of them attentive to him. He outlined graphically just how he would kill the next fool to touch the maiden. He roared, and they cowered before him, as well they should. He once more bared his fangs and stalked off. He headed to the stream and dunked his head under the cold water. Raising his head, he shook it scattering the water. He was hoping it would clear his head. He had been aware that his blood was coursing with the desire to mate. He should not be going into rut. Something in the grasblett's potions had upset his balance and he was losing control of his desires. The dynoi female was entering her fertile cycle. Of this he was sure. Despite her unbathed body or maybe because of it he could smell it. That sealed her fate. Without that he could have used one of the rizi females, as distasteful as that was, to blunt his needs. It was not so much that taking the dynoi was not desirable. It was the fact he would have to kill that damn old man. With the old man's death, the connection to the huldra would be lost and he would fail his clan. His orders had been clear, he must trace the enemy to its lair. Whoever they were it was clear they had been involved with the enslavement of the lyion yetann in Torion. The Cyngor Volstan (governing council) had selected him for this assignment because of his stability. And look at him now!

The wind carried her smell to him. He wanted to taste her, taste her fear, taste her submission. Shaking his head, he tried to bring his thoughts into submission. He had known that tracing the huldra would be dangerous, but he had never imagined how the strange drugs he had been subjected to would affect him. He determined to do his best in not killing the grasblett. "I'll cower him, twist the location from him. Then kill him." He thought

Singa found himself back standing near the female. He looked at the other yetann. He snarled at them and they turned their eyes down and backed away. Bending low he sniffed her. "Hmm," He thought "she was ripe, almost ready. Tomorrow, yes tomorrow. He bent lower, his nose almost touching her, his whiskers brushed her face.

She must have drifted off to sleep. Thorn had been tormenting her again, he was such a bully. This time when she complained to papa, he taught her a little trick. Warning "Use this carefully." It was a little secret about the lorki. Now when Thorn threatened her, he would get a sneezing fit like something near her made his nose itch. Something tickled her ear and she swatted it away. Suddenly she was flying through the air! She landed hard and then the great yetann was over her. He rubbed the base of his paw over her chest, rubbed his chin in her hair. Then he knocked her around a bit more. Pissed on her and turned away seemingly satisfied that she was properly marked.

Her eyes grew wide. He was marking her! Whether she was to be a snack or something worse she couldn't tell. She lay where she had landed. Bruised and battered and now for the first time truly frightened. A sob escaped, and tears began to fall. Well her dream had given her a clue to at least pay the beast back even as she died. She would die fighting. She had a weapon, a tool against them. She would die but at least that beast would feel a great deal of pain, especially if he ended up eating her.

Tears began to fall again. She couldn't help it. Life had been too short and too restricted. "No hope" she whispered.

There was a scratching sound. Did it say "hope"? Opening her eyes, she saw a small broken and trampled sapling. "Child," it rasped "help is coming. Hope. At dawn, help will arrive. You are not alone. I'm here and others are on their way."

Slowly Catherine pulled herself to a sitting position. The old grasblett averted his eyes when she looked at him. He was now just a frightened old man. This stranger who had unleashed this all on her now knew he had no remaining control of the encampment. He also could end up a ney snack.

Hiisi gave a glancing look at Singa. He didn't dare look long. He did not want Singa to think his look was a challenge. Not in the mood he was presently in. Eye contact could lead to a duel. And that would end badly for him. Taking this contract had been a mistake. It was troubled from the beginning. Oh, but the promised pay, when they reached the seior's destination (wherever that might be. The old man had not told them where that might be, yet), was enough to buy a den and live modesty for the rest of his life. Even after buying a wife and a maidservant. Two females to bear his kits. He looked up at the bluff above.

Nothing would be left of the woman after Singa finished with her. Not that he would share if there was. He made up his mind. When Singa began his rampage, Hiisi decided he would kill and eat one of the pyris. This was the third day with only water. No game was near enough to hunt, and he would not sate his hunger with the seior's drugged food. Then he would try escaping this trap by climbing that bluff. Perhaps if he acted fast a female rizi could be caught and tied to his back to later satisfy other hungers that had been awakened. Treasa would have to find his own way out of this mess.

*

The forest grew very still around the green man. Then the branches rattled with a very angry dryad's voice. "That horrid monster! Pull that kilt tighter it's about to fall off. Hurry green man. We need the felag. We must hurry!"

*

It was midafternoon as Jae sat and watched the spot he had come out of the grove. Yes, there had to be some kind of magic working against him here. He had never been lost before. And he got lost every time he entered that grove. He blinked his pile of stones, were gone! No, they were obscured by something. There before his eyes, something appeared to materialize. How had the grove hidden such a large person? He blinked; this man was green! Almost as tall as he was and over a hundred pounds heavier. The square jaw and other facial features reminded him of the drawing at the academy, the ones of the ancient gods. The gods that had abandoned Ymir thousands of years ago. Odin, Thor, Frigg, the whole pantheon had fled. All that remained was the

16

gifts of Yggdrasil, the long-dead great tree. And those gifts were few and far between, mostly just myths and legends. And here before him stood a legend! A green man. He was turning to call Crispin when it spoke.

"Hello, the felagi." He called, "May I come in? I have need of aid. Will you help me?"

Drew stood and took his ax in his hand. Eric strung his bow. Jae noticed Elgar didn't move. His facial expression didn't change. You would think he saw green men every day. Slowly rising to his feet, Crispin motioned for the others to stand down. "Greetings, stranger", he began.

"Stranger than most, I would wager. If you will pardon my strangeness and poor use of your tongue. I will pardon your staring at my greenness." A smile came to his face as the green man took in their camp. "The dryad sends her greetings as well. She has tried to speak to you, but you are rather far from her grove. She's a lady and prefers not to shout."

Jae considered this revelation. A dryad, that would explain so much. But if she had wanted to speak to them why not talk to him as he wandered through her maze of trees? There's more to the story than the green man was saying.

"Come in and sit with us," Crispin responded. "We have some trail food. I will beg your indulgence for that fact we have no proper meal."

"You've kept a cold camp, so not to alert the raiders to your presence, I take it?" The green man stated. For though it was worded as a question. He spoke as if he knew that this was the fact. "The wind blows up the valley now. And you will need a good meal. If you are to help me with our task. Start a fire. I believe there is rabbit on the menu this afternoon." He lifted half a dozen rabbits by their ears.

So, began the process of building trust between them. It was after the meal when the green man's plans were revealed. "With the dryad's aid, we will travel through the night and be sitting outside their camp. As near to the maiden as possible, while still being in the protective cover the dryad will provide. The yetann and etunazi should not be aware of us until I reveal myself. Stay hidden, ready with your arrows. We must take down the yetann. Then the etunazi will be easy to deal with."

"Someone will need to get to the maiden before it begins," Jae interjected.

The green man responded. "The dryad told me she has an agent in the camp. A rizi, dynoi breed."

"You think that a mortdingya will be of any help?" Eric spat out what almost all the felag thought. "Those halfbreeds, those roach dung's are notoriously unreliable."

The green man sat his gaze on Eric. Then he looked over the others. "The dryad speaks very highly of this youth. She has told me, that despite the danger of aiding the maiden, he has provided clean water and fresh food to her. All before the dryad asked for his help. If we fail at the rescue, he will be among the first of us to die."

"Well, I for one, wish that the dryad would speak for herself. As it is, we only have your word, stranger. You could be leading us into a trap." Drew threw out.

A whisper came across with the breeze. "I resent you questioning this man's honor." A stern toned voice came drifting from the grove. "As you argue with him, you further endanger the young woman I've listened to you brag about saving. The yetann are growing more restless. And from the behavior I have observed, she will not be alive noon tomorrow!" The voice seemed to come from the shaking of the aspen leaves and the rubbing of their branches. "It takes a real effort to project my voice so far, especially when you all have such dull ears. I attempted to speak to the vanir who tried to traipse through my grove. I think he thought my noise just his imagination."

Jae's ears reddened. He hoped no one noticed. He remembered that first exploration and the strange sounds from the trees. He hadn't looked for meaning in those sounds. He was so intent on making no noise of his own and hearing anything that might be approaching. He had discounted as his imagination the archaic words he barely understood. "I beg your forgiveness, my lady. My mother would be ashamed of my rude behavior. Please forgive me."

"I won't tell your mother if you don't." The whisper came back. "I will endeavor to use your newer language while you travel through me this night. I know I was using an ancient language at first. I am still learning yours."

It was as if she read his mind in her response. Jae smiled at this. He believed that he could like this dryad. Well, why not. She had a sense of humor. Unlike the ones in the storybooks of his childhood.

*

It was during this time that Ruskea the etunazi johtaj (officer) kicked Lauloi in the side. "Wake up you ney bait, why do you get double pay if I can't trust you to be awake! You saw what I saw. The yetann are disturbed. They've let us be and not made demands of us for the past two weeks. That's changing now. Rouse the company. Tell them to sharpen their blades and prepare their armor. There's a battle coming. Have them raise their guard. Move it dog. Inspection in a shadow's mark (a unit of time, about an hour).

Ruskea watched his second rouse the men. He fully intended that his rabble would be standing ready between him and the yetann the next day. It was always best to be on your guard when yetann were about. Now as he watched the one called Singa going into rut, it was doubly important to be ready. He hoped his men could at least deflect a raging yetann and give him time to escape. Besides he had detected a scent he did not recognize last time he was at the stream. It seemed strange that the yetann had not. But whatever had brought the lead yetann into rut might confuse their noses. He would wake his men early the next day. He would be ready.

He glanced over toward the seior. He felt no loyalty for the dynoi. The person who had paid the commission fee for his band had told him that the guide was the one to listen to. The seior was just another hireling as far as Ruskea was concerned. He had been ready to obey the old man's orders after the guide's death, but none came. The seior had not assumed command, had not even tried to dissuade the yetann from heading up the mountain. Ruskea knew that the guide had been correct that they should head downslope. But he had also been a fool to think that even a drugged yetann would ignore a fist stuck in his nose. The guide was disemboweled before Ruskea could blink. The largest yetann had backhanded the younger yetann and stared him down afterward. Then he asked the seior for orders but received none. So up the mountain, they headed, till they happened upon this grove and they had been stuck here now a five-day. The freshwater and a few bites of food with none of the seior's medicine had canceled what little effect that medicine had had on his band.

Ruskea drilled his band until the sun began to set. It felt good to at least pretend they had a plan.

*

Cu lain lay on his back. Out from the camp so that the fires would not hinder his view of the night sky. There to the south, just as his father had taught him, bright Asgard showed itself at dusk. South was where home had once been. He was amazed at how much he remembered. He was just a cub when his father died in a battle during the ill-advised war Khann Kiernan led to expand the power of his city, Tawnia.

His mother must have been a willing participant in Cu lain's creation. She shared many fond memories of his father. As his mother told the story, her son was a descendant of nobles. On both sides of the family, though her lineage was vaguer than his fathers. As Cu lain remembered the story his father's grandfather was the bastard son of a samir rizi prince who had a dalliance with a woman who happened to be a j'ss rizi. Although the woman's family was of minor nobility, the prince wanted no part of her or the half breed child. The noble's family bribed her family to ship the woman off. The incident was soon forgotten by the noble family. But the child later rose to fame in Tawnia as a mercenary. His son, Cu lain's grandfather and later his father followed in the mercenary trade.

She made it seem all so romantic even though his father had purchased her from the Tawnia slave market. He had treated her well, she was a full wife and unlike many of his fellow soldiers, his father had refused to take another wife. Cu lain remembered her tears when his father departed for the war. He remembered his own, which his father tenderly wiped from his face before he turned and strolled out in his new armor. It was the debt of that armor that would cost Cu lain and his mother their freedom. Two years after his father had marched off to war, he was in the battle that ended the war and made the city of Tawnia a subject of Torion.

Cu lain's happy childhood ended with his father's death. The losing side very seldom fully pays their mercenaries. And when the disaster on the battlefield led to the death of Tawnia's king and it's absorption into Torion. Well, there was no pay for any of the defeated army and even less for the dead mercenaries and their families. His father had unknowingly pawned his wife and child to equip himself for battle and the usurers were quick to collect what was owed them. That was how he and his mother became the property of the potion mixer. And from the time they had become the property of that wicked old man his mother spent the nights with the old man. All would work out for the good she had told her son.

Prysivolar made his living by selling potions and love charms. Both worked equally well. Which meant not at all except in the imagination of the buyers. Well, it was true the old man did have two potions that worked well. One for fevers and the other for stomach cramps. Cu lain suspected that the one made to abort a child also worked. Though in the case of his mother he believed that the bastard had given her too large a dose. He could only speculate. By the time his mother died, Cu lain was thirteen and being drugged. It seemed the old potion maker had acquired an ancient book. And by some wicked twist of nature somehow Prysivolar was able to translate it. The potions created worked beyond expectations. And the ones that made those who imbibed them highly suggestible and docile were the most profitable. As Cu lain reached puberty a new spice was added to their food. The old man had insisted that it go in all the food they ate. The old potion mixer must have had an antidote he took because it hadn't affected him. But both Cu lain, and his mother lived in a haze because of it.

To his shame, he found that even though he burned with anger when he walked in on his mother being used by a clevoki, as the old man watched, he was helpless to intervene. The old man saw him and ordered him away and he had just turned and walked away. Tears sprang to his eyes. He knew it was the resulting pregnancy that had led to his mother's death a few months later.

The new potions were a great success. They were sold for a very high price to very wealthy patrons. It gave them more control over a recalcitrant wife, a rebellious daughter or son, or a reluctant lover. One of them worked very well to control the giant yetann that were used as private guards. The old fraud soon styled himself Seioknar Prysivolar.

A few months ago, Prysivolar appeared to gain a new patron. One that seemed to be offering both a large reward and the threat of some harm to the old man. So off they journeyed on an expedition. They had sailed from the docks of Tawnia. They and all their baggage changed ships in some port whose location Cu lain could not even guess. Between the drug and seasickness, he had spent most of the trip in a daze. On reflection, it was apparent that Prysivolar varied the dosage he gave Cu lain depending on what was desired of him. When skilled work or attention to detail were desired Cu lain must have received very little. When all that was desired was obedience and subservience, the dosage must have been increased.

Shaking his head Cu lain got up and looked around. The camp was quiet. It was sufficiently dark that he could roam further without being noticed by the old man. The yetann had long ago decided that the drugged Cu lain was not a threat or an escape risk. So, they ignored him. But now Cu lain was free from the drug. The rabbits and later the rats that were too small to interest the yetann or the etunazi fed Cu lain. The food and the freshwater from the stream meant that he no longer needed the old man's prepared rations.

The night was dark, only Asgard shone, the other moons would be dark for most of this night. He knew that with his head clear he could flee the marauders. The forces which entrapped him while he was drugged could not keep him here. Cu lain was certain that the yetann and etunazi could leave without much effort, too. If they were not so blinded by their nature. Yet, the dryad had spoken to him. She had asked his help for the maiden. He had fed the girl some rabbit and rat when the grasblett was busy elsewhere and had received a smile. It was clear to him that during the last three days the drugs the old fart had force-fed her had lost all their power over her. She did not deserve the death that was stalking her. Singa had taken a dangerous attitude as his mind was freed for whatever drug the old man had used on him. He was going into rut. Cu lain had heard of such things but had never seen it. Often the guard yetann were not only drugged but castrated, to protect from such dangers. Though the dryad had promised help, Cu lain did not see how anything, but an army could save the young woman. And him if he dared attempt to help her. Well, there were worse ways to die. Maybe, in whatever afterlife there might be, his father would greet him proudly.

Cu lain set his face to meet whatever would follow. He decided, help or no, he could not leave her to die without any aid. He stretched and began his slow walk to be near her and ready. The dryad had promised that at dawn help would arrive. Well, he would be ready. He had his whittling knife in his belt and that at least could cut her bonds.

CHAPTER 3

From the lecture series "Myth and History" by the learned Ljot Jartasen

The Great Tree: Yggdrasil is the mythical parent of all who dwell on Ymir. He meets his death battling the god Fenrir. With all the myths and legends swirling around Yggdrasil his historical existence has been called into question. With the new information provided by Karl Greenman, we can, without doubt, confirm his historical existence.

*

Ruskea awoke to the call of his bladder. The old trick had worked. The large drink from the stream late the night before roused him awake. He walked over to where he would want the men to gather after he woke them. He emptied his bladder at the spot. The smell of his urine would help gather the men to where he wanted them. He wouldn't have to say anything. No need to let the yetann possibly overhear orders. When he was a young cub, he had no idea that the games they were taught in childhood would turn into warrior tools. Yes, even the foolish game of baiting bears, increased their fighting skills. He smiled as he shook his head. Huijat, fool that his name suggested, had won his bet with Olut. It was very brave of him to grab the captive's breast and lick her face. And very lucky that the yetann backhanded him instead of using its claws. Huijat would collect his bet if they survived the large yetann's rut-rage.

He started to kick Lauloi awake once more then thought better of it, leaned down, and shook him awake. He motioned for him to wake and prepare the men to move. Then he heard a grunt behind him, Hiisi, the yetann made the exaggerated yawn that meant he had caught a scent. Ruskea raised his nose, opened his mouth, and drew in a breath which he exhaled through his nostrils, Yes, there was some new smell in the air, what he could not tell. Hiisi walked closer. "Do not move your men away. Move them closer to Treisa's assigned position. Singa's rut is not our only concern." Ruskea nodded his head. He knew an order when he received one. He quietly moved through his men giving them new instructions. They dressed and moved toward their new position.

As it began to dawn the green man walked out of the grove. The yetann had noticed almost from the moment he appeared. Slowly they took up positions between him and the sorcerer. The largest stayed next to the captive, the other two slowly separated to the right and left and began to close on the stranger.

"What do you want?" growled the largest yetann in passable daonna.

"I'm here to let you know what the dryad desires."

"I am Singa Raion of the Rahvas. Warrior and battle tried. I make scat of my enemies! Who and what are you, that I should speak with you, Green-man?"

"I am the son of The Great Tree, Yggdrasil, and a green man as you have observed. Come for peace but knowing war. I take scat and make life."

"The great tree is long dead and no longer is worshipped or feared." spat Singa.

"So, I have gathered, but I do have a way off this mountain."

"What do you want?" the yetann asked, again.

"To tell you what the dryad wants and what she is willing to give. She has allowed game to pass by your camp and water from her stream for you to drink. Your head has cleared because of the food and drink she provided. She wants very little in return" The green man nodded toward the girl. "Just the ney snack. I can get gold to buy the grasblett if he's cheap." The green-man smiled a tight-lipped smile and glanced at the seioknar.

"Ah, the ney snack." Singa pulled her to her feet, placed a claw under her chin to lift her head. The etunazi want her use."

He sniffed at her running his snout over her breasts. Slowly, he turned his claw downward and began to tear her blouse. "Maybe I'll take her first."

Then with a swift movement, he tore the blouse open and ran his rough tongue up her body over her breasts, up her neck forcing her chin up as he finished. He cradled her head in one great paw. His extended claws securely held her head, she could not move as he forced her up almost lifting her from the ground. Bending down, once more his tongue traveled up her body. This time the stiff hairs on his tongue brought blood. Which he swallowed. Aroused he lifted his kilt.

She had him! This final insult mingled her lorki with his body. Catherine trembled with anger; she had had enough of the weeks of mistreatment. And now with her head cleared, she saw how to take this wretched beast down. Closing her eyes, which the yetann took for fear she reached out.

Singa roared. Then he made a poem (a very poor one but it was a poem in his native tongue, nevertheless) "I'll take this snack. This snack will take me all inside. Her body my toy. I'll eat a salad after from a green body. And after he is dead. I'll burn the dryad's grove."

Camouflaged by the dryad grove, Jae and Drew carefully aimed for the eyes of the yetann holding the maiden. They knew they would only get one chance before the battle raged. Crispin and the rest of the scouts readied themselves as they watched the other two yetann close on the green man. They waited anxiously for his signal.

A roar of conquest began but it was choked off, causing the other two yetann to turn and look. The etunazi were running toward the battle their weapons at ready. Singa released his victim, dropped to his knees clutching his throat with both paws. He then rolled on the ground in agony. An arrow flew by striking the grasblett in the shoulder.

Cu lain had worked his way close to Catherine. Now he ran forward and cut the rope binding her arms. He threw his cloak over her shoulders. Grabbing her arm, he pulled her up and pushed her towards the grove. "Hurry while they are distracted. You must reach the grove. You will be safe once you reach it. The dryad has promised!"

That's all it took. Even though she felt drained she gathered Cu lain's cloak around her and began to run into the grove as the battle unfolded.

Cu lain, paused reached down, and drew Singa's short sword before running it through his spine. This yetann would never threaten anyone ever again.

Their target gone, Jae and Drew took sight on the scar-faced yetann who was closest and as he turned back toward the green-man released their arrows. One took out an eye, the other pierced his snout. They would argue for years over who got the eye. As Jae readied another arrow, Drew threw down his bow, took up his ax, and charged the wounded yetann. Shaking his head Jae sent a shaft through the yetann's throat, then joined the others in taking account of the etunazi.

Cu lain looked up and saw Drew running toward Hiisi. Hoping to distract the beast he threw his tiny blade at the yetann. As expected, it bounced off the back of Hiisi's armor, but it was distraction enough. Jae's arrow entered the yetann's throat through the opening made when he turned his head slightly as Cu lain's knife bounced off. And it was enough distraction to allow Drew to slide past the yetann's guard and mercilessly hack Hiisi's left leg. The yetann fell and Cu lain turned and ran into the dryad's grove.

The last yetann grabbed the green-man trying to tear out his throat with his fangs. He was over two hundred pounds heavier than his opponent. He bore the green man down and ripped his flesh with his massive claws. They tumbled together.

Treisa hit the green man with all his weight. He had conquered many of his opponents this way. Knocking the wind out of them this way usually led to a quick battle. As Treisa bore the green man down, he expected his opponent to pause. It was a surprise that during their fall a breath shattering blow struck his gut. So, this would be no ordinary fight.

The green man imagined that this was what being struck by an avalanche felt like. He managed a blow as they went down. Though the blow had given the beast a pause, its massive claws began tearing at him. He gave a jab with his left fist to the yetann's nose. The massive creature struck back with his clawed right tearing the muscles of the green man's left arm from his shoulder. It fell useless to his side. Luckily the knife he held in his right hand struck home into the yetann's left shoulder. The blood spurted out in pulses; he had hit an artery. The knife slipped out of his hand when the yetann rammed his forehead into the green man's nose breaking it. The yetann raised up preparing to tear the flesh from the green man's chest. Two things happened then that turned the tide. The green man felt his useless left arm rise off the ground. He felt the dryad's roots begin to secure it vertically. Then an aspen sapling slammed into the yetann's head. As the yetann fell forward the green man forced his fingernails to grow into sharp stakes while he extended roots from his elbow to entangle with the dryad's. As the yetann fell from the dryad's blow the green man's fingers found a gap in its armor and pierced the yetann's right shoulder. His fingers sent shoots into the shoulder socket. Then as rapidly as he could he grew them out, sent roots into the wound causing the yetann bellow with pain. Drawing strength from the earth and the dryad, the green man struck the yetann's left forearm breaking it. Then while the beast tried to pull away from his left hand, the green man grabbed him by the jaw, giving it a twist to the right. The green man surprised himself when his right arm grew longer with enough thrust that with a crack the yetann's neck was broken. The yetann collapsed upon him.

Crispin motioned Elgar and Eric to target the approaching etunazi with their bows. Slowly walking out of the grove, they fired several volleys. Then they dropped their bows and drew their swords. The remaining etunazi were struck down. This was much easier than Crispin had expected. The etunazi lost their footing just as they were about to strike. That saved Crispin at least once. Looking up he watched as the pyris scattered down the mountain. Easily passing through the scattered trees that had confined them.

Something cracked, and they saw the green-man start to untangle himself from the dead yetann. Standing he nodded at the fleeing grasblett. He tripped over a root and fell to the ground.

Glancing at Singa the green-man commented "What an interesting use of the art. Very effective. I've never seen it used quite that way."

The comment was lost to the others until later. Their attention was fixed on the appalling condition of the green man's left arm. It appeared like most of his bicep muscles had been shredded and detached from his shoulder. Seeing them stare at him, he looked down at his arm. Shaking his head, he gathered the detached muscles into his right hand. He then moved the detached ends to his shoulder. He held them there a moment. After lowering his right hand to his elbow, he slowly moved it up his arm, pausing several times to squeeze and massage his arm. When the right hand was once again at his shoulder, he lowered it and flexed his left arm before raising it. Both hands moved to his nose covering it, there was a small snap, and when his hands were removed his nose no longer appeared broken. "That's one of the benefits of my greenness. I heal quickly." He calmly stated.

*

Prysivolar lay where he had tripped and fallen. Curses poured from his lips as he wept in anger and pain. He had stood there unable to move as he watched Singa rage. It was fascinating watching the yetann in rut attack the girl knowing that if he perceived you as a threat you would be laid open with one swipe of his claws. Standing as still as he could, had seemed like the best defense until the beast was fully occupied. When the monster fell, he was shocked to realize that it was that girl and not arrows that had laid the yetann low. The huldra had not warned him that she was a danger. He had thought this was only a political vendetta or a gathering of breeding stock. Then as he started to turn and run, an arrow had passed through his shoulder knocking him to the ground. When his head cleared enough from the pain, he had gotten up and ran, only to trip and fall again. Pain had seared through his shoulder as he hit the ground. He was faint from blood loss; of this he was sure. And that cu dhear (damaged dog) had betrayed him, cursed dog that he was. In horror, Prysivolar had watched as cu dhear ran a sword through the yetann's back. Shudder, he could be next as he lay helpless on the ground.

This was supposed to be a quick kidnapping. Planned out, and carefully executed. But no the yetann and etunazi were more difficult to control in this wild environment. It didn't help the huldra's handpicked guide had baited the yetann from the start. The fool had gotten them lost. Such an arrogant bastard. Prysivolar had bitten his tongue when his skill with potions was attacked. Trying to shout down a yetann who had pointed out how lost they were, had been the agent's last mistake.

As they finished their check of the enemy dead, Jae glanced up to see the waif and her konkur walking from the grove. She looked awful pale under the dirt. He watched as she paused and almost fell. The konkur steadied her as she sat down. Jae was moving to her before he even thought. "Are you injured? Can I do anything?" he started asking when her green eyes caught him. He stopped short unable to move in the intensity of those eyes.

"I need something to eat, a fruit, dried is fine, anything sweet if possible." She responded. "It drains a person when one uses the lorki so intensely, and I haven't had much nourishment for a long time."

Jae blinked and reached into his travel pack. "My mother sent these." Handing her some greased paper wrapped bars. "She calls them travel snacks. Just dried fruit, berries, apples, and plums I believe. They have some parched grain all held together with a honey syrup. I hope they help."

"That was kind of your mother, tell her thank you when you can." Catherine ventured a smile. She felt an attraction to this stranger and here she was a stinking filthy mess. All attempts at conversation ceased as she began to chew the tough bar. She could feel the sweetness begin to appease the lorki. Her heart was slowing down to a near normal pace. She could not remember being so frightened or so angry. She silently studied what had happened and what she had done. This would take some thought. What happened would be hard to duplicate, but she knew she would have to try so she could understand the process better. She watched the men move across the encampment. They were gathering the supplies into one area. The refuse into another. Cu lain sat beside her watching the strangers and surveying the scene. In some ways, he behaved like an abused and frightened animal. But he had exhibited, what she felt was exceptional bravery and foresight. From the first time he shared some food with her, she knew he would become a friend. That small bit of food had helped her and her lorki defeat the grasblett's potion.

Her eyes focused on one of the strangers. He was green! A green-man. Some hint of a memory rustled through her brain. What was the old nursery rhyme? The green man and the dryad danced in the grove... something. They angered Yggdrasil... maybe later she would remember. The green man and another man approached.

"I'm Crispin, I see you've met Jae. My friend here seems to have no other name than what you see. And you are?"

Catherine looked up at the brown-eyed daonna. She studied him for a moment. "I'm Catherine" She responded.

"Catherine, what can we do to help now?" Crispin asked.

Catherine considered. What did she need? A bath, yes, a bath even if it must be in that cold mountain stream. Clothing, something not so filthy and frayed. "I need to bathe. And I need some clothing. Something that fits better than the cloak Cu lain has so kindly loaned me." She said as she realized that Cu lain though taller was a sparer build than she was, and his cloak barely covered her. She adjusted her grip on the front, hoping to cover more.

"Elgar" Crispin called. "Can you loan this young woman your extra shirt? I know it's clean, I saw you tending to it yesterday."

"Aye, she can have it if it pleases her." The older man responded. He then turned and searched through his backpack. Pulling out a shirt. He approached and handed it to her. Nodding his head in thought, he reached into his pack again pulling out a leather pouch. "I've scissors, needle, thread and a bar of soap, in here. Use whatever you need, lass."

His warm rumbling voice reminded her of her father's. That and his kind and gentle looking face made Catherine feel a bit more secure. "Thank you, Elgar."

As she began to stand up, Jae reached out his hand to help and Cu lain touched her elbow to steady her. She stifled her initial response of "I don't need your help". Their aid had been and still was needed. She felt drained of energy. Not only the energy she had expended today in her wild grasp at defense but the past several weeks had drained her. She looked down and said, "Thank you both."

Jae blurted out, "You can have a warm bath. I found a pool of dragon piss in the grove. I can show it to you."

"I'll go too" Cu lain said looking at Jae.

"What did you find in the dryad?" The green man asked. "A pool of dragon piss?"

Jae's ears reddened. Drew stifled a giggle, only he and Jae probably had ever heard that term. And though they were friends, Drew enjoyed seeing Jae's discomfort.

As his ears grew redder Jae stammered, "I'm, I'm sorry, that's what we called the hot water springs back home. There's a fine hot spring flowing into the stream in the grove not far from here."

Leaves rustled, and a laugh came out of the grove. The dryad was amused. "Dear Catherine. I can show you where it is. I know the spot well." Directing her comment at the almost too helpful boys. "I believe Catherine would love some privacy, some time to herself. Am I right?"

Catherine just nodded her head as she chewed another bite of trail bar. The thought of some privacy after all the time that she had had none, was a need she felt almost as much as a bath. She steadied herself and shooed the men's hands away. They might be friendly and not intrusive, but she had enough of male hands for a while. She took a few wobbling steps. Stood still for a moment. Then she took a few steps toward the grove, where she saw a single tree trembling.

"Ma'am? Might these fit you?" A voice interrupted her progress. She turned and looked at who the voice was coming from. At her direct look Drew grew embarrassed. He held in his extended hand a pair of moccasins that appeared like they just might fit her. Drew was glad his dzwerc heritage kept his blush from showing. Having the full intensity of those green eyes directed at him disturbed him. The warm "Thank you, I believe they will." Didn't help his composure. Drew prided himself on being unaffected by females. He had always been amused at Jae's uncertainty with attractive girls. And he didn't care for Eric's casual use of the poor girls that fell for his charms. He steeled himself and looked directly at Catherine. He handed her the moccasins, turned, and walked away.

What a strange guy this dzwerc was, Catherine thought. Then she turned and walked into the dryad grove.

When she entered the grove, a voice whispered. "I hope my presence here will not disturb you. After all, I am everywhere in this grove"

Catherine thought as she continued to follow the dryad's signs. "Dryad," She finally responded, "I think that the presence of another woman will be a comfort."

Cu lain noticed the grasblett begin to rise from where he lay. His hand went to the blade he now carried. But before he could move, he heard Crispin. "Eric, gather that man in. I want to question him." Glancing at Cu lain, Crispin quietly said, "I know that fellow owes you a lot. But you need to consider your friend. We need to learn why they picked her. What motivated this raid. Do you know? Any thoughts on it at all?"

Cu lain shook his head. Until they had reached this grove, he had been in a drug-induced daze. Most of the journey was just a fog. If he had heard the plans being discussed, he had no recollection of them. He realized that if they had stalked the lady Catherine specifically that she could still be in danger. "The debt he owes me can wait. Thanks."

Crispin considered the young konkur. He was small for a konkur. Apparently, he had been in the grasblett's control for a long time. For one who had been drugged and malnourished, he showed promise. Crispin wondered if the king would let him take the boy into his training program. There were places a konkur could go unnoticed that a daonna or a vanir could not.

The day passed quickly as the green man directed them to space the dead etunazi at the edge of the grove. Near the center of the open field where the raiders had camped, they dug three large holes to bury the yetann. Sometime during that labor, the dead etunazi disappeared into the earth.

With Cu lain's help they then divided the pile of supplies into usable and worthless. They paid particular attention to Prysivolar's personal baggage, much to his discomfort. Prysivolar sat silent when questioned by the green man and Crispin. Most of his time was spent glaring at Cu lain. Elgar had tended his wound and stayed the bleeding. But the green man had insisted to Crispin that no more than the minimum should be done. That Catharine needed to lend her hand to the criminal's healing.

It was past noon when Catherine walked out of the dryad grove. She felt better than she had for weeks. Almost herself again. The dryad had supplied her with some fruit and nuts. She did not recognize either type of fresh berries, but they were good. The dried grapes were a total surprise. There were pinion nuts, walnuts, and some sort of acorn that unlike those in Boer Akarn were sweet with just a hint of the bitter tannin.

The pool that the dryad had led her to, was hot. Wonderfully hot. After she had scrubbed all the filth from her body she worked on her hair. Once it had been a beautiful braid of auburn. Now it turned out to be in an impossible mat. So, she hacked it off. She cut it until she could comb her hair out with the comb that had been hidden in Elgar's kit. So short that it would be a scandal in Boer Akarn.

Then as she soaked in the hot pool she and the dryad talked. "So, this must be like having a mother or a sister." Catherine thought as they shared their stories and tears. Catherine cried much more than the dryad. The flood of tears seemed to cleanse her. She did what she thought would be impossible before her time with the dryad. She was freed from the terror that had gripped her from the moment she was grabbed until now.

As she dressed, she thought how outraged the villagers of Boer Akarn would be. Elgar's shirt reached just below her knees until she cinched it with the belt Cu lain had handed her. Then it was above her knee. Scandalous! She smiled. she would not return to her old life in that village. She made sure the scabbard with the yetann dagger was securely attached. Then she sat and firmly laced up Drew's moccasins They were soft leather and calf high. She wished her old shoes had been as comfortable.

She strode out of the grove with a bounce in her step. Her inner confidence was a warm fire in her heart. She felt better about herself with her rough cropped hair, dressed only in a man's shirt and moccasins, than she ever had in Boer Akarn. That village was full of so many restrictions. Everything was governed by their traditions. How long a skirt or dress was, how much of a maiden's bosom should be exposed. Enough to prove she had one but not enough to make a man stare and some men stared no matter what you wore. Then her duties as healer confined her more. She must look sober. She must, oh she must so many things. When widow Sturlasda was alive things had been better. She had learned and practiced healing free from the demands of the old women. The elders deferred to the widow. And the men were not always trying to get Catherine alone. They didn't dare with the widow watching. The wives and mothers were jealous of the freedom Catherine had been afforded while the widow was alive.

The dryad had agreed with her that she should never go back to that place to live. The dryad suggested she join the felag that had rescued her. A thought she was just now emboldened enough to consider. She would have to see how those men behaved the next few days. Before she made that decision.

Eric was first to spot Catherine as she came out of the grove. "Well," he thought, "that turned out better than expected. She fills out Elgar's shirt quite nicely." That thought made him sorry he had not been in the right spot to see her bare chest. She was plump for Eric's taste but well, given a chance he might make an exception.

Jae looked toward where Eric was staring. What a confident walk he thought. Not many men could have recovered so well from an ordeal like hers. She was beautiful. And her hair was red! Even with her hair a ragged mess, he thought she was beautiful. She was taller than Drew by more than a head. To his eyes, she was nicely rounded. It crossed his mind that he would have to bend to kiss her. Now, what brought that to mind? Then she looked at him, raised an eyebrow, and gave him a look. A look he didn't know the meaning of. He looked away while his ears got redder.

She gave a small smile to the world. When she had given, what she meant for her "Yes, what do you want" look. The tall Vanir's ears had turned a bright red and he had turned away. She appreciated that his look was a different look than the looks some men gave. His ears turning red was kind of cute.

She walked over to where Elgar and Cu lain were talking. As she handed Elgar his kit. He told her. "Let me trim up that hair. I used to cut all my brother's hair when I was at home. I think I can trim it so it will grow out nicely."

"What if I want to keep it short? It's so much easier to wash that way." She asked.

He smiled at her and responded. "That I can do, too. I believe I can make it so you can do whichever you prefer."

She looked at Cu lain. "The dryad thinks that you need a good scrubbing. Do you think you could take something clean with you? I believe you've lived in those rags long enough."

"Since we left Tawnia. These and that cloak are all I have." He lowered his eyes and looked down. "I know I stink. My cleanliness was not a concern of that old man." He glanced over to where Prysivolar sat tied.

Crispin was glad that someone else had decided to tell Cu lain to bathe. He walked over and handed Cu lain a robe, pants, and a nice pair of boots. "The grasblett's feet don't look much bigger than yours. Though I would bet the old man hadn't worn these for years. If they are too big, we can find something else, later. Go on now, get bathed. You've helped enough for now."

There was no argument from Cu lain. He would wear those boots even if they rubbed his feet raw. He loved the idea of the discomfort and anger that would give the old bastard. Taking the articles from Crispin, he turned and walked in the direction Catherine had come from.

Catherine sat on the box Elgar had indicated. He shook out a large cloth he had obtained from the baggage. He stepped behind her and settled the cloth in front of her. Then he pinned it behind her (His small kit was almost magical in what it contained). Only after this preparation did he begin to comb through her hair. His hands were gentle. It was not long before Catherine was able to relax. Elgar treated her as a sister or daughter. He directed her to turn her head left, right, up, down. Stepped away walked around her, then gave a nod. From somewhere he produced two mirrors. She later learned that the larger one was the grasblett's scrying mirror and the smaller Elgar used to shave.

As she examined her new hairstyle, she noticed how different her hair looked. Besides being cut short it was no longer her familiar auburn. Her hair now was definitely red. Not the orangish-red of her childhood. It was flaming red. She also noticed a hint of freckles across the bridge of her nose. She hadn't had freckles since she was nine summers old. She turned her head left then right examining them. Some might call them cute. Maybe when she was eight, they were. Well, there was nothing she could do about it. Was there? She noticed Elgar's expectant face.

"Thank you so much!" she beamed at Elgar. "I love it." Elgar cleared his throat and tried not to look too proud of his job.

While Catherine's haircut was being accomplished, Crispin called Jae and Eric over to him. "I need you both to take that grasblett over there near the grove. There are things I don't want him to overhear. The dryad has assured me that no matter how good his hearing, over near her she can interfere with any attempt of his to listen. When you have him over there, you can untie him. Let him walk about some. Find out how the containers marking his supplies are marked and offer to bring him some food. If he refuses, give him some of our leftover rabbit and some water to drink. One of you needs to stay with him at all times. I don't believe he could escape the dryad, but it pays not to underestimate the enemy. I'll call you back when we want him."

Jae and Eric walked over to where the old man was tied. They released his bonds and led him to the place they were directed. On the way, Jae offered him his canteen. Which Prysivolar batted away. Eric's offer of food was ignored. The young men tried to start several conversations. All offers to fetch him his personal supplies were met with a grunt. Soon all attempts at communication stopped. When they reached the dryad's grove, they stood glaring at each other. The old man acted as if the short walk had exhausted him and lay down in a soft spot and at least feigned sleep. Jae was sure that his breathing betrayed that he was still awake.

When Crispin surmised that the old grasblett was far enough away, He began, "We found this charm on that fellow. He gave some protest about it being stolen from him, but we persuaded him that it should be in our care for the time being." With these words, he opened his hand to reveal a charm that had been attached around the old seior's neck with a chain.

Catherine took it from him and examined it closely. "What strange markings. They look like they might form words, but they are like nothing I've ever seen before. Maybe Cu lain can tell us something when he returns."

The green man rubbed his head. He then produced a matching

necklace. "I have this from a seior I met once. As for the meaning of the words. Well, at one time I knew that language. But I've forgotten it along with considerable other things. Some more important things. Hanging his head, the next words were barely audible. "An important friend, I believe."

Crispin looked up at the rustle of the leaves. "Dryad, do you recognize these?" He asked.

I recognize the green man's charm. The scar I bear came from the one who carried it. I knew that language as well, but like the green man, I too have lost its meaning. Somewhere in my scar, some kernel of memory may bring back that knowledge. But that area bears a dangerous poison. Even after over a thousand summers, I can just now reach into its periphery. It could be another thousand summers before I regain memories from there." She paused. "I would prefer that no one mention the presence of a dryad. I still bear the scars of my last encounter with a seior."

"May I hold them?" Catherine asked. Both men handed them to her. She carefully examined both one at a time then together. "They look almost the same, but they are not. The one the old grasblett had is a poor copy. The letters are poorly engraved, some so badly that their forms are obscure. One other thing, the other has a hint of power. I can barely perceive it, but it is there." Shaking her head at the mystery she handed the charms back.

"I think I know of someone who might be able to help. He is one of the king's advisors, a seioknar who is a scholar of ancient script." Elgar told them.

Then turning to Catharine, Crispin asked. "Will you kill that old grasblett, if I place him in your care?"

"I may hate that old goat. I have the right too, you know. But I made promises as a healer, that I don't break very often." She responded. "I won't kill him. I do hope my presence will make him uncomfortable."

"Oh, I do hope so. I do hope so." Crispin gave a wicked grin. "He deserves more discomfort than I and my felagi appear to give him. We need to gain some answers. Until we know why he targeted you. Catherine, this band of raiders targeted you specifically. All the evidence we saw at Boer Akarn points to that. Until we know why you are still in danger. You will be till we trace the reason to its roots."

Catherine shook her head in disbelief as Crispin continued. "Make him uncomfortable. Treat his wound. But, don't ease the pain too much. we need to get him to tell us what he knows. I don't believe he knows all we want to know, but he knows enough to help us find the source. I hope he believes you can deal him torment without killing him. Maybe some fear will loosen his tongue. If not, maybe we can favor him with his own potion."

"Cu lain may be able to help. He was that wicked old man's servant for some time I believe." Catherine said. "Is his wound serious? Does he need immediate treatment, or can we wait until Cu lain has returned? I think Cu lain's presence will help bring that cur to heel." She smiled. She liked that play of words. She remembered how Cu lain was tormented by that old man with that word. She believed she would only address the sup-posed seioknar as cur.

She liked what she had on now. There were some modifica-tions she would like. The shirt needed to be shorter. With pants, she would have more freedom of movement. She began to look through the pile of clothing the men had gathered. Was there anything she could modify to fit her? While she was at it, she made a pile of clothing that might work for Cu lain. He needed a civilized selection.

"Jae, did you notice how much a bath improved that girl's looks? Eric asked. He noticed a little red begin to creep up Jae's ears. So, he had noticed. He was wondering how far he could carry this theme. He was about to see when Jae changed the subject.

"Did you see what took down that large yetann holding the girl?" Jae asked.

"I had thought that you or Drew got a lucky shot. But then I noticed, that there was only a little blood around his mouth. An arrow up his mouth would bleed much more. So, what do you think happened?" Eric responded.

"I don't have to think. I know." Jae smiled. "He got too fresh with Catherine. She's what took him down. I imagine anyone who got too fresh with her would reap her wrath. I wonder what she does to people that only annoy her?" The grin faded from Eric's mouth at that. So, Eric and Drew weren't the only ones who could make others uncomfortable.

Eric wasn't the only one to give pause. The old man stopped his attempt at escape. His face became even more sober if that was possible. Jae had been watching the old man edge his way into the dryad's grove. He had no idea how impossible escape through that would be. And now he had even more reason to try. A woman with real power and an ax to grind with him.

Prysivolar backed slowly away from the two vanir. Maybe if he were careful, he could disappear into the grove like they had appeared. The harder he tried the harder it became. He tripped over a root and crashed into a limb. No matter how he tried he could not silently fade into the surrounding trees. Well, he had never been comfortable in the wilds. He only spent time in the forests of Tawnia, when he had no choice. When the cur dhear's mother was alive he had no need. It seemed like she knew all the plants of those woods. If she had been afforded an education in potions, she might have been one of his rivals in the trade. As it was, she bartered her skill for better treatment for her son. If he had known that she would die in the experiments with the docile potion, he would have bought another woman to use instead. The huldra paid well but he was always frugal. It paid to conserve his resources. The little mongrel had been useful, else he would have been sold upon his mother's death. But he knew the herbs almost as well as his mother and his woodcarvings sold very well as magical charms.

Anyway, with these wilderness scouts, his escape through the woods would not be possible. So how would he frame his story? How much truth should he tell? What could he fabricate that that cursed mortdingya could not refute? Hopefully, his being under the influence of the spice would help Prysivolar's case.

Thankfully he had swallowed his ring before they had tended his wound. It should be another day or two before he would need to retrieve it. Maybe, by that time he would be near some ally the huldra had in the area? Otherwise, it would be wisest to swallow it again.

He watched as a young woman walked out of the grove. No! It couldn't be. He had almost not recognized her. Her confident walk was impossible. She had been under the influence for four weeks. No one recovered so quickly. No one. At least no one, he remembered. Yet he had never heard of any slaying a yetann with just a look. He shuddered. He remembered hearing that she would need to examine his wound. She was a læknir, they told him. If true that might explain the huldra's interest in her. That and the signs she carried of a heritage they coveted. Yes, that was it. He was just a pawn. If he played it right, they might believe that he was under the spell of some other drug. He, too, was just a victim.

While she waited for Cu lain to return from his bath, she rummaged through the stacks of armor and clothing the men had collected. There was very little of the clothing that she considered salvageable. Maybe a couple of shirts that might fit Cu lain, but nothing that came close to fitting her. Then she spotted some unusual garments. They appeared like the nightshirts she and widow had worn, but they were huge. Holding one up, she rubbed her fingers over it, it had an unusual texture, the threads did not appear to be spun. She could imagine a dress or robe from them. She noticed Elgar close by and asked "Elgar, do you think I could cut one of these up to make me some garments?

Elgar shook his head. "You could læknir (a respectful title for a healer) Catherine, but I wouldn't advise you too. Those are made from a rare and expensive fabric. I believe they call it silk. It is valued by warriors because it does not easily tear. When you're struck by a weapon that breaks through your chain mail an undershirt made of this will usually allow you to pull the fabric from the wound bringing the broken bits of mail out with it. Infections are less likely when you are dealing with a clean wound. Whole those shirts are worth more than the armor they were under. To the right dealer, they would sell for double that. You have my support if you want to claim those for your share of the plunder."

"Why should I get a share? I'm the reason you all risked your lives. I don't deserve any of this." Catherine argued.

"No, you killed one of the yetann. Take those as your bounty. We are in the king's service and any plunder we retrieve will first go to the treasury and then we will receive an allotted share. You and the green man should split the armor. You take the shirts and he the armor itself. The king's scholars will want samples of the grasblett's potions. We will get an allotment from the value they perceive from those. To my eye, there is nothing else worth carrying away. As the king's agent, that is my decision" Crispin interjected ending her argument.

"Cu lain should have a share." The green man spoke up. "He can have most of what you allotted me. I'll need a little gold for clothing if I travel down the mountain with you. I will not need more."

As he finished speaking, she spotted Cu lain emerge from the grove. My, he looked like a different person. Dressed in a fine robe, pants that though too large for him in circumference were cut to a length that with the boots made the ensemble complete. If Elgar did not volunteer to tailor those pants for Cu lain, she would. She suspected that Elgar would do a much better job. She only sewed because that was the only way she had of having clothing that fit to her liking. She refused to dress like an old woman (the widow's preference) or a piece of merchandise on display (Like the eager to marry young women of the village attempted).

She knew she was avoiding dealing with that old cur. Maybe later she would argue with Crispin. Later then. She got up. Laid the silk shirt with the small pile she had gathered. Then brushed the dust off her outfit.

"Green man, would you come with me." I'm ready to attend to that cur." She said as she began to relish the irritation that calling that supposed seioknar, cur would give him. She waved to Cu lain to join her. Then walked to where the old cur was.

"Please, send Jae and Eric back to me, while you treat the grasblett." Crispin requested as Catherine and her entourage began walking to her patient.

"I will," Catherine responded.

As they walked over to where they were, she noticed Cu lain chewing on what appeared to be a stick. "What are you eating?" She asked.

Cu lain pulled the piece of plant from his mouth and looked at it. He thought a moment, then responded. "I don't know what this is. It grows near the stream. It has small purple flowers and it seems to satisfy a hunger that I can't place."

What kind of hunger do you mean?" Queried Catherine. "Is it like a sweet?"

Shaking his head, Cu lain got a quiet look on his face. "No, it is a hunger like I've not known before. Before I began chewing on its stalks, I was getting nervous and sometimes my hands would start to shake."

The green man held out his hand requesting a sample to examine. As he looked over the remains of the plant. Catherine said. "I knew an old man that widow Sturlasda was treating. He had a hunger for the concentrated sap from a red flower's seed pod. He had lost his home and family while living in the dreamlike state induced by the potion. He usually smoked it. Now that you've mentioned it one of the components in the grasblett's potions was quite similar."

"I know what this is. We called it the mountain poppy. Its sap can be used to produce a pain killing potion and if not carefully administrated can become very addictive." The green man broke in.

Catherine stopped and turned to Cu lain. "I believe this plant's sap is keeping you from having a bad reaction to not having the old man's potions. It would make sense to introduce a substance into a potion used to subvert another's will. They would more readily consume it if it induced a hunger that could only be sated by it." She took Cu lain's hand. "Sit here with me." She said as she lowered herself to the ground facing him.

Cu lain quickly sat facing her, unsure of what she wanted. The green man sat a short distance away. Wanting to observe without interfering. He was curious at what limits this young woman might have.

As soon as they were settled, Catherine took both of Cu lain's hands into hers and looked him in the eyes. "I'll need your help with this. You must desire to truly be free from this hunger. If you harbor a secret desire for the feelings induced by this plant or the grasblett's potion, we will be laboring in vain.

When Cu lain looked up into her eyes, she noticed that his dark brown eyes had small greenish flecks. "I want free of all the shackles that old man has laid upon me. I'll do whatever I can to be free of the remnants."

"Good" Catherine nodded her head and continued." We are going to attempt to call your lorki to battle. Move your thoughts to a pleasant memory if you can. Slowly close your eyes and picture that memory, hold it in your thoughts as you slow your breathing, calm your heart." She waited as she felt his pulse slow. The present disappeared to her, only her patient remained. She searched through Cu lain for his lorki and when she was touching their presence, she asked Cu lain. "Reach your thoughts out, look deep into your body, become aware of the smallest part you can." Cu lain caught his breath. "Easy, friend," Catherine responded.

"There are countless numbers of some tiny life in me." Cu lain's voice was full of wonder. Catherine recognized that Cu lain had the potential to be able to enlist his lorki to his aid. With desire and training, he might even be able to influence another's lorki. She had only met a few who could. Her father, widow Sturlasda, A holy man from up the mountain and herself. She suspected that she was just now starting to explore her limits.

"Cu lain, desire to be free of the hunger. Release the hunger and desire it gone." She kept just the faintest tendril of her presence as Cu lain's lorki began their labor.

The sun had noticeably moved when she stood and touched Cu lain's shoulder. He looked up at her and smiled. "That's amazing! Would it do any harm if I searched my lorki out from time to time?" He asked.

She smiled. "No harm. I will tell you that learning to listen to your lorki is probably most important. A mentor to help you learn more of the lorki ways could be helpful. You have a gift for it I believe." She got up off the ground where they had been sitting and continued, "For the time we are together, I would like to show you how you and your lorki can detect harmful substances in what you are about to eat or drink. With practice, you can tell what your lorki can handle and what you should not ingest.

"I believe that Crispin would love to have you sit with him and his men and cover the same training with them. I think that they would find such skills very useful if any of them have a talent for it." The green man said. Then he started a new thought. "I do believe I would like another name to be addressed by. Don't you find green man a bit, I don't know, distancing maybe? I believe I want my friends to call me Karl. Karl means a common man. I know I'm quite uncommon. But, call me Karl if you will, læknir Catherine and friend Cu lain."

Cu lain and Catherine both nodded to this. "Karl it is." She smiled at the green man. "Karl Greenman has a nice ring to my ears."

The few feet left between them were covered quickly. As they approached the three men, Catherine began to study the old man. Trying to discern his condition and attitude. It didn't help that for some reason, her eyes kept finding Jae.

Jae saw her approaching and gave her a smile. "It's a good thing Crispin wants Jae with him." She thought. It appeared to her that at least for the next few days, Jae would be a distraction. She didn't need distractions when examining a patient. Especially one she had hostile feelings for, one she knew was her enemy. She knew she not only needed to help the man heal, she also needed to get a handle on his motives. She needed to gauge his emotions when she and Cu lain were near him. There were many questions that needed to be answered. She doubted that they would be extracted easily.

She smiled at Jae. To tell the truth she found it hard not to. "Crispin wants you both to go to him." She paused. "Would you be so kind as to pass on to Crispin that I have some knowledge I want to share with the felagi?"

"I will læknir Catherine," Jae responded. The smile she rewarded him with made him glad that he heard as well as he did. He had been watching the trio approach, he wouldn't admit that it was Catherine he had been watching and listening for when he heard the green man address her as læknir. He had noticed how that seemed to please her. For some reason, he wanted to please her. And addressing her with a status that he was sure she fully deserved, well that took very little effort.

Catherine then turned to Prysivolar. "I'm læknir Catherine. I've come to examine your wound. I want to make sure that it is healing properly. May I examine you?" All thought of calling him a cur, or in belittling him in anyway fled her as she assumed her role as healer. She was læknir and that filled her. "By what name may I address you?"

Prysivolar wrestled within himself. Part of him feared her touch. Part of him wanted to feel the touch of her power and thus learn from it. There was a part that wanted to demand he be called Seioknar Prysivolar, or at least Seiknar. But he knew that if he did the chances of his acquiring some kind of understanding of her abilities would be lost. He had been thinking of this for some time. And when she and Cu lain sat together on the ground, he saw Cu lain being freed from the last vestige of his potions power. He knew he had to learn more. She appeared to have real power, power he had only heard rumors about. So, he calmly looked her in the eyes and said. "Please address me as Prysivolar. A name I've been known by for almost a hundred years. I'm afraid I wouldn't recognize another." A small attempt at a smile cracked his face.

"I understand that an arrow pierced and then traveled through your shoulder, and Elgar has cleaned and bound it. Am I correct?" She asked while she tried to sense what motivated this change of mood.

"Yes, læknir. That is true." Prysivolar tried to keep his voice neutral. It pained him to give a title of honor to this child. He watched her. He wondered why he had never noticed the intensity of those green eyes. Green eyes, now what was that a sign of? What had green eyes? Then she touched him, and he jumped. His thoughts had drifted off.

"So sorry to startle you." The girl addressed him. "I need you to take off your shirt, so I can examine the wound. It would also be helpful if I could touch your shoulder. That would make it easier for me to see if your lorki have mustered to healing properly."

He glared at the pleased look Cu lain gave him as he winced while removing the shirt. She asked again. "May I touch you?" Prysivolar nodded his head. Then he tried to follow what she was doing.

Catherine slowly and gently brought her hands in contact with his shoulder. Then she slowly moved her hands closer to the wound. She began to probe searching for the lorki and their activity. Trusting Karl and Cu lain to watch over her she kept only a minimum awareness of the world outside herself and the wound. There, there they were the lorki and the bodies other defenses were hard at work.

Prysivolar watched as the girl began her process. He felt the warmth of her hands on his shoulder and prepared for the pain that would occur when she touched the wound. Only that didn't happen. No one could be so gentle. What was she doing? He started to ask her, but she spoke first.

"Prysivolar, I would like you to help with mustering your lorki. If we can motivate them to be more active your pain will lessen, and the wound will heal quicker" Catherine looked up at the grasblett and caught the quickly hidden confusion in his look. Was it possible he had no idea of how to work with the lorki?

Prysivolar was torn, admitting that he didn't know what on Ymir she was talking about would shame him beyond endurance. But, the secret to why the huldra wanted this girl so much that his years of quiet service in Tawnia were tossed aside to acquire her, might be held in this lorki mystery. It wasn't like he didn't know about the lorki. He knew of them and some of their attributes and the theories of how they worked. But none of the seiors he knew had any idea of how to muster them to their service. And this child seemed as if she was old friends with them and could easily bring them to service. So reluctantly he told the truth. "I have never been instructed in this technique."

"Are you aware at all of your lorki?" she asked. He shook his head. At his negative response, she looked at him and then said. "Then all I ask is that you relax. Clear your mind of thought as much as you can and let your consciousness drift to your wound. It may be that you can gain some insight as I attempt to attune your lorki to care for your wound better. She turned her head and her eyes shut as she drifted back into full awareness of his lorki. After a short time, she moved her hands off his shoulder. Sitting up straight she addressed him. "There, you should regain full use of your arm in a few days. Don't overstress it for a week or so. And don't be concerned if you can't gain awareness of your lorki. Yours seem healthy enough. You can put your shirt back on now."

He pulled his shirt over his head and mulled about what he had discovered. This child possessed remarkable skills. She would be a remarkable asset if she could be brought back to the huldra. Little chance of that in the current situation. But, perhaps? He hadn't tried in years. Do you suppose?

He settled his shirt back into place, reached his hand out as if to touch her sleeve. "Læknir, thank you for your care." He leaned toward her and reached out in thought. He could feel the power rising. She shyly dropped her eyes. Oh, it was working. He had her!

She could almost taste the force of the attraction this old

man generated. So, the old fool did possess an inkling of how to direct his lorki. He was a charmer. He might have been a powerful charmer at one time. Maybe he still was. An unguarded person might succumb to his attack. But she wasn't unguarded. She silently thanked her father for one more lesson she had almost forgotten. She looked up at him and let her face take on the calm look of one enchanted. She was surprised at how easily it was working. The old grasblett was focused upon his prey. She could tell he was gaining confidence that the charming was working. She leaned closer and touched his hand. The touch shocked him, he almost pulled away. But he didn't. He was much too sure of himself. Gradually she changed the direction of the forces interplaying between them.

*

When he saw Catherine becoming charmed, Cu lain almost ran to her. He feared her coming under the old man's influence. But as he started to move the green man touched his arm. When he started to pull away, the green man whispered. "Don't underestimate the lass. She's in control of this. Let's see how much she can learn."

So, Cu lain waited. His hand on his sword. Watching.

"My dear Prysivolar, what do you want with me?" she asked. He just smiled and increased his effort. Catherine hoped none of her new friends interfered, for the old man was almost in her thrall. "Where are you going to take me?"

Prysivolar, still thinking he was enthralling her, whispered. "I don't know, the huldra didn't tell me. We were heading for a rendezvous with a ship."

"What ship?" She whispered back.

A confused look crossed Prysivolar's face. He shook his head. "Child, come back later, and I'll tell you more." Something was wrong. He had said too much. Then it struck him! Pulling away from her. "You witch!", he said.

She glared at him, her anger rising. "You, old goat, then hold your tongue until the king of Alfheim tosses you in a dungeon to be questioned."

Prysivolar shuddered at that thought. He well knew of some of the methods being used in dungeons.

As Catherine backed away the green man touched her shoulder. "You've done very well." He said. "Tell me how did you come across how to do what you just did? There are very few that can turn a charmer's tricks back on him."

Catherine took a deep breath and tried to calm herself. "My father was a healer in Kalfa. Once someone brought a nymph for him to treat. She looked very young, but father told me that she was very ancient and very ill. The man who claimed to own her had moved her from her source spring so he could use her gift for gain. My father helped her escape. He pressed the constable of Kalfa to arrest the man as a slave trader. And while the man fought the charges, my father sent her off. Why I just remembered. Widow Sturlasda took her in her cart, just like she took me a few years later! I must have been around 6 summers old.

While the nymph was at my father's he took me to see her. He talked to her and she sent a tendril of her charm at me. Father showed me how to guard against it. He told me a girl could not be too careful. She needed to be aware that villains could be as charming as this lost artifact of the gods. I thought it strange that he called the woman an artifact as if she were some kind of construction like a wagon?"

"I don't recall ever meeting a nymph. They are very rare. I have heard of them. Some of what I heard could lend credence to what your father said." The green man commented. "I would have to meet one to say for sure." He shook his head, "You could consider the dryad and myself to be constructs as well. I have vague memories of being a man. Something changed me. I believe it was Yggdrasil's doing. And you could call him a god. According to some of the stories, all Ymir is a construct for the entertainment of the gods. Who knows?"

He then turned to Cu lain. "Would you bring me that rope? We best tie our prisoner. Wouldn't want to have him roaming about lost, would we?" Together they tied Prysivolar hands together leaving a short piece of rope to guide him with. The four headed for where they could see the others preparing a camp as the sky began to grow dark.

Crispin and Elgar had their heads bowed together as the young men approached. Drew was pacing a few feet away, trying to work off some of his impatience. The day was waning, and he wanted to be about the business of selecting and preparing a campsite. He had no time for lectures and if the expression on Crispin's face was any indicator, a lecture was forthcoming.

"This has been a long couple of days. I dare say none of us has slept since we began our trek through the dryad's grove." Crispin stood as he began. We still have a camp to prepare and watches to set. I'll be brief. After a battle, there is the necessity of studying it so you can learn from the errors and successes of both sides. What lessons can we take from this your first battle?"

"I'd say we whipped their ass," Eric responded.

"Sent them straight to Hel's realm." Drew chipped in.

Crispin looked the boys over. They were very young. The excitement of their victory was still pumping in their veins. Even as exhaustion tugged on their bodies, they felt that they were ready for more. He didn't want to shame them. For a fact, they had done well, but they needed to understand some things. "Alone we had no chance. We five would be feeding the dryad's grove not them. We were more than lucky this day. Even with surprise, we would have lost. And did we surprise them? With all the cover the dryad gave us, did we surprise them?"

Jae shook his head. He spoke softly. "No, it was not a complete surprise. The one with Catherine was surprised by it all, he was so lost in his lust. He hardly saw anything. But the other two ye-tann were getting prepared. They had caught something in the wind, so they were gathering the etunazi. They weren't ready, but they were not surprised."

"Well spoken." Elgar put in.

"We had help, and I'm glad of it. But we won, didn't we?" You could tell Eric was a bit puzzled. Were they about to be reamed for doing a good job? It seemed to him, trainers and teachers were too focused on errors and not on progress. This was his first battle and he carried some pride in the fact his arrows and arms accounted for more than one enemy death.

"Eric, your arrows didn't start flying till Elgar nudged you. You were so intent on what was happening to Catherine, you lost sight of the battle. The etunazi had moved ten feet before you struck a target. And you're the best archer present. As it was, we went to swords long before we should have. I had expected you to take down three before they were close enough for swords."

Crispin's words struck Eric like a dagger. Yes, he was too lost in trying to see what was happening to the girl to focus on his marksmanship. "Did Crispin say he was the best archer here?" Well, that was some salve for his wounded pride.

"Don't look so smug Drew" Crispin's attention turned to Drew. "You and Jae accounted for yourselves very well, until you threw down your bow and ran toward your death. That yetann wasn't slowed by your two arrows even with the loss of his eye. He had you. I saw your death as his greatsword began its arch down. If Cu lain hadn't thrown his knife at that beast causing him to hesitate, Jae would not have had the chance for his lucky shot. You would be dead and buried, to be mourned by your friends. Battle instructor Brand had told me of your wild charges. Wild charges like that may work on your fellow trainees. But, to battle-hardened warriors like those yetann we fought, they are not even a distraction." Crispin shook his head once more. "You're not alone. If the dryad hadn't tripped that first etunazi charging me, I would have joined you in the grave. You will not fight another battle like this one. Between the yetann Catherine took out, the one who the green man battled, and the interference provided by the dryad we fought a battle where we lost no one. I had expected to have lost at least two of you. It seems that in every battle I've fought I've lost at least one felagi (companion). Think on what I have said. You still have much to learn." Crispin paused. "You did well. I've seen older warriors falter worse in battle than you. Now let's prepare the camp. Drew you will sleep in Eric's tent tonight. Jae take Cu lain in with you. That will leave Drew's for Catherine. I will take first watch tonight. The regular rotation will follow me. Any questions?"

The young men shook their heads. The day's toils had finally hit them. They would be lucky to get all the work they had to accomplish finished before they dropped. As they moved off to their assigned duties the green man approached and asked. "What's for supper? I'm sure everyone is famished. The felag gave him a look that showed they had given no thought to a meal. The toils of the day had drained them of an appetite. Together they realized that their desired for sleep would not be complete for truly they were famished. The green man cocked his head. "Is there a pot among the spoils clean enough to cook in? Get it or make one clean enough. Fill it with water and place it on the fire. As it begins to boil break some handfuls of your jerky into it. I saw some field pots (a wild herb with large starchy roots) growing in the meadow. I'll gather some for the pot."

"I saw some ney roppa (cattails) downstream. The growing stalks should be tender this time of year. I'll go get a batch." Cu lain headed down to the stream. The thought of a good meal made his mouth water. He turned and headed downhill to where he knew they were.

Drew placed the pot of water he had intended for drinking on the fire. There was a full waterskin hanging from a branch where he had placed it to cool overnight, so drinking water was not going to be an issue. Jae and Eric began breaking up the jerky. A real meal. Yes, that was what was needed.

Catherine found herself alone holding the grasblett's rope. Wrapping what she held around the old goat's neck entered her mind, but she quickly dismissed it, no matter how satisfying that might be. She was relieved when Elgar took the rope from her hands and directed Prysivolar to sit on a log near the fire. Elgar offered him a drink and when Prysivolar was seated, he dropped the rope, gave the old man a stern look, and walked over to Catherine. He wiped the mouth of his waterskin took a swig of water, then wiped the mouth again before offering it to Catherine. She gladly drank the cool water. She hadn't realized how thirsty she was. Elgar grinned, watching as she lustfully chugged down the water. Now there was a woman to challenge any fuddy-duddies' perceptions. For his money, Elgar believed the world was in need of more women like this. Strong and able to take on the challenges of the world. If Crispin didn't ask for her to train with them, he would lose some status in Elgar's eyes.

*

Asgard was becoming visible in the clear night sky and the air was crisp as they finished the stew. Catherine sat between Elgar and Cu lain as she finished her share of supper. Her head was clear and her belly full. Something that had been missing in the weeks leading up to this night. She still had no idea why she had been kidnapped. The little she was able to glean from the grasblett only seemed to cloud the issue. From listening to Crispin and the others she gathered that the king of Alfheim would take the raid deep in his territory very seriously. If they so easily gained access to the hinterlands of his realm without a hint of warning until after the fact, what else could they accomplish? The yetann with the raiding party were especially troubling. Aside from a few raids on the borders of Vestan the yetann had been quiet. There was an unacknowledged peace between the folk and the yetann.

Catherine watched as the grasblett was led to his tent. At first, she thought it strange that he was untied and given the largest tent. Then she noticed how the tent's walls had various pots, pans, and metal utensils strung around them. If the old man attempted to leave his shelter the noise would alert more than the sentries.

She caught herself looking at Jae in the firelight. He was laughing at some joke Drew was telling when he looked toward her, and their eyes met. They held each other in a gaze and then embarrassed they both ducked their eyes. Catherine got up and excused herself, claiming, truthfully, exhaustion. She slipped into her assigned tent. Thankful for the felagi's kindness for this was the first shelter she had had for more five-days than she could remember. Wrapping herself in a blanket she was soon asleep.

*

When Jae grew silent in the middle of Drew's telling of his favorite story. Drew turned to see what had caught Jae's attention. Drew being Drew started to see how bright a red he could bring to Jae's ears. Then he thought better of it. Besides, Jae's ears couldn't glow in the dark, so he would never be able to tell just how red they had become.

The camp soon grew quite with only Crispin and the green man sitting under the stars. "Tell me," The green man began. "What brought your small band here to battle the yetann and etunazi alone?"

"It was never my plan to battle the raiders," Crispin answered. "When we came across the raiders' trail, I sent a felag to backtrack the trail, while the rest of my tyge followed the raiders. It was noon when we entered the village of Boer Akarn. I sent Elgar, Drew, and Jae to scout the surrounding area. I then noticed a man exiting the healer's house from a door that had been obviously torn from its hinges. He was carrying a small box. I arrested him, sighting the king's law against scavenging a victim's property. Seeing that the village had no place to lock him up, after a stern warning I released the man to Elder Oysten's custody, seeing that he was lodging at the elder's home. Then I assigned a felag to guard the house and keep it from being disturbed further. I took the little box and locked it in a closet that had a key then I nailed it shut and placed the king's seal on it.

I requisitioned two horses and sent my two best riders to alert the garrison at Goa Vollar to the raider's presence.

Elgar reported that the raiders seemed to know exactly who they were looking for. The healer's house was the only one attacked. They had passed by several others on the way to it. Somehow, they knew where to find their intended victim.

As we followed the raiders from the town, we came across a woman wailing over her dead husband. He and a dead cow with

56

a rear quarter removed lay in their mingling blood. I sent Asleif back to the village to bring the poor woman some aid. Nine of us then continued behind the raiders.

Days later we came to where the yetann and etunazi joined a group of pyris at an aspen grove. Four were sent to backtrack that group and report to the field officer from Goa Vollar their findings.

Instead of retracing the path of the pyris porters, the group headed toward the north. I thought then they were heading toward an escape through the wilds and then south. That seemed strange but not knowing what motivated the raid I couldn't judge their course of action."

"I believe a daughter of mine decided to misdirect their path." The dryad interjected. "She and her sister thought the maiden would have a better chance to escape if I were involved."

"So, the grove where the body was, is your daughter?" Crispin asked.

"Yes, she is. It was she who alerted me to the bandits and then directed them north to my valley." The dryad confirmed.

"I had wondered why the band headed north. I knew of no way out of the mountain range they were entering." Crispin said.

"There is only the pass to Niflheim, a western pass to the next valley and the way they came in, south down the mountain." The dryad informed him.

"This area is almost unknown to us, being part of the wild. Some of the ancient maps give some indication of the terrain, but they are more art than information." Crispin acknowledged before continuing his answer to the green man's question. "If we had not lost contact with the raider's trail, I would have sent Jae down the mountain to bring the king's forces to deal with the raiders. But, once we entered this valley, well I believe a dryad had her own plans."

"I'm sorry, I was afraid you would madly rush to the maiden's rescue and die in the effort. I've seen men do such foolish things.

I also knew Karl was coming down the mountain. Karl is the name you've chosen, isn't it, my dear?" replied the dryad.

Karl, the green man, nodded his head in the affirmative. Then the dryad continued. "I knew with his help your felag could mount a successful rescue. It was apparent that the maiden's time was running out. The grasblett's potions were having effects on his yetann that he had never expected. They may have turned against him even if I hadn't interfered. I can't tell. I hope my interference did not endanger the child more." The dryad grew silent.

"They may have escaped with her if you and your daughters had not involved yourselves in her rescue," Crispin told the dryad.

They then sat in silence until almost the end of Crispin's watch, when Karl stood and told Crispin. "I believe I will spend the rest of this night with the dryad." He then turned and walked into the grove.

"I was wondering if you would sleep with me this night." The dryad chided him.

"I didn't want to appear rude. I wanted to give the man the opportunity to ask his own questions. Though to tell the truth I'm glad he didn't. I might not remember what he would ask." Karl told the dryad. "Might you share a memory of us before we share dreams?" he requested.

"I will." She responded. "Seat yourself, my dear. Let your roots mingle with mine."

"Dear dryad will you tell me your name?" He asked as he seated himself and began to extend his roots to mingle with hers.

"No." She said. "You need to remember my name. You need to find me in your heart. Even if our hearts are no longer flesh. I need you to remember me."

He sat silently in the dark as their roots intermingled. As their roots intertwined, he teased her for a memory. "One of my favorites." The thought echoed through his mind.

*

They stood in a large bright hall. The music was lively, full of joy. He asked her to dance and she took his hand. They moved to the music as they whispered into each other's ears. The music slowed, and they clung closer together. Their lips met for a moment. When the music paused, she pulled him out into the night and wrapping her arms around him. She kissed him, giving herself up to the passion. He pulled her close and held her. Then hand in hand they left the party and entered his private room. Was this a shared dream or a memory? He couldn't tell. "give me more." he begged.

He felt a wave of emotion, something between joy and regret. "No darling no more. I could not stand it. If you find your half of this, I will know it's a memory and not a wished-for dream. For the rest of the night, it's only dreams we share."

CHAPTER 4

From learned Alphere's first year lectures on required knowledge of a warrior

The Dragon's Spine mountain range dominates Midgard. The spine runs West to East across Northern Midgard for thousands of miles before it turns South forming the Eastern border of Midgard. North of the spine is Niflheim a land of ice. The Spine's highest peaks occur where the Spine turns South. There may be passes over the mountains in this area, but why would anyone care? They would only lead to death. If the cold doesn't kill you the ice giants or great white bears will. South and to the east of the Spine is Vedrfolnir, the great desert. Some legends tell of a great lost city of mirrors somewhere in the eastern desert.

*

Light was just peaking over the eastern mountains when Karl spoke again. "That was a wonderful night. Though I don't believe we slept at all. I want to spend the summer like this. Intermingled with you, dearest dryad. I don't want to leave you ever again. Even if I remember nothing more about you. I know we belong together."

"Yes, my darling. I've missed you so." The dryad responded. "But I know."

"Yes," he interrupted, "I have to go with them. We need to determine if this could be a threat against our existence. I need to discover if this is an old enemy or the shadow of one. I tend to believe it is only a shadow and not a real threat. I can't believe any group could survive unchanged for as long as I was away."

"They do not appear to be of the same lot as before." She replied. "They are imitators, I believe. But the danger this huldra present is to more than just us. The world we live in. The folk who live in it. You know we have a responsibility to them as well."

"I seem to remember a very similar conversation, my love," Karl told her. "Isn't that strange? The memory is there but it is so dreamlike, the edges are vague."

"I understand. Many of mine are that way. There are some from long ago that are very clear. And others little more than dreams." The dryad told him.

As he withdrew his roots, she added "Promise me this time that you won't be gone so long. Return to me as soon as you can. I'd travel with you if I could."

"I know you would." Karl rose to his feet. "I hope to spend this next winter with our roots intertwined."

*

Cu lain woke in a panic. "How could he forget!" His head bounced off the canvas of the tent. Jae was on watch so Cu lain's struggled to get out of the tent didn't wake him, much to Cu lain's relief. Still, Cu lain was cursing himself. He had forgotten the old man's potion book. He knew that it had to be somewhere in the old seior's baggage. Why hadn't he thought about it yesterday while the felag searched through the spoils? Prysivolar didn't seem worried about it, so he must know where it was and possibly have it well hid. That book might be some help in spoiling the plans of those who wanted Catherine. It could hold a trace of where and who they were. He suspected that Catherine could garner many useful things from it if she could decipher it. That's something he would never be able to do. He had watched with envy as the felag sorted through Prysivolar's papers. They read most of them with ease. The ones written in other languages didn't stop them if one couldn't read it, another could, or if that failed together, they could puzzle out some meaning. The pen scratches were meaningless to him. What little his mother had taught him of reading he seemed to have forgotten.

Cu lain rushed out of the tent only to turn and reach inside to grab the robe he had forgotten. One night in a warm tent and now he wanted a robe to keep warm.

As he settled into his robe. "His robe, that sounded nice." It had been a long time since he had anything, he could consider his. Across the fire from him, Jae and Catherine were sitting close to each other. They were almost, but not quite touching. It was obvious they had been sitting together for some time. As Catherine stirred the fire she glanced up and noticed Cu lain. She gave him a warm smile.

"Good morning friend Cu lain," She said. Cu lain noticed Jae move a little further away from her. If she noticed, she didn't show it.

"What strange mating rituals the vanir must have." He thought. "But, what did he have to compare them to. In his native city men usually bought their brides, following more the customs of the yetann than the folk. Any custom would be better than that."

"Morning to you," Here Cu lain hesitated, "Friend Cu lain?" she had said. She tossed that out without a second thought. He smiled and finished, "friend Catherine."

Jae stood and looked at him. Then he stepped closer. Cu lain wasn't sure what to make of his approach, was he jealous? Jae reached out his hand and placed Cu lain's hand on his elbow while he took hold of Cu lain's. With a shake, he said, "Shall we be friends too?"

Given pause by this strange ritual, Cu lain bowed his head then deciding that he should act like the free man he now was, looked Jae in the eyes, and in a husky whisper said, "Yes, I would be honored."

"Why don't you and Jae go down to the stream and see if you can catch some of the trout, I saw in it yesterday? That would make the breakfast I'm hungry for." Catherine asked.

This and the rumble in his own stomach made Cu lain almost forget what had startled him awake. "No, I mean wait. We need to find his book."

"Whose book?" Jae asked.

"The old grasblett's. The book of potions. It has to be somewhere in his gear. Where did you lay his stuff?" Cu lain looked about trying to figure out where it could be. "Crispin said something about taking his potions to be studied so someone could figure ways of counteracting them. The book has all the information about the potions. It might even have the antidotes for them."

"We put his gear in that chest over there. Let's go look through it and see if we find that book. I don't recall seeing a book in the stuff. I did see a plank of wood with a cloth cover." Jae responded.

"That's it!" Cu lain almost shouted. "He called it a book, but all I ever saw was that plank of wood. Except when he was using it, then it had strange lines and marks that moved across it."

They walked over to the chest and Jae opened it. After some digging, Jae pulled out the cloth covered plank of wood. He turned it over in his hand and pulled back the flap of cloth covering it. There it was, just a piece of polished wood as far as he could tell. He handed it to Cu lain with a shrug. Then he heard a squeal and looked up to see Prysivolar twisting Catherine's arm behind her back while holding a knife (where did he get that knife?) to her throat.

"It's poisoned, you know." The old man said. "Don't try anything girl, wouldn't want to cut you by accident, now would we?"

The look on the old man's face was grim and determined. Jae and Cu lain both froze at the word poison. Catherine started to struggle again when the old man added. "Your lorki can't react fast enough to save you, wench. It's a very fast acting poison."

Catherine stopped her struggling as her lorki began to piece together the nature of the poison on the knife's blade. It was indeed very fast acting. A scratch on her arm might be dealt with after days of struggle. A cut on her throat would spread to her mind and heart much too quickly for her to counteract it.

Jae saw Eric and Drew walking back up the hill with the string of trout they had left to catch on Drew's belt. He turned to face

Prysivolar, hoping his momentary look down the hill did not alert him to what Jae hoped would be help. Now if only Eric and Drew noticed the danger and calmly acted, they could move into place, and Eric could pierce the old man's head with an arrow and end this trouble.

"You've no place to run you know," Jae told him. "You can't hope to get away. If you kill Catherine you've lost your leverage. And besides that, you're lost. You would wander this wilderness 'till a bear ate you. Your little knife probably wouldn't get through a bear's fur let alone pierce his hide."

A look of doubt crossed Prysivolar's face. When he had heard Cu lain yammering about his precious tablet he had panicked. That was his private treasure, he had spent all his fortune for it and indentured himself to those dreadful huldra. All to gain that ancient artifact and the key to access the knowledge hidden within it. Everything he had worked for, all the honor he was to receive for aiding the elite of Torion. The power that wealth would bring him. All lost. He had foolishly played his last hidden hand. A movement out of the corner of his eye alerted him to someone approaching. He pulled Catherine in front of him as he turned and saw Drew drawing his bow. Drew nodded to his right and when Prysivolar turned his head in that direction he saw Eric standing with his bow drawn ready to kill him. Then he heard that cursed green man say, "You wouldn't want to die the way you would at the dryad's hand if you harm that young woman."

Prysivolar moved his knife from Catherine's throat and released her arm as he backed away from her.

What an idiot he was letting that wretch bully him into leaving his safe home. How many years had he lost studying the ancient knowledge? How easy his life would have been if only he had not taken this journey. Well, they would never torment his secrets from him! He looked around one last time. Then before anyone could move to stop him, he plunged the knife in his chest. As they watched, he sank to the ground, fell over, and with his eyes staring into the sky, took his last breath.

"How did he get that knife!" Crispin demanded as he approached the camp. He and Elgar had been scouting the path they were planning to take down the mountain, today. Now there had been a serious breach in discipline. At first look, it appeared that Jae had neglected his duty to the felag and Catherine and had let the old grasblatt gain possession of a knife; a poisoned knife at that. Such carelessness was unlike Jae, but Crispin had not failed to notice the chemistry between him and the young woman that could account for his failure. This incident could cost Jae a career in the king's service and the king a valuable man.

Cu lain was staring at his dead tormentor. The bane of his youth. It was hard to believe the man who held title to him was dead. There was no one in the world who could claim rights to Cu lain any longer. The day might come that he could travel back to Tawnia to visit his mother's grave. As the issue of where Prysivolar had gained possession of the knife swirled around him, Cu lain was lost in, was it joy or relief? Cu lain could not tell. Looking at the corpse he noticed that the robe the old man was wearing was hanging strangely. It had fallen open as if part of its structure was damaged. The old robe was almost identical to the one he wore. He fingered the front of his robe. Down the left side of the opening was a stiff rod that appeared to strengthen the attachment means of the fastening loops. That stiffener appeared to be missing from the left side of the robe Prysivolar was wearing. It was now that the conversation concerning the knife penetrated his mind. Opening the front of his robe he noticed the top of a rod in a small slot near the top of his coat. This was what held the front stiff. He could barely grasp the top of the rod. But with a little effort, he pulled it out. It appeared to be a half-fingers breath round piece of black wood about two hands long. There was a line half a hand down from the top. He pulled it all the way out. Grasping the top and bottom of the rod he gave a little twist to the left and pulled out a knife just like the one the old grasblett had been holding. Holding the knife up he said. "I believe I have an identical knife here."

The camp grew silent as the group turned and looked at the wicked blade Cu lain held. Catherine left Jae's side and asked. "May I hold the blade?" Cu lain handed the knife to her. She carefully brought the blade near her face and inhaled through her open mouth. She crinkled her nose and made a face. "Yes, this blade is covered in the same poison as the other."

"I inspected those robes," Elgar said with a puzzled look on his face. "I thought they were just a style of Seior robes from the south. I had seen robes like these at the port in Kalfa. The formal military coats of the Duchy have stays much like these. Who would have thought an old grasblett's robes would be an assassin's coat?"

Crispin shook his head, then gave Jae an apologetic look for the reaming he had been about to give him. They needed to look through that old grasblett's things a lot more carefully. He would need to carry this lesson back to the academy. The king's bodyguards would also need to know just how easy it was to carry an undetected blade into a room.

"That's an assassin's blade for sure," Elgar noted. "See how it has no edge, just a needle-sharp point. Used by someone practiced, it could be slipped through several layers of cloth, prick the skin and hardly leave a mark. With the right poison, it could be a day before the victim died."

A shudder ran through Jae. He had forgotten that the old man had asked to leave his tent to attend to his business. That's what he had said "his business" meaning he wanted to defecate in private. Something Jae was glad to allow. The evening before Crispin had no difficulty allowing the old grasblett his privacy to relieve himself. So, this morning Jae thought nothing about it. And then Catherine had come out of her tent. All other thoughts fled Jae's mind when she sat beside him almost touching. They had been talking about Jae's family when Cu lain came bolting out of his tent.

Elgar stooped over the dead man and with his fingers closed his eyes. "Can't bear to be stared at by a dead man" he said. Then he ruffled through the front of the old man's robe. He pulled out a stay from the other side of the robe. "Here Cu lain this will make your robe right. I dare say Crispin will want both those assassin's blades locked way." He handed the stay to Cu lain. He then pulled the dagger from the dead man's chest. As he did, he noticed that the blood was already congealed. "Stopped his heart right quick." He observed.

Glancing up he stated "Drew, you and Eric can stop staring. Get about making breakfast or we won't be on our way before noon. What with another body to bury." Then he turned to Jae as he wiped the blood from the blade and placed it in its sheaf. "Grab a shovel, you've dawdled long enough."

With the dryads help, he and Jae would make short work burying the old grasblatt. Then they wolfed down what was left of breakfast.

Crispin had wanted an early start, but all thought of that disappeared with the grasblett's death. In his planning, he had allowed for Catherine and Cu lain to be able to sleep longer. He felt that after their ordeal extra sleep would be appreciated. Catherine had surprised him that morning. She was up and warming her hands at the fire as he and Elgar started to scout their trail down the mountain.

It was obvious to him that he needed to reassess what they needed to take with them. He had thought that the grasblett's chest could be left behind and forgotten. It had appeared to him to be nothing but cryptic journals and an old man's keepsakes. That funny piece of wood that was a dagger had changed his mind. They had to take the chest and all its contents. Someone more studied than he would need to decipher its contents. Now, what should he leave behind? Could he pack two of the prepared food jars in with the other things in the chest and leave the two packs he had so carefully prepared? If Cu lain was right, and there was no reason to doubt him, more knowledge resided in that plank of wood than they could gain from a few jars of tainted food. That would lighten everyone's load and let them carry a few more articles of clothing just in case they found any of the pyris on their journey.

Eric and Drew had the fish and the mashed field pot cakes fried, when Jae returned alone from burying the grasblett. "Where's Elgar? Did you bury him, too?" Drew called out.

Jae just shook his head. "Elgar found something on the old man, he told me he needed to wash the stink off and headed for the stream. I was hungry and smelling that fish now I'm famished! I'll grab a bowl and tell you what I know after I've had something to eat."

He started to help himself to the fish when Drew slapped his hand away. "Let the læknir get hers first. You unmannered lout what would your mother say?" Drew said with a smile as he watched Jae's ears redden. Jae's ears grew even redder when he heard Catherine's laughter.

Much to Drew's satisfaction, Jae's whole face turned the most exquisite scarlet when Catherine tussled Jae's hair as she stepped between them. She still had a bite or two of her breakfast in a bowl. "Drew likes to put you on the spot doesn't he Jae?" She said with a smile. "This is my second helping, and there's some covered by the fire to keep warm. Grab the fresh ones before Drew eats them. What is it, Drew? Thirds or fourth helpings?" She added as he pushed Drew over to make room for her to set between them. Drew moved over so they weren't touching. But Jae sat where he was, so red, he almost was glowing, but his thigh was touching hers and he wasn't moving. Catherine started to move over some, but she didn't. The two looked at each other and Catherine's cheeks took on a slight reddish hue as if she might have gotten a little too much sun. They both were feeling awkward, neither willing to retreat, but not sure what to do about it. They were rescued by Elgar walking up examining something in his hand.

It was Cu lain who spoke first. "That's the ring Prysivolar always wore on a chain around his neck. The few times I actually saw it was while he prepared to use his book. He would close the door when he saw me watching."

"It was on his left little finger when I saw it. Still had feces on it. I think he must have retrieved it this morning when he went out. He didn't have the stomach to swallow it as it was and the commotion about his strange wooden plank stopped him from doing something about it. So, he left us an unintended gift." Elgar concluded.

*

As final preparation was made for their journey down the mountain, the green man walked over to the dryad. "Well, it is goodbye for now. I will try to be back before winter, my friend." He said.

"That yetann kilt is much too large for you. I can't even see your knees it's so long. I can see Catherine's. Yours are as nice to look upon." The smiling voice of the wind teased.

"I have to wear something. That bit of bark tore off before the battle even started. I needed something to cover me." He responded.

"Well you didn't have to grow everything, now did you?" She asked

"It's a habit." Was the gruff reply.

"Well, my dear I know with a little effort you could grow a fine kilt." She teased again.

"It takes an effort to grow such things and then you have to maintain them. That's the reason I didn't grow hair. I hope you don't mind. The lack of hair that is." He responded.

Well, I suppose you have a fine enough head to not need hair. What color would you make it if you did? My sweet." She questioned.

"I'm going to miss you, dear, dryad. I will surely miss you." The green man told her. "The camp is ready to go, so, so must I."

"Hurry home." Whispered the wind.

CHAPTER 5

From learned Alphere's first year lectures on required knowledge of a warrior

A perfunctory knowledge of the different kinds of Yetann will be helpful to a warrior. There are Three kinds of yetann extant in Midgard. That is unless you include the mythical haf yetann. Imagine a yetann swimming in the ocean. The idea is myth. Ask Ljot Jartasen if you are curious about them. To continue with the yetann you may have to deal with. The great yetann are found west of Vestan and Northeim which still experience random raids. Their cousins the idalyon and the plains yetann are counted as the same kind. The plains yetann is found in the Kentta as such you will likely never deal with them. The great yetann are the largest of the yetann standing up to 12 feet tall and over a thousand pounds. Then come the mountain yetann. They attain a height of eight feet and a weight of up to six hundred pounds. The east and western mountain yetann have maintained a close relationship with each other through the aid of their pilgrimages between the two. The skogr or forest yetann are the smallest yetann seldom growing over six feet in height and three hundred pounds. They can be found in the eastern reaches of the Obygo.

*

The camp was bustling in the early morning light. It was still dark when Crispin had roused them. He was determined to make good time today. All that they could pack the night before had been packed. There were cold fish and leftover field pot for breakfast. No fire and no hot food.

Where yesterday they had followed the stream, today they

would cut across the country and not follow its winding course. Crispin figured that it could save ten or more miles of travel, a day saved. He was concerned with the weight they had to carry. The grasblett's chest, pots, and pans, jars of tainted food, yetann armor and additional clothing that they might need (those were being carried at Catherine's insistence. The pyris they would encounter on their journey down the hill being her concern. All added to gear and other supplies they were already carrying slowed them down. He was thankful that Karl insisted on carrying the armor, the clothing, and even the potion laden food. That moved most of the extra weight to him. Then with Catherine insisting on carrying her own tent and the pots and pans and Cu lain carrying two tents and a few other supplies, he was able to send two of his felag out scouting without any burden on them. That meant they could cover twice the ground than the rest of the group could. And that added security to the group and the opportunity to possibly gather in the fleeing pyris.

Jae and Eric had left an hour before scouting the path the others would be following. Then they began their crisscross of the valley covering as much ground as they could. They were looking for sign. Sign of possible danger, a bear or yetann, or even a mountain cat. And sign of pyris lost in this wilderness.

Crispin and Elgar lead the way. They would exchange packs every shadow and the one with the lighter pack would move ahead of the group, looking for anything that might hinder their journey. Twice they had to circle rock outcroppings. Once they had to skirt a beaver with its dam across a stream feeding into the dryad's.

Today Drew was given the tasks of watching their back trail and keeping the new members of their party moving. When the green man told Drew that he had an eagle watching over them and there was no need for constantly looking over his shoulder, he let himself be drawn into the conversation Catherine was insisting on starting.

For most of a shadow Drew was able to keep the conversation centered on Jae and his adventures as children and young adults. Most of which ended with Jae in a humorous incident. Almost unaware of the fact, Drew told of how his father had died in a mining accident when he had barely been weaned. He then told of how difficult it had been when he was six summers old and the man who became his step-father began courting his mother. The trouble he caused in the dzwerc school lead him to be placed in the vanir school where he met Jae. If he could have, Drew would have blushed when he told how his step-father won him over and helped him through the grief he had been holding after the death of his father.

Much to his surprise, he related how much he valued his friendship with Jae. Though he teased Jae mercilessly, he knew that in Jae his back was always guarded. He then admonished Catherine and Cu lain, since he was standing there, that if a word of this ever reached Jae's ears they would pay dearly!

Catherine laughed at this, to Cu lain's confusion.

It was then that Catherine opened up about her own story. She told of never knowing her mother. How abandoned she felt when her father sent her way with widow Sturlasda. How she had resented the widow for stealing her away from her father. The years of kindness that the widow showed as she was taught the art of healing. She told of the loss of her second mother. The widow was beloved by most of the village having been in the village of Boer Akarn for over fifty years. No one in the village remembered the widow ever being young. The oldest woman in the village told Catherine of her moving into the house she shared with Catherine.

Cu lain walked silently, listening to the banter between Catherine and Drew. He wondered if he ever would understand this culture in which he found himself transplanted. The ease with which they teased and traded stories was a mystery to Cu lain. The only companion he had ever known was his mother.

They walked in silence for a time. Then Catherine gently urged Cu lain to tell what had brought a tear to his eye. So, he told of roaming the forest with his mother and at times his father. The joys of the family picnics. The warmth he observed between his father and his mother. He related the shock and despair as he watched his mother mourn the death of his father. And then the end of his childhood as he and his mother were sold into slavery to pay his father's debt. Catherine touched his arm. He noticed tears in her eyes as he raised his head to look at her. On her other side, he saw Drew's sober face contemplating the fate of a child born in such an unforgiving culture.

The green man and Crispin trudged on ahead of them giving no clue that they had been listening.

The band walked silently, the conversation changing to thought. It was several shadows before anyone spoke but the birds.

Around noon they stopped and unburdened themselves of their packs. As they sat resting. Drew began to speak to Cu lain. He spoke so quietly that the rest of the group felt like they were intruding on a private conversation. "I've been told," he said, "that you saved my life. That won't go unpaid."

"I did nothing." Cu lain responded.

"Oh, you did. The flight of your little knife distracted the yetann." Drew told him. "I have it. I picked it up where it fell, intending to immediately return it. Well, Crispin gave me a lecture. This time I listened. I kept your knife as a meditation focus. I want to exchange this blade for your blade" He said as he extended a small knife toward Cu lain. "As a felagi token. I keep your blade as a reminder not to wildly charge an enemy. You keep mine as a reminder of my pledge of friendship."

Cu lain was stunned. Where did this come from? This pledge of friendship. This exchange of blades? Was Drew's unseen meditation so powerful that it required so profound an action? Cu lain realized that if he took this blade, he would be bound to a code of honor that he only vaguely glimpsed. He was not such a fool as to not take it. The words jumbled in his mouth. "Jarl... ah, friend Drew. I, I am, honored is not as fine a word as I need. I will stumble learning your ways. I, Thank you, my felagi. Is that right?"

Drew gave Cu lain a sage look as Cu lain took the blade. He slapped Cu lain on the back. Then he turned, walked over to a large rock that he climbed up before he sat looking out into the distance, silent.

This confused Cu lain even more. He looked over to Catherine. Who shook her head, before she said, "That dzwerc is a confusing fellow. You think you've figured him out and he surprises you with something like this."

Karl walked up to Cu lain and patted his shoulder and said "Relax into it like you do with your lorki. You'll do fine." He then sat down and ate his share of the cold lunch.

Drew sat looking out into the distance. He couldn't say what had drawn him this rock outcrop. But this was the place he should be. He planned on returning Cu lain's knife. Somewhere within him the desire, the need to keep it emerged. He was uncertain about what drove that need he was not sure. Some of the odd mutterings of his grandfather had drifted into his mind while they had traveled down the mountain. Traditions and rites of the ancient dzwerc that his grandfather had tried to pass down. An ancient chant his grandfather had taught him circled in his mind. His distress at having pledged himself to this konkur receded in his mind and he found himself in the elsewhere, A place he only knew from the myths his grandfather imparted.

The world changed and he saw or knew. His eyes had little to do with what he saw. Shades and shadows, raw iron, a coal seam deep below where he sat, off to the west steel. Man crafted metal. This far in the wilderness. Strange.

Then it was over. He once more sat on an outcrop of sandstone. His felag and the others eating their noon meal. His grandfather had tried to explain how the ancient dzwerc miners could follow the seams of iron and coal that they so often were charged with finding. Now some of what he had taken as nonsense he understood.

He left the rock and joined the others.

CHAPTER 6

There is an old saying that instructs one on how to deal with each variety of yetann.

When you encounter a mountain yetann say "arm maetipp" that is blessings of the peaks. And you will pass in peace.

When you encounter a forest yetann say "hea jaht auvaern" that is, have good hunting honorable one. And you may share meat.

When you encounter a great yetann let him speak while you prepare for battle.

*

As his contingent of men marched back to Boar Akarn, Thane Awrick Baldursen's thoughts rattled about his head. He was concerned for Crispin and the felag with him. His contingent had followed their trail until the rain began. Then three days of rain wiped out any sign of the raiders or Crispin's felag. He assigned two of his best officers with two tyge to remain at their last known location, an aspen grove where two unnamed streams joined to create the Laek Gritter.

He had decided to return to Boar Akarn with the remainder of his men. He needed to question the tinker who was apprehended as he tried to gain entrance to the victim's home a second time. He knew his tyge and the felag Crispin had left behind would keep the house secure. But this raid was especially disturbing. What did the presence of etunazi and yetann portend? Was there some new alliance in the works? How did these raiders intrude so far into Alfheim without being confronted?

The questions seemed to multiply. Was there an enemy in the mountains they had not encountered before? What especially worried Awrick was that this raid appeared to indicate that there were enemies hidden within Alfheim.

Awrick was feeding his mount Yorliek a measure of grain while they took a brief rest. Yes, he knew that he was spoiling Yorliek. But that horse had saved him more than once and besides, he liked the stallion.

"Thane beg your pardon, but you are needed."

"Yes, Arin, what do you need?" Recognizing the voice of his aid he turned to address him. Standing behind his aid was a young vanir. She looked like she had been running for days. Her legs trembled with exhaustion. "Arin get the fra a place to sit! She looks to need one." He ordered. The young woman tried to speak but he hushed her until she was seated and looked to have caught her breath.

"What is your name and what brings you to us in such a rush?" Awrick questioned her.

She ducked her head and replied. "I am trainee Asleif of jarl Crispin's tyge. I was left in Boar Akarn with the felag. Carorek our point and Herr Lyos sent me to inform you that they discovered Asvald the tinker was no longer in elder Oysten's house. He apparently left in the night. Herr Lyos sent Carorek and his felag to attempt to track him and sent me to inform you." She paused to once more gain her breath. Asleif was rather proud of herself. She had made better time than she could believe. The telling of her run should impress the other felagi. Possibly even Jae when he heard of it. And she would be sure he did.

"Damn!" she jumped at the thane's roar. She almost sprinted away when he fixed his gaze at her.

Seeing Asleif almost jump to her feet at his roar, Awrick took a deep breath and calmed himself before he spoke again. "I'm not angry at you fra Asleif. Hopefully, Carorek and his felag have already captured him, a part of a night would not be too great a lead. Now, will it?"

"The trouble is sir," Asleif explained. "We did not discover he was gone until at least two days after. Herr Lyos went to inquire of elder Oysten about some hams he had for sale. After agreeing on a price for three Herr Lyos asked to see the tinker. He believed he could perhaps persuade the man to explain his actions. The elder offered Herr Lyos a mead and started asking if the scouts could use some bread. He told his daughter Frida to go fetch the tinker at which point she confessed in tears that he had left the house through her window. When I left, elder Oysten was chained to the hitching post in front of Biorn's pub."

The picture of the pompous elder chained to a hitching post amused Awrick, but not enough for him to let it show. They were still a three-day march to Boar Akarn. Would Lyos leave the man there until he returned? Knowing Lyos, he probably would. That would most likely outrage the village. Would that lead to action against the king's men by others in the village? He thought Lyos and his tyge able to handle the villagers if there were. He decided not to take the horse and rush to the village. Maybe when he arrived with his men the elder would be more willing to cooperate than he was when his dirfylk first arrived. "Arin fetch a horse for fra Asleif. After such a run she will ride with us back to Boar Akarn." He then handed her his water bag. "Rest while you can fra. We will be moving again shortly."

*

Trestein, like its name suggested, was a stone house in the forest. The old castle seemed to squat on a ridge almost lost in the trees. The owner seemed unconcerned with upkeep. The stone walls were covered with moss and lichen. Wild grape and other vines covered the south side of the building where the ancient gate stood open. A trail led down the hill to the better maintained village.

The twenty or so buildings were surrounded by a wood palisade. Its single gate faced north toward the old castle. That gate also stood open, though two guards in the green and gray family colors stood at the gate. You could see places where the palisade had recently been repaired. The rumors of a yetann raid had reached the village not two days ago. Two buildings stood outside the wooden wall. The mill which supplied the lumber that financed the noble family and the village, and the market where fresh produce was traded for flour and other goods this village did not produce.

The villagers were thankful that the Hilmir was not a greedy man. He barely charged his tenants' rent. The low rent and the plentiful trees meant that they were better fed and housed than many who lived on wealthier estates.

The old gold mine, the reason the great great-grandsire of the family located here still produced a few ounces of gold each year. Half belonged to the Hilmir and half went into the village treasury providing for maintenance and guards. The steward who served the Hilmir was an honest and hardworking man who had served their lord and the village for over fifty years.

The Hilmar was seldom home. He served the king in Arnarhvall. The villagers took a certain pride in the old man who they served. His father had at first discouraged his son's interest in the lorki and magic. But seeing his son's determination he had sent him to study at Virkiflyot. Now he was a well-respected Seior.

The castle cook, wife of the steward, was at the market today. The master had arrived two weeks before. His mind, occupied by some esoteric subject. He had tried to enlighten two of the villagers who greeted him the day of his arrival. They excused themselves as soon as they deemed polite, their heads aching from the confusing conversation on a subject, they had no talent or interest in. This had not bothered Seior Lyos, he had become used to the quick departure of those uninitiated in the arcane arts. He had laughed to himself when the villagers departed recognizing that at their polite greeting, he had launched into his lecture mode, which only the most devout students did not sleep through.

Seior Lyos had returned to his estate to have time away from the bustle of the capital and college. He recently acquired some artifacts and desired time alone with them. He had brought several others with him. He couldn't travel without at least five artifacts even though only one had ever worked for him. He still attempted to activate them.

This day the steward and his wife were in the village. She was looking for some fresh lamb. Her lord had mentioned his hunger for some of her lamb stew and her husband had been politely asked to help her find some. One guard stood just inside the castle door in an alcove placed there for that purpose long ago. The others had been dismissed for the day. The Hilmir desired that the building be as silent as possible. A difficult feat even with no people present. The young swallows kept up a constant cry for more food as their parents swooped through the air capturing insects for their meal.

Seior Lyos sat at the table that held the one artifact that had ever responded to him. What looked like an ancient mirror was a scrying glass. He had placed it in direct sunlight the day before knowing from long practice that this enhanced its abilities. Today in a darkened room he sat trying to see where the kidnapped maiden might be. Being a little over a five-day's journey from the king's hunting lodge he had heard the news days before most others in the area would. It didn't hurt that he had traveled part of the way to his estate with the king. Awrick had been heading to his hunting lodge hoping to surprise the students with his presence. That hope had been dashed by the raid. Not knowing where the raiders were headed, the commander of the garrison at Goa Vollar had sent riders to warn the area of the yetann presence.

As he studied the ancient glass, he noticed a faint pattern north and east of lake Vollar. Suddenly, as he tried to bring that area into closer view, a point of light flared. For a moment it almost lit the room with its intensity. Then it faded until only a bright point appeared. Some ancient artifact must have been activated. Lyos knew that had to be it. He was so excited that he almost danced. He had never seen anything like this.

Whatever artifact that lit up his glass it was powerful. And Lyos knew that anything that powerful was a danger. He must warn the king! He called for his steward and when he did not appear, Lyos remembered he had sent him on an errand. Well, he should be back soon. That gave time for him to decide what to bring with him. It also gave time for Lyos to decide where he would find the king.

CHAPTER 7

From learned Alphere's first year lectures on required knowledge of a warrior

The pyris are best known for their large, upturned canines that give the appearance of tusks or gith as the pyris call them. Their clans and tribes are scattered over the planet. Their native language is known as Kanader. Unlike the other languages of Midgard, it requires a talent for melody for an outsider to develop skill in Kanader. Some tribes have allied with the different human races. While others have allied with the various yetann clans. There is a scattering of independent pyris states as well.

*

Valmi squatted outside the thicket of brambles. The little female had run into the brambles to avoid his attentions. If he had some food it would be easier to entice her out, but he didn't have any. A fact his stomach was reminding him of now. But if he left to search for food, she might avoid him altogether. And she wouldn't want that, now would she. When they were that young, they hardly knew what they wanted. A little dalliance with him was just what she needed. Well, it was what he needed. She was a pretty little thing. He had been eyeing her for some time now. But, with a full belly and the other pyris around, the desire to have her did not drive him as it did now. "Come child, I won't hurt you. Let's go find something to eat. I saw some ney roppa sprouts by the steam. Maybe we can catch some fish to go with them."

"Go away, I didn't like the way you touched me." Came a trembling voice from the thicket.

"I only want to teach you to purr. Oh, you'll purr, yes, you'll purr. You'll like what we will do. Oh yes, sweet one. Come out, we'll go find some food, and then we'll teach you to purr." This line of seduction had worked for Valmi before. It might well work again.

"You promise you'll stop if I say too?" Came the voice from the brambles. "I am so very hungry. Promise we'll eat first."

"Yes, of course, we'll eat first. Purring's so much better on a full stomach, my sweet." He lied.

*

Jae had heard the sing-song voices of the pyris long before Cu lain did. Crispin had sent them out together to see if they could find any of the pyris who had scattered from the camp during the battle. So far, they had not found any, and this was the second day of their journey down the mountain. Jae couldn't understand what was being said. It sounded like a chorus of tree frogs, but he could tell there were words floating about in the muddle. Suddenly Cu lain's head jerked up. He stood still for a moment listening. He then motioned for Jae for silence. A hand signal he had learned just this morning. Jae nodded his head. Then Cu lain quickened his pace as he headed for where the noises were coming from.

He stopped as they topped the hill and saw a male rizi squatted in front of a bramble thicket. When the warble of his voice stopped a small head appeared from within the brambles. The head looked like it must belong to a child, Jae thought.

It was then he noticed that Cu lain hadn't stopped with him. He was already within an arm's length of the male. Cu lain raised his foot and gave a boot to the squatting rizi's backside.

Something hit Valmi from behind. He tumbled over himself a couple times before he stopped and faced his assailant. Why it was the little mortdingya who ran the seior's errands. Valmi growled a curse at the wretch. He started to rise and teach the dog some new tricks when he noticed that the mortdingya was carrying a sword. That gave him pause. The roach was dressed differently and there was something about his demeanor that caused Valmi to hesitate. "I'd teach you some manners in a fair fight, mortdingya. But you have a sword and you'd just cut me down, so you could play with the maiden. I wouldn't be above sharing but by rights, I should get her first."

"I knew you were lying, Valmi. I'll not be shared or used by you." came an indignant voice, now completely hidden in the thicket.

"You want a fair fight, rizi?" Cu lain asked. Then turning his head, in the daonna tongue asked Jae. "Will you lend me your sword. I have a matter to decide with this rizi."

Jae could tell that Cu lain was struggling to control himself. It was hard to believe that Cu lain's dark skin could show a blush. Jae believed that he would avoid a fight with Cu lain when he was this angry. "Yes, you may have it," Jae said as he unbuckled his scabbard.

Without hesitation, Cu lain removed his sword and tossed it at the feet of that reprehensible male. "A fair fight it is then." He said as he turned his back on the rizi and walked to where Jae held his sword out to him.

Valmi looked down at the sword at his feet, it was a ye-tann's dagger. This mortdingya was carrying a yetann's dagger as a sword! Suddenly he wasn't so sure he was taking the right course of action with the breed. A person could die when blades crossed. And Valmi was sure that if he crossed blades with that male, he would be the one injured. "Oh, aw, let's not rush into anything. The female is yours. I've lost all interest in her. Please forgive my rudeness. I was just shocked when you kicked me." Valmi lowered his forehead till it touched the ground. This couldn't be the seior's slave. He tried to still his trembling. "Please, master mercy!" he wailed.

At this Cu lain winked at Jae, then turned and retrieved his sword. "Dog, you can carry for us and if you promise to pretend you are a gelding, I won't make you one."

"Thank you, jarl. You won't regret your mercy." Valmi was sure that the young male meant what he said. He almost fainted at the thought. He kept his head to the ground. He dared not move until his new master told him too.

"Stay away! I won't let you touch me. I can stay in these brambles till they have berries." I can!" came a plaintive voice from the thicket.

"You're safe now," Jae told her. His rizi was poor he knew some of the intonation was beyond him. But he was sure he got that right.

A giggle came from the brambles. "What's the vanir mean, I juggle eggs?" came a query.

Cu lain stifled a laugh before he said "He is trying to assure you that it is safe for you to come out of those brambles. No one will harm you."

"How can I be sure that you won't molest me like Valmi wanted too." She asked.

"All we have is our word and Jae's honest face" Cu lain told her in rizi. "Just look at that face. You'll see it's safe to juggle eggs."

That earned him a small laugh and the girl's head poking out of the thicket. "The læknir will want to clean those scratches on your face. She will also want to help you and this cur get free of the grasblett's drugs."

"You have a woman læknir?" I've never seen a woman læknir?" The maiden poked her head out a bit more. "Maybe I can follow you back to your camp, at a distance. Then I can discover if you're telling me the truth" She responded.

"I am Cu lain and this is Jae. What is your name?" Cu lain asked her in daonna.

"I'm known as Ceri, jarl," Ceri told them as her head hesitantly reappeared at the edge of the thicket. There was a strange lilt to her words. But Jae had to admit her daonna was better than his rizi.

Ceri slowly untangled herself from the bramble's thorns. Her blouse was torn, and her shorts ragged. Scratches covered her arms and legs. There were several across her face as well. Jae wondered how young she was. He had never seen a rizi without their characteristic tusks. Cu lain had a prominent set in spite of his dynoi blood.

"How old are you Ceri?" Cu lain gently asked.

She hesitated then told them. "I believe this is my twelfth or thirteenth summer." Then she again added "jarl."

That brought a small smile to Cu lain's lips. "He was a jarl. Indeed, by the laws of the pyris, he had been born free. And now he was free. Truly free."

He looked down at the rizi with his face still touching the ground. He wasn't sure what he wanted to do with this man. He considered that it might be that Prysivolar's potions could play with a rizi's mind as it had the yetann. But he doubted that was the story here. Still, he decided to give his prisoner a chance. "What's your name?" He asked then when he got no response he added "Rizi male, face down, is that the name I shall call you, or do you have one your mother would know?"

"I am Valmi, jarl." Valmi looked up slowly as he spoke. When he saw that the Konkur no longer wore his anger he sighed with relief. He would live another day. He promised himself he would be on his best behavior while this jarl and any of his friends were near. He suspected he had best be. He didn't want to be a eunuch.

"Get up." Cu lain told him. "I expect you would eat if we fed you. How many days has it been without food?"

"I think two, master" Valmi answered. "Do you have any of the food we carried? I seem to crave it as awful as it was."

"You won't eat that again any time soon," Jae told him. "Læknir Catherine will want to tend to your health. I expect she will want to purge you and Ceri of the grasblett's drugs. You'll feel much better after, I promise."

A large pot of fish stew was bubbling on the fire when Jae and Cu lain walked into the camp at dusk. Valmi was now a few steps behind them. While Ceri was walking beside them, her fear of them assuaged during the walk to camp. She was asking Jae why he had no gith when her nose caught the aroma of the stew. At which point she forgot about the nature of Jae's curious mouth and headed toward the direction the smell was coming from. She stopped astounded as she watched Elgar handing Catherine a bowl full of the stew. What a strange world she had stumbled into. Not only did it seem that the young woman (she was the only other female in the camp, so she had to be) was a respected læknir, but a large burly male was handing her a bowl as if they were equals. The wonder of it almost made her forget her hunger, almost but not quite. She took a small step back as the large male approached her. He smiled the strange smile of the unfortunate without gith. Then handed her a full bowl. Which she took eagerly. He then pointed to a seat next to the lady. There she sat as she watched the others circle the pot filling their bowls. It was no big surprise to her when Cu lain told Valmi to sit as he handed that wicked male his meal. The felagi spoke so quickly that she had a hard time following Jae's telling of the story of their encounter. She looked to where Valmi was sitting. How would he take being the butt of the joke? He looked as confused as she felt. This was the first time either had encountered friendship. When she finished her bowl she was offered more, which she eagerly took. Her head nodded as she relaxed for the first time in months. The first time since her father had sold her as a pack beast. It was her bad luck to be the fourth daughter in a family with no son. At least he had not sold her to the brothel, anything was preferable to that.

CHAPTER 8

From Larea Visiput's "Etytha Kendt Verden" (Study; the Known World).

The Obygo is a large expanse of forested wilderness occupying an inland portion of the dragon's belly. It contains the area east and north of Vior to the Dragon's Spine and the haunts of the Skogr yetann and south to the border of the Kentta plains.

*

She woke as the sky began to lighten. A tent stretched over her head and the læknir was sleeping beside her. As she watched, green eyes opened, and a smile stretched across the young woman's face.

Catherine lay on her blanket waiting for the rizi child to wake. She hoped her presence in the tent with her would keep the girl from panicking. Why would a child be here? Could it be she was one of the porters? Catherine opened her eyes and saw Ceri laying across the tent from her. She was still dressed in the ragged clothing Catherine had first seen her in.

Sitting up, Catherine began to talk to the child. "Did you sleep well?" Ceri nodded her head. So, Catherine continued. "I cleaned the scratches on your face last night after you were asleep. Now it is time for me to examine your other wounds and make them right. Please take your blouse off. No one but myself will see you, but I do need to see your wounds."

Ceri hesitated for a moment, then complied. The young læknir had a very kind face, Ceri felt that this was a person she should trust, but trust came hard for a female from Torion and its slave markets. Looking at her torn blouse as she held it in her hands, she realized it was not only filthy but torn so that it left very little covered. Looking down at her shorts, tears came to her eyes. She had been practically naked when she walked into camp. That she had not been passed around camp last night might only be because of the presence of the læknir. Sadly, she realized the examination might be more for the protection of the men while they used her than protection for her. A sob escaped her and then her tears flooded out of her eyes.

"What was wrong with this child? What have I done?" Catherine wondered. The child was sobbing uncontrollably.

"Ceri, what's wrong?" Catherine gently touched her shoulder.

"I, I … I don't, I don't, oh please, I don't want to be a camp wench." Came between her sobs.

"Oh, poor child. I'd never let that happen. I don't think that misusing you would cross any of this felagi's thoughts." Catherine consoled the young rizi. What kind of world did this child come from?

Catherine wrapped her arms around Ceri and held her as she sobbed. Gently patting her back like she would any distraught child. Rocking her gently Catherine hummed a lullaby she remembered from her childhood. Slowly the sobbing stopped.

"I'm sorry mistress, I'll do what I must. I was foolish to let a dream misguide me." Ceri sobbed once more and grew silent.

"Ceri, it may seem a dream, but here in this place, you are safe. Those are good men outside this tent. They will defend you like a sister. That you can trust." Catherine told her.

A sad look crossed Ceri's face. "That's small comfort she thought." She knew of a third daughter of a neighbor's family who had been shared by her brother with his friends not so long ago.

A thought crossed Catherine's mind. Maybe being a sister isn't as safe as she was raised to believe. At least not where Ceri had come from. "Ceri, believe me." She said as she released her from her hug. "You are safer with these men than a bear cub with his mother at his side. You know how ferocious a mother bear can be, don't you?"

Ceri shook her head no. But then ventured a tentative smile.

She would trust this stranger until she was proved otherwise. What choice did she have? It was possible that she had found herself in a world better than she could fantasize.

She sat calmly through the rest of her examination. The ointment the læknir used on her scratches was soothing. She was naked now. So, when it appeared that the laeknir was finished with her care, Ceri reached down for her clothing. It was then that a gentle touch stopped her. She looked up to see that the læknir had something in her other hand. As she looked, the læknir displayed a blouse and pants. A confused look passed through Ceri's face. They looked to be slightly used clothing, but they were clean and would give her proper covering.

"I'm sorry, these will probably not fit properly but they are all we have at the moment," Catherine told her.

"These are for me? What must I do to earn these, mistress?" Ceri began.

"Ceri, I am Catherine. Call me Catherine. And these are a gift to one who needs their use. A poor gift, I must say, but all we have at the moment." Catherine told Ceri. "The time will come when you will be given chores and work to do. We all must work to provide for our needs and for the needs of others at times. But now is not the time for you to worry about that. Get dressed. Crispin, the leader of the felag that rescued me has allowed us extra time this morning. But we need to be traveling down the mountain. We have far to go till we get to the closest village that might have supplies we can purchase." Catherine turned toward the tent flap, looked once more at Ceri, and said. "Finish dressing and then we can eat before we travel."

Ceri wondered whose clothing this had been. She had no doubt that these were among the supplies that she and the other pyris had abandoned when they had fled the battle. Well, even if they were a bit large, they were better than she'd had in a very long time, maybe ever. She slipped the blouse over her head and pulled the pants on. As she tied the cloth belt, she slipped out of the tent to a camp busy with packing.

Catherine was sitting with Valmi apparently tending to his

health. The handsome breed was watching them closely. The large man from last night noticed Ceri standing in front of the tent and motioned for her to come and eat. Then, after he had made sure she had food and some water to drink, turned his attention to taking down the tent the læknir and she had shared the night before.

Rallying the lorki of the male rizi was more difficult than Ceri's had been. Catherine was encountering resistance from the male. She supposed it was a mixture of distrust and fear. She had been able to work with Ceri's lorki last evening as the child slept. The poor girl had been exhausted. Imagine using a child as if she was only a beast of burden. Catherine shook her head. Having accomplished all, she could with her uncooperative patient, she handed him a bottle and instructed him to drink it all. He complied, only because Cu lain was standing there threateningly. He made a face, the potion she had been able to cobble together from the grasblett's supply was very bitter. She hoped it would ease the pain of withdrawal that the male rizi was experiencing. Using the patient's lorki would have been much more effective, but a healer did what she could.

As Ceri finished her meal she noticed a pot of water sitting next to the fire with various bowls and utensils immersed in the hot water. Taking her bowl over to the pot she washed it out, sat it on a nearby stone, and started on the others. She had a stack of ten and she was looking for something to dry them with when a towel dropped into her lap. Looking up she saw the big burly man they called Elgar smiling at her. He then turned and continued with the packing that had been occupying him. When Ceri had finished washing and drying the pot full of dishes, Elgar stopped in front of her and placed a pack at her side. He smiled and said. "I believe you'll find space in here for those." As she packed the bowls and utensils into the pack, she considered what she was seeing. This group of men was different from any she had ever seen. Here they were doing, what for her countrymen would be considered slave or worse women's work. There was no hesitation or evidence that what they were doing was demeaning. Even the leaders took part in the work. It was evident to her that Elgar and Crispin were the leaders and she could not tell which outranked the other. This was almost too much to comprehend. She decided to try to learn these new ways and see where they lead her. After she had finished packing, she tied the top of the pack, and seeing that it was fairly light, threw it upon her back. While trying to settle it on her back she discovered two straps which; when she placed her arms through them, made the pack almost comfortable on her back.

Elgar walked up and dumped the water from the pot onto the fire then he dried out the pot. As he dropped his pack to tie the pot to it. Ceri grew bold. "Jarl Elgar, tie that to my pack for now, please. I think next time I will be able to get that in this pack too if I put it in first."

That earned her a big smile from Elgar. "Lass, I believe you will do fine. Turnabout and I'll tie it on. Let me know if it gets too heavy or cumbersome and we can try something else."

Ceri turned around as instructed and waited. The large man gave her a gentle pat on the shoulder and walked away. She was pleasantly surprised that he had not fondled her bottom like so many of the pyris males had done. Læknir Catherine must be right about her estimation of these men.

Where Ceri was beginning to enjoy her new companions, Valmi was not. He did not dare let his eyes wander to the two females, for his fear of what jarl Cu lain might do. And he was forced to do women's work. True he was a slave purchased to be a pack beast, but some things were not right. Imagine being examined by a woman (who he could not fondle) and having to address her as læknir. The potion she gave him almost gaged him it was so bitter. All he wanted was some of the Seioknar's prepared food, that would set him right. That would cure his headache. It had the last time he had gone a day without it. And now he was burdened with twice the weight of all the others. (Unknown to him, his pack was barely ten pounds heavier than Ceri's) "At least I'm not dead yet." He thought.

Crispin even while he packed his kit was watching the whole

camp. He was quite satisfied with how they were functioning today. True they were getting a late start but the new additions to his band were showing themselves for who they were. Cu lain was right in his assessment of Valmi. That rizi would need to be watched like he was a captured enemy. Whereas the girl rizi, Ceri, if treated well, as he intended, could be trusted. At first, he had trusted Elgar's and Catherine's judgment on this. And now he saw for himself, in her behavior this morning.

He had sent Eric and Drew scouting ahead for any pyris or other potential surprises. This was wilderness and now they were two days away from the dryad's help. He had hoped to reach the dryad's daughter before noon today. But it appeared they would not arrive there before two shadows after that.

They paused around noon and ate the last of their trail rations. Now they needed to hunt as well. Crispin feared that this would slow them even further.

A smile crossed Elgar's face. Crispin turned to see what had attracted Elgar's attention. Catherine and Jae were sitting near each other talking. They had passed the initial shock of the strong attraction between them. Crispin hoped they were becoming friends. He had observed that the strongest couples were those who managed to meld friendship with a strong mutual attraction. Time would tell.

They emerged through the mountain pines and the valley opened before them. They could see below them a sparse growth of trees between them and a glade that opened between the dryad grove and the other trees. Beyond the cliff, the dryad grove sat on was the mixed forest of Alfheim. The stream flowed to the right of the dryad before tumbling down into the valley below. Crispin dreaded taking the group back down the trail they had taken up. But from here he would see no other way back down the mountain. For now, the trail they followed gave them an easy walk. It looked to him that it would take another two shadows to reach the dryad. Then it would be best to rest the night before taking the steep trail further down the mountain. The burn areas where the raiders camped were still visible.

Further to the right of the dryad was a small hill of rock almost lost in the pines. For a moment, he thought he saw movement there. Maybe some deer or a bear.

It was three shadows past noon when they arrived at the dryad's daughter. The trip had been uneventful. The male rizi was a slow walker. That he was alive and able to hinder their path, indicated to Crispin that he had not slowed the advance of the raiders. The threat of a yetann's claws would increase the speed of anyone.

Crispin had hoped that they would meet a contingent of the king's warriors when they reached the dryad's daughter, but he was not surprised that they had not. The trail his felag had taken up the mountain would have been difficult to follow. Combined with the signs that it had rained in the area after they had ascended the mountain, almost made it certain their trail would not be followed.

Crispin judged it warm enough that they could sleep without the tents. He intended for a very early start. The path down to the dryad's second daughter was steeper and farther. He wanted the most difficult part of the descent while they were fresh from a night's sleep.

Karl spoke to the dryad when they first arrived, but only silence replied. He tried gently coaxing her to reveal herself, to no avail. After a period of time, he excused himself and then walked into this dryad's grove. He would remain there until the sun was beginning to set.

It was almost four shadows past noon when Drew and Eric returned to the group. They almost strutted in. They had not discovered any other pyris while scouting the area. But they carried between them a small dressed deer.

Now they needed a fire. So, Crispin volunteered Valmi to help him gather some wood. The rizi balked. "I'm dead on my feet." But Crispin roused him at the suggestion that Valmi being fed depended on the wood being gathered. No wood no supper. Grumbling, he left with Crispin in the search of some fallen wood. There was forest all around them. It shouldn't take long.

Jae and Elgar gathered the water bags and headed for the stream to replenish their supply.

So, that left Drew and Eric with instructions to guard the baggage and the others of the party. His last glimpse at the camp as he followed Valmi into the forest in search of firewood caused him to smile. There on a flat rock outcrop Cu lain, Catherine and Ceri were cleaning it of debris. They were preparing a place that would contain the fire that would roast the deer.

CHAPTER 9

Karl had a solemn look on his face as he walked out of the dryad grove. He quietly approached Crispin who was watching the fire being built by Jae. Elgar was carefully placing the dressed deer on skewers to roast. The leg roasts were set so that they could be rotated as they cooked. When cooked they would be saved for breakfast, lunch, and possibly dinner. That depended on when they made it to the dryad's other daughter.

"Something is disturbing the dryad. I can't get her to speak to me. Not a twig or leaf responds to me. From what her mother told me I expected this one to be the most vocal of the two daughters. I'm going to try something else during the night. I won't be much company tonight." Karl told Crispin. "Oh, before I forget. I retrieved this from a body on the other side of the grove. It's another copy." He said as he handed Crispin another charm. With that, he turned, walked over toward the grove, and sat down and appeared to sleep.

Dusk was upon them as they sat together eating. Jae and Catherine were laughing at something that had passed between them. Then Jae grew silent. He nudged Drew and nodded his head in the direction across the fire and whispered. "We have company." It was then that they heard Eric, who had the watch. "Hello, strangers."

At the sound of Eric's voice coming from the stranger's right, they all gave a little jump and the smallest one took a step back. Crispin turned and there standing just at the edge of the firelight stood three male pyris. He had a momentary opportunity to observe a change of expression on the pyris faces. They had become bland. He wasn't sure what it had been before. Was it predatory or hunger? They would bear watching.

He waved them over. When they hesitated, he picked up three skewers of meat chunks and walked over and handed them each one. With only a moment's hesitation, they took the skewers and devoured the meat. They managed to eat three more each before Elgar cut them off. He wanted food remaining for the next day and Eric had not yet had his share.

When asked, they gave their names as Brast, Wedi, and the smallest Blewg. Nothing more was to be learned from them. Though they did admit to being some of the porters that fled the battle after Ceri told the band she recognized Brast as being of the group. When questioned about any other pyris in the area, they shook their heads "no".

Crispin gave up. He hoped they would be more trusting the next morning. So, he instructed Drew to give them each a ground cloth while he settled the others in. Jae and Catherine settled in with their heads almost touching. While Cu lain laid down on Catherine's right and Ceri on her left. Crispin smiled at this. Cu lain and Ceri had become Catherine's guards and un-intentionally, by their effort to protect Catherine, kept her and Jae separated. Nevertheless, Jae and Catherine had a brief con-versation where their hands almost touched. Then they turned over to sleep.

Quiet settled over the camp as all but the watch slept.

Y'dalir had set and darkness enveloped the camp. After circ-ling the camp for the second time during his watch Jae sat down with his back to the dryad grove. Mistakenly believing that this protected his back. He purposely settled in opposite where the newcomers were sleeping. They had laid down near what now looked like a large rock. Jae knew that this was where the green man had sat earlier in the evening. After a time, Jae's head dropped down, an outside observer might mistake him to be asleep.

Maybe watching the yetann slaughter their guide had trau-matized the dryad to silence. To Karl that did not fit what he knew of dryads. He was perplexed. The only thing he was certain of was that the dryad has judged something dangerous about. So, he sat watching the darkness. His senses stretched out to the surrounding area. Trying to see what possibly could be out there. What had so frightened the dryad? He was so focused on the area away from the camp that he almost missed the movement next to him.

The pyris who had been sleeping beside him had begun to stir. There was an energy about them he had not noticed before. He thought it strange that they ignored him. Usually, the pyris had decent night vision. They should see him as a man, but like the dynoi who could barely see during a dark night like this, they seemed oblivious to his presence. The three near him began to draw knives that had been hidden in the folds of their clothing. He noticed movement behind Jae. Was he asleep on his watch? That's what it appeared to be. Now the quandary. Warn Jae and give up his opportunity at surprise or hope Jae was aware of the enemy behind his back and flank the enemy between him and the sleeping camp?

Now he noticed all five moving figures had a malicious glow about them.

Crispin lay awake. His dreams had been troubled this night. That was a rare occurrence. But it was one that he took seriously. More than one bad dream had alerted him to danger. But from where? He had been staring at Asgard when a movement on his left caught his eye. He turned on his left, hoping that whoever was watching would assume that this was just the movement of a sleeping man. How he wished his night vision was as good as Jae's or Drew's. The three pyris that had just joined them were stirring. It appeared that they were preparing to move against the camp.

Jae closed his eyes and as his grandfather had taught him stretched out his senses so that he could focus on his thoughts and not be caught unaware. He had much to think about. He knew the attraction between him, and Catherine was mutual. But what was he to do about it? He was still obligated to four years of military service to the king of Alfheim. And Catherine had the mystery of her kidnapping to solve. For a time, their paths ran together. But they could diverge at any time after they left this mountain. He was just beginning to puzzle out the situation when something impinged upon his awareness. Something or someone was behind him. No, there were two behind him. Stealthily they approached him. But they were no vanir, the noise from the leaves and twigs as the approached let him know their approximate positions. If they had been friendly or benign, they would be making more noise. His hand tightened on the grip of his sword as he waited for them to draw nearer.

Two sets of feral eyes watched Jae. Ready to kill. Ready to present his blood to their master. To feed it with the panic and pain they planned to inflict on this camp. All that lacked was the signal from the others.

As Brast rose he waved the now glowing blade of his new dagger. He stretched as tall as he could so the two assigned to kill the watcher would see. Hopefully, the watcher would see it as well. That would be a satisfying distraction. The blade desired panic and pain. And he willingly would comply.

Jae was not distracted by the blade's glow. His eyes were closed. But when the enemy behind him began to move closer for the kill, he rose and swiftly turned. He drew his blade in one fluid movement, just as he had practiced a thousand times both in body and thought. His blade caught the first rizi's neck smoothly cutting its jugular. A very lucky blow Jae thought as the blade continued on to confront his other attacker. There it met more resistance as it struck the hand holding an ancient sword. The guard of the sword kept Jae's from removing the thumb of his remaining attacker. That rattled the rizi enough that he stepped back and stumbled. That gave Jae the chance to call out "To arms! To arms!" A shout he heard echo from Karl at practically the same moment.

Then he drove his attack against his assailant. Their blades struck each other as they parried and thrust. Jae had the advantage of his training and soon took advantage of an opening. The rizi's eyes grew wide as Jae's blade sliced open his belly. Looking down he saw his bowels spill out of the cut. Then before the pain could begin Jae thrust his sword into the rizi's heart.

He then turned and began to move toward the camp.

When Karl saw the rizi begin to wave his blade, he reached out his left hand and grabbed the rizi's extended arm at the wrist. He then stood and raised the rizi from the ground. Seeing that his captive did not drop the knife he squeezed his enemy's wrist crushing it. The blade made a satisfying thud as it hit the ground.

Brast screamed in agony as his wrist broke. He also felt the blade's pleasure at his agony. Obeying its desire, he kicked at his assailant landing a firm blow to the gut. Strangely this did not seem to have any effect on the large stone that had become a man. His next attempt at kicking found his leg firmly held in the big man's other hand. At that moment his wrist was released, and he felt himself rapidly swinging around until his body met Wedi's. A moment later his head met Blewg's causing both to never feel again.

Brast's scream caused both Wedi and Blewg to hesitate. Then Wedi felt himself fly through the air until he landed with enough force to knock his breath out. Blewg felt nothing his skull crushed by the force of impact with Brast's head.

Wedi began to push himself up. Then a foot was firmly planted on his back and a sharp blade set against his neck. The cursed blade no longer in contact with flesh released its hold on him and with that the energy that had empowered him left. He sobbed for the loss of power and lay still.

Crispin knelt on the rizi's back and swiftly tied his hands and feet together leaving him lying on his belly looking at the blade that had fallen out of his hand just out of reach near his head.

The rizi secured, Crispin walked over to the still faintly glowing blade and began to stoop to retrieve it when two voices loudly said "Stop!" He looked up to see a panicked look in both Karl's and Catherine's faces.

"That's a very dangerous artifact," Karl told him. "Best not to touch it with bare hands, if at all."

"Can't you feel it's malignancy?" Catherine asked. "It feels almost like heat from a flame. Only cold, no, I can't describe it. But Karl is right, we should not touch it."

Drew threw a skin over it. Then hesitated to pick it up.

"Wait just a moment Karl said as he walked over to the pack with the cooking utensils. He was opening it when he noticed Ceri's sitting next to it shivering in fear. He touched her cheek and said. "Dear child you're safe now. Whatever it was, it is defeated now." An attempt at a smile crossed her face as he took a pot that looked to be the right size.

Karl gingerly picked up the skin covered knife, wrapped the skin around it securely, and lay it into the pot. He then bent over the sides and taking a rock did his best to seal its opening. Then he took another piece of skin and wrapped it around the reformed pot. "Best I can do for now. If I knew how to destroy this thing I would." He said.

He knelt by the prone rizi and asked. "Where did you find your weapons?"

Wedi stayed silent. He had heard the sound of hammering but knew that the ancient blade could not be harmed by such effort. If only one of them touched the blade. Silently he waited for a chance to once more experience the power the blade gave.

The glow of the malignant blade now hidden; Catherine noticed that the glow of two dead pyris' bodies had faded. She wished her night vision was as good as a vanir's or a dzwerc's. But she had other ways of seeing. She expanded her awareness and what she found disturbed her. The glow was the pyris' lorki being consumed. The force was abated and the remaining lorki were not being affected. She turned to examine the rizi Crispin had tied. The glow of the dying lorki had gone dark on the rizi. But, his remaining lorki were injured. They appeared unable to replicate themselves like healthy lorki would. Whoever created that blade intended for death to take both those served to it and those who served it.

She turned her attention to the green man. Karl seemed unaffected by the sinister magic. From a quick examination, none of her friends had been damaged by the forces contained in that blade. She hoped that Karl's effort to keep the blade from touching one of them was effective.

"That's very disturbing." Catherine began, and the eyes of her companions turned toward her. "Whatever forces that blade releases destroy the lorki of the ones using it." Nodding her head toward the prone Wedi she added. "The lorki remaining in him are stunted and will not grow more. Almost any illness will be dangerous for him. A simple scratch can turn malignant and infect the whole body. Without his lorki working to keep him healthy, he will have an early death."

Karl was barely listening to Catherine. His eyes were scanning the camp as he noted where everyone was. Jae stood near his dead attackers still watching the area between him and the grove. Elgar, Eric, and Drew stood near the perimeter of the camp watching different areas. Cu lain stood near Catherine with his blade ready. Both Ceri and Valmi were huddled in their blankets afraid to move. It was then that the words, lorki, and death broke into his thoughts. There was something there tickling his brain. Something he should remember. For about two heartbeats he left the present and saw. Or was that remembered?

He shook himself bringing his attention to today. "I believe I remembered something about this blade and its sisters." Seeing that the group was listening he continued. "Long ago, sometime after the gods fled Midgard there came the Tynagloggr, those who were to clear the errors of the gods. They created the Thrir I'hraezle, in the old tongue. The three that set terror in motion as we would say today. The three were Fyorendir – life ender, Ondbane – breath of death, and Fyorlag – deathblow. Egon Vaskre defeated the bearer of Ondbane and took it to Valhalla. He hoped to destroy it in the volcano created by Mjolnir's fall. His success is unknown and he and his deeds are lost. Asdis Sigrider captured Fyorlag high in the dragon's spine. The Tynagloggr pursued her deep into Vedrfolnir. Where the legend says they all perished, the pursued and the pursuers. For a time

Fyorendir brought terror into the world until somewhere along the dragon's spine the armies of three forgotten kings battled for control of the cursed blade. The legend ends with the armies lost in the wilderness and never heard of again. I believe we have found Fyorendir."

"I've never heard that story before and I've read all the legends found in the books in our school back home." Jae, with the always listening ears, injected.

This brought a laugh from across the camp. Drew well remembered Jae scavenging for more books with the ancient legends.

"The stories of Odin's clan and their adventures seem more to the taste of some. I remember my great grandfather telling something of the Thrir I'hraezle. Mostly to scare us, boys, into staying in at night. It was at night when we got into the most trouble." Elgar added.

Crispin bent and picked up the sword lying at Wedi's head. He examined it carefully. "I've not seen workmanship like this." How long do you suppose it has been out exposed to the weather? Look there is no sign of rust or any corrosion. A winter out will damage most blades today." He said.

"Hard to say," Karl replied. "The Thrir I'hraezle was the first attempt to make Ymir safe for the gods again. Those blades could have come from the forges of Asgard. If so, they are almost two thousand summers old."

"We'll have two on watch the rest of the night. The rest get what sleep you can. We need an early start tomorrow." Crispin told the camp.

Karl motioned for Catherine to follow him. Then he turned and approached the dryad. "Can you see better than me?" he asked her. "Something appears wrong with the dryad. I hadn't noticed it before, but now I see something different than it should be."

Catherine using what some called the healing sight, but what she believed was just her bond with her lorki, examined the dryad. Walking up to one tree in particular she ran her hands over it. She removed her hand and showed it to Karl. There was sticky sap on it. "The lorki in this tree are damaged. It appears to me that she has been attacked with that cursed blade."

She concentrated for a few moments then turned to Karl and said. "Tree lorki are so different from mine I can sense them but not quite tell how to focus them. And I'm not too sure on how they should be directed. How familiar are you with the healing forces of the lorki?

Karl looked at her, then released a sigh. "I know mine very well. But how to read another's let alone help direct them in healing. I've never tried. At least as far as I can remember."

"Well, take my hand and we'll both touch the tree that has been cut with the blade. Extend out your desire for healing as I do mine. Together we may be able to help." Catherine told him.

Karl reached out and took her chin in his left hand. Turning her head to face him he said. "You trust me this much, do you? You're very brave or foolish. You've known me, what? A little over a five-day. And for this stranger, you put your life on the line?"

He grew silent and took her right hand in his left. Perhaps new legends were getting ready to be told.

She smiled at him and placed her left hand on the damaged tree as he placed his right on it. They were motionless for a time. Then they both released their hands and stepped back from the tree.

It was then that Karl spoke. "Dryad, we are sorry for the pain you have been caused. What we are about to do will also be painful. But it must be done for you to heal. This tree must be removed from you with some of its roots. Forgive us for this pain."

Karl squatted next to the damaged tree and wrapped his hands around its base. He wiggled the tree beginning to break it away from the earth and it's attaching roots. Then he slowly began to stand pulling the tree up from its roots. The other trees in the grove that were near them shuddered. As the damaged tree began to release from the ground Catherine knelt by its roots tenderly as possible breaking each root from the tangle of its sisters' roots.

They returned to the camp exhausted. Catherine was possibly the only member of the group who slept uninterrupted through the rest of the night.

It was a nervous camp that night the least sound would rouse one or another. A night bird calling, a wolf howl, the crackle of the fire's embers, things they would barely have noticed before, would wake them.

Karl spent the rest of the night contemplating the evil blade he had contained for a time. How should he dispose of it? "Never," he pledged "would it fall into the hands of man again." He then remembered the clay where they had extracted the diseased sapling. That should work. It would be the best he could do with what was available. He broke the green sapling into pieces and laid it on the fire. Then he trudged into the dryad grove. As he returned, he gathered dead branches and even came upon a rotten tree trunk that wasn't wet. He piled the wood he had gathered on the fire and as it began to burn, he fashioned the clay he had gathered around the bent-up pan he had placed the blade in. Yes, that would do. Carefully he placed what he had made into the fire gradually easing it into the hottest part of the fire. Unseen by the others he also placed the rock he had covered with clay. Unless examined carefully they appeared identical.

CHAPTER 10

From Larea Visiput's "Etytha Kendt Verden" (Study; the Known World).

Vanaheim is composed of the islands at the mouth of the Elfra. It is made of twenty large islands and hundreds of smaller islands. The waterways are shallow with shifting mudbanks. Making the karf the perfect vessels for navigating between the islands. The main current of the Elfra passes to the east of the islands.

*

As soon as it was light the camp was busy readying for the next leg of their journey down the mountain.

Karl stirred the ashes of the fire. He gingerly picked up the still warm lump of clay. He walked up to the rock outcrop and dug out some rocks from its base revealing a crevice just large enough for the clump of clay. He then carefully replaced the rocks he had removed. "Well, that's taken care of for now." He said to no one in particular. He then turned and walked into the dryad grove. He was gone the better part of a shadow. He then walked out of the grove and gathered his share of the gear.

Wedi stood with his hands tied in front of him, as Elgar tied a heavy pack onto his back. Elgar in his most solemn voice said to Wedi "If you carry your share and give no trouble during the rest of the journey an opportunity for mercy will be given. However; the first time your actions endanger the group, you're dead. Do you understand?"

"Yes, jarl" Wedi dully answered.

Valmi gave no complaint this day. Though he had not slept well, it appeared that the terror of the night before had silenced him for the time being.

As Crispin began to instruct Eric and Drew on where they would be traveling as they scouted the path back down the mountain, Karl interrupted.

"Friend Crispin, may I intrude?" He asked.

Crispin looked at him and simply nodded his head in affirmation. He had some questions about Karl's display this morning but had already decided that a private conversation would best suit what he wanted to know.

"The dryad was able to speak a little to me this morning." He began. "She and I believe she will fully recover from the damage inflicted by Fyorendir."

"I'm glad to hear that," Crispin replied. "What else is there?"

"She told me that we should go a little left of her and follow the deer trail we will find there. We will have an easier journey down the mountain following that path than we will have if we follow the path you took up the mountain." Karl informed Crispin in a voice that carried across the group.

"That sounds like the path to take then." Crispin agreed. "Eric, Drew take that path. You know our needs."

With their orders clear the two set out in the direction indicated.

"Shall we take the rear guard today, friend Karl?" Crispin asked.

Karl smiled and readily agreed.

Unknown to Karl and Catherine a shy creature had watched them as they extracted the diseased sampling from the dryad. As the dryad cried in her wounding the creature sent calm and peace and whatever comfort she could. She watched as they struggled to heal the dryad. She started to reach out and then hesitated. She stayed back and watched. It couldn't be, could it? Not the child from long ago. Possibly. What should she do there's too many men, too great a chance that her routine would kick in.? No! Never again she promised herself. She had been given tools that allowed her to sidetrack the impulses and desires. Tools that were safeguards against hunters that might come through. She had places to hide. A set of rules that the healer in that city long ago had given her, had taught her, had instilled in her. She was not the same slave she had been. And the desires for the pain had been removed by her new routine. She was diseased, retched, and dying when he first touched her. He had great strength against her charm. Something that she had no control over at that time. But years of practice, years of meditation had given her control. Besides the green thing whatever it was looked like a man but wasn't. There were others out there. There were real men out there and she had felt that old routine in the pit of her stomach, so she withdrew and thought.

Now these two men. Two viral young men. Ah, what a danger. Almost desiring it. But no, she had other things to do. She had animals and plants and friends. That she-bear was a friend. Her two cubs had been longed for by the bear and now they were a reality. And the nymph had been helping her. This was her first cubs. They were growing fine and now these young men wanted to travel the path that their eating blocked. And they debated whether to kill her and the cubs to protect the people following. But there was a stubborn desire in them not to harm the she-bear and her cubs. So, they waited and watched, and the nymph watched too.

She talked quietly to the she-bear in their own special language that those men could not hear. She reminded the she-bear of an old tree that had fallen last year. How fat the grubs would be now. She could teach her cubs how to dig out the grubs and how tasty they were. There by the old fallen tree was a thorn berry patch. Those berries should be sweet, sweeter than these half ripe berries they were now eating.

The she-bear shook her head rue to abandon these berries to those strangers up the hill. True, she had hidden her cubs when the yetann passed through and crossed the stream and didn't go back to avoid them. But these were not yetann.

Yes, that old tree would have some tasty grubs and the cubs did need to learn to tear rotten trees to gather grubs. And those berries would be sweet. So off she went up the hill away from the men. To a place, two or three rests away. The cubs would be very happy learning to tear trees apart. True it was a dead tree but still yet, cubs got great joy in tearing things up and learning what to eat.

As the she-bear traveled away from the trail the nymph withdrew keeping a tendril of awareness out there. Quiet and unobserved.

"Eric, the bear has moved on. How long should we wait?" Drew whispered.

"Not much longer. Something is out there, maybe." Eric whispered back. "I couldn't tell you why that bear abandoned those berries. It seems to me, something more than our presence encouraged that she-bear to leave with her cubs. I'm glad we waited and didn't have to kill her."

"Yes, I really didn't want to get involved with that bear and her cubs," Drew said.

"So, have you noticed Jae? Have you ever seen him act this way?" Eric changed the subject.

"What way?" Drew asked.

"Smitten, that girl has got him. She's got him. Now me, I'd let her have me." laughed Eric.

"Oh, after all the things you said about Alvar Dansen's daughter, how she was much too fat for you?" Drew poked at Eric.

"Well, she is. And a girl should wait to be pursued. The chase is half the fun." Eric grew hesitant in his words.

"You've got a one-wheel wagon there. You know that. It's the only thing you seem to think about. Unless we are out and alone in the wilderness. And even then, you can't avoid the subject" Drew harried him

"You know better than that. I have my fun. But I have other things on my mind. I'm a good archer. I'm going to take the prize at the next competition." Eric bragged

"You think so? You think Asleif is going to let you have it?" Drew asked

"She won't have any choice. You heard Crispin I'm the best archer." Eric told him

"He said you were one of the best and you are. But you'll have competition from other felag as well as Asleif." Drew told him

After a bit more, banter they grew silent and proceeded down the path. They would miss nothing that would endanger the others.

*

Bui was not sure what to do. The king had not been pleased by the last meal served. To be honest it wasn't that he was displeased. It was that he was preoccupied by the raid that had occurred on the new moon. Nothing was pleasing him now. Nothing would please him until he knew that raiders were captured or destroyed. Knowing King Awrick as he did, Bui suspected that the king would not be pleased until whoever or whatever had instigated this violation of Alfheim was duly punished.

The king had been in a particularly good mood when he had arrived at his hunting lodge. There had been a hunt planned. With a party afterward. The king had set aside time to spend with his eldest son. And then what the king considered the best part. The testing of the new scouting felags. Rumor had it the king had a bet riding on how far into the lodge's grounds Crispin's trainees would get. The two tyge of the guard units were readying their traps and watches in anticipation. The exercise had already been set when the news arrived that there had been a raid on the nearby village of Boar Akarn. It had been all he and the others in the staff could do to keep the king from mounting his horse and entering the chase of the raiders. The king was trembling in rage as he walked back into the lodge. Bui suspected that the king was now impatiently pacing the floor of the great hall at this moment waiting for news of Crispin and his lost felag.

Ari sat watching his father, the king, pace the length of the hall and then turn and return to where he had begun. He had counted, this would be the twentieth crossing of the room, this morning. General Gudbrand was laying a map of the area out on the large table in the middle of the room. Ari was thankful that the general had finally arrived. Now there was another person to share the king's rage. Ari had never seen his father so distraught. Today Frou Eir Ulfdot would be arriving with Baldur Unison. With them would be the king's secretary and possibly a representative of the Gafur, the king's watchers. They and the additional troops that were bound to arrive would perhaps give him the opportunity to requisition a tyge of horse. Because Ari knew that would be the minimum his father would want to travel with him. And then he could head back to the palace. Of course, then he would have to listen to his mother scold him for not having more with him. If he dawdled, he could stretch the journey back to two weeks. No, he better not, a week at most or both his mother and father would be on his case.

Ari stood and slipped out of the room as his father started another round of the room. Perhaps Verdandi would have some of her butter and nut cookies today. He had requested some the day before, but she had been overwhelmed by what she mistook for the king's displeasure with her when his breakfast had been returned untouched. Some fresh milk and those cookies would clear his mind. He understood his father's mood. He too was troubled by this attack. Maybe he should stay and stand by his father as the situation developed. Someday the crown would weigh on his head. Hopefully many years from now. He wanted the opportunity to court a maiden or possibly two. He knew he would have to consider the politics of the times when choosing a wife, but he hoped he did as well as his father in finding one who would share love as well as politically strengthening the realm.

Awrick watched his son slip out of the room. He remembered the times he too had slipped away when his father had been pacing the floor. The political turmoil of his father's early reign was forefront in Awrick's mind. He had hoped to present a much more stable world to his son just as his father had him. The foundation of the Free State alliance had been the labor of his grandfather and the solidifying of it the work of his father. Now with his wife's influence on her father and the duchess' support he had hoped to put in writing a more formal organization. This raid could portend an effort to weaken the Free States. Only time would tell.

He took a deep breath. Pacing the floor was a poor substitute for a long fast ride on horseback. A love both he and his son shared. He remembered how much he treasured the memories of riding with his father. Convincing those responsible for his safety that he needed a long ride alone with his son was impossible at this time. He was sure this was an isolated incident. He was almost positive that whatever was the reason for this raid the presence of him and his son at the lodge had nothing to do with it. From what information he had at this time, the raid was the main event, not a distraction.

He walked over to the map and let Gudbrand point out all the areas his patrols had covered around the lodge. Only one wayward poacher was discovered. No activity was discovered that would lead one to believe that the king was the target. From the reports from the scouts who had been sent to backtrack the raiders, they appeared to have traveled from the almost isolated western through the Etunazi occupied hills. A wild landscape of cliffs and rocks with only a few spots suitable for a landing. The exact spot that the raiders had landed had not yet been determined, but Awrick was sure they would know that soon.

Studying the map Awrick could see where the raiders should have crossed the Laek Gritter and headed south back to the coast. Why they had turned north and headed up into the mountains of the Dragon's Spine was a mystery. One he hoped Crispin could answer once he appeared. In spite of the pessimism of many of those around him, Awrick was confident that Crispin would appear out of the wild with all of the felag he had disappeared with. And with him the answer to the many questions surrounding this incident.

*

The light was fading as they finished the climb down the deer trail. As the dryad had told them, the journey down the trail was much easier than the one they took up the mountain. Still, they were another day from the dryad's other daughter and the Laek Gritter. From there it would be another three days until they, at last, returned to Boar Akarn. Once there Crispin planned to question the tinker and the elders of the village, for he had many questions he wanted answers to.

Including the strange sense that they had been watched as they drew near the stream at the base of the waterfall where the dryad's stream cascaded over the cliff above. Catherine and Karl had stopped and watched letting the others pass by them as they studied the area trying to discern if indeed there was a watcher. They dawdled there until Crispin had to send Jae back to get them moving again. Most of the journey that day was spent in discussion over whether there had been a watcher. Both Catherine and Karl were certain there was, which for Crispin meant that there was one. Thankfully it appeared that it was not a hostile one. After they left the immediate area the sense of being watched faded away.

He gave Jae first watch and lay down to sleep as Asgard's light began to shine. He planned to have them all up before dawn. Another four days. A journey like this was hard even on wilderness hardened scouts. The others in the group were doing better than he had expected. He hadn't pushed them hard because he knew how difficult even journeys on good roads were for those unaccustomed to it. As he drifted off to sleep, he could hear Jae explaining to Catherine how to navigate the wilderness with the aid of Asgard and the stars.

CHAPTER 11

As the sun peaked over the mountains she awoke. Well, she prepared to interact with the world. For truly she never slept like the others did. The moving water constantly replenished her, so she had no need of sleep. Most evenings she spent talking to the night hawks or the bats. Last night was spent reviewing her impressions of the maiden who was the healer's daughter from long, long ago. How else could you explain how the small child she had helped teach defenses against charmers was now a grown woman. Yet she knew it had only been around 10 summers ago that the old woman brought her here and planted the artifact that empowered her life.

Upon this reflection, she remembered: "Yes, that was my name, the one the healer had given me." If she had remembered it while the maiden was close, she would not have been afraid to allow her presence to be known. Her name gave her strength. She must endeavor to remember it for the next time the folk journeyed through her wilderness. By the healer's words, she was Diana the huntress.

The dryad was chattering now. She kept up an almost constant conversation even if the nymph didn't participate. This brought a smile to the nymph. Her friend was apparently fully recovered from the evil blade's wound. She listened for a bit and discovered that her friend the dryad had something to share with her. Actually, some sort of request that required the nymph's presence in the grove. So, the nymph began her climb up the falls.

Long before the nymph began to stir Crispin had roused his band. They had heated the last of the deer and with a pot of wild mint tea made a breakfast for them all. They had Cu lain to thank for the tea. No one else was watching the plants around them. Jae and Eric had just finished first watch, and Catherine was acquainting Ceri with her lorki. Drew was sharpening his ax as he guarded the rizi named Wedi. He and Elgar had just built the fire to warm the deer meat when Cu lain sat a pan full of water by the fire to heat. He then had walked a short distance to an outcrop of rock where he gathered the herb which he steeped in the pot until Elgar had declared the meat ready to eat. Cu lain then carefully filled each person a cup from the pot. The tea was a welcome treat which everyone except Wedi and Valmi thanked him for.

Wedi was watching for an opportunity to escape. The hunger in his eyes could not be hid, even when he attempted to, which wasn't very often. Wedi lusted after the blade that had shortened his life. That he thought he knew where the blade was seemed to stoke his hunger. Crispin was glad that Karl had used a ruse to hide what had really happened to that cursed blade. Crispin was thankful that he was an ally. He hoped there would never be a reason to find out what being an enemy to him would cost.

Their morning meal finished, Cu lain, and Jae set out to scout ahead. Cu lain had much to learn but he was eager to be of value to his new friends. From what Crispin had gathered these were the first friends Cu lain had ever had. If his word mattered, and it did, Crispin would have that young man enrolled at Virkiflyot by this fall.

By noon the trees had gotten larger and the land leveled out. They followed the stream down the valley. Once or twice they had to detour to find a way across the streams feeding into it. As they topped a hill, a valley stretched out before them. There, where the Dryad's stream met another forming the Laek Gritter, stood the other daughter of the dryad. And camped in a clearing near the dryad were two of the king's tyge, about forty scouts.

Crispin unpacked one of the yetann's undergarments and tied it to a long sapling Elgar had cut down for this purpose. He and

Elgar waved their flag until Crispin saw a contingent of horse mounting. He then repacked the shirt and waited with the others for help to arrive. The hardest part of their journey back to Boar Akarn was over.

As Crispin and Elgar were waving their flag, the nymph was complaining to herself about the filthy task her friend had talked her into. The bat guano stank terribly. She took sand and massaged it into her hair. Then she once more plunged her head beneath the waters of her stream. Well, the job was done. If a man ever found his way as deep into the bat cave as she had gone, he would die of the stench. As it was, she would be rebuilding her reserves for a week. Yet the task was, to be honest, a necessary one. The spot she hid the clay casket of the cursed blade would be dry enough to preserve it. And no living thing but the bats and the cave bugs would ever find it.

*

The hymriursar was puzzled as he stood in the snow of the high mountain pass. Below stretched a valley and green was everywhere. For a creature accustomed to shades of white, this was astounding. The only green he ever remembered seeing was bits and pieces of lichen or moss, and they were scattered and rare.

He had no interest in descending this side of the mountain. The temperature was already too warm for his liking. The sight of all that green had caused him to forget momentarily why he had journeyed up this mountain. He might be repaying a debt, or he might be hunting. That depended on who or what the trail he was following led him to. Someone or something had left him a gift of meat. It was hard to tell how long ago the gift had been left. It wasn't too old. Not as old as some he had happened across. This meat had a different flavor from the walrus and the seal. It reminded him a little of the great white bear. But the body had been much more delicate than that. The bones had a nice crunch. His ancestors had told stories of being hunted and hunting gods. They too had been covered with strange removable fur. They were very dangerous to hunt; hard to get close to.

They could throw their fire. Yes, according to the stories they threw fire at the hymriursar that they hunted. If a hymriursar could get close and take advantage of their ability to give an unexpected burst of speed the ancients claimed that the meat of the gods was the best eating imaginable.

The trail of the thing he followed was meat and not meat. Something he did not remember smelling before. The thing could be very dangerous. So, the gift he brought, an ancient artifact he had found in the high frozen desert of Niflheim, was either bait or repayment for the meat given. What it was he would never know. The valley and the land spreading from it would be too warm even in the midst of its winter. So, he dropped the ancient artifact and slowly turned, adapting the slow methodical walk of his kind, conserving his energy until he needed speed to capture a meal or avoid being a meal and returned to his world of ice and snow.

*

It had been a long four days. Over twenty years since thane Awrick's last full campaign. This had been a brief reminder of how difficult a military life could be. He missed his wife. If the training exercise had gone as planned or even if it had had its normal delays, he would be retiring to bed with his wife instead of riding into this hamlet that was the center of the crisis. His detachment had been in Utroor when word of the raid arrived. He had sent a rider to the king's lodge and a small boat across the lake to Goa Vollar notifying them and then marched his men to Boar Akarn. Now over four five-days had passed, and he hadn't had a warm bath the entire time. And his cook had. for reasons of his own. stayed with the contingent left at the source of the Laek Gritter.

He knew the king would be sending, if he hadn't already, a rider for word of Crispin and the raiders. Hopefully, the king was still at the lodge and not waiting for him at Boar Akarn. At this point, he had no idea what had happened to Crispin or the raiders. No doubt the garrison at Goa Vollar had sent forces east along the Laxvik to intercept the raiders if they had

116

headed south. Awrick for his money felt that they had gone up the mountain following one of the two streams that merged to form the Laek Gritter. But all sign had been washed away with the rains and short of sending men up both streams there was little he could do now. Crispin would not have led a lone felag into confrontation with a band of yetann. Why he had not sent word back to them was unknown. Well, if Awrick had to face the king's wrath so be it.

For his money, Boar Akarn was a miserable little hamlet. It claimed to be the source of the best hams in Alfheim. True the hams from here did grace the king's table. but the hams sold to others were not the same quality. They were overpriced to Awrick's mind, and no better than any other he had tasted.

His horse shuffled to a stop as they approached the lone tavern in the town. No one was shackled in front of it. So Lyos was no longer keeping the man chained there continuously. This pleased Awrick, Lyos could be overly strict in his interpretation of the rules. This showed growth in his judgment.

Awrick called over a man and sent him to find Lyos as he dismounted. Oh, he was sore from this ride. Yorliek seemed glad to be relieved of his burden and gave his head a vigorous shake. While he waited for Lyos' arrival he walked over to the man standing at the door of the tavern. "Do you have a hot bath available?" he asked him.

"I can have one ready in a shadows span." He answered.

"Get to it then! And after that's started, bring me an ale. I'm dry from the journey." Awrick told him. He called Lini over and gave him instructions to have the camp prepared for the night. It was then he saw Asleif leaning against a tree. She had only ridden the first day, claiming she preferred walking to bouncing. She was no horsewoman that was true. There was something about the lass that reminded him of his daughter, lost those long years ago. "Asleif, come here." He called. At his call, she straightened and ran to him giving a salute as she came to a halt in front of him.

He almost offered her his bath. Then thought better of it.

Some would suspect him of giving this young woman special treatment. And if they did, they would suspect, he was preening her for something more intimate later. That had not crossed his mind. It was just that she bought his daughter's memory to mind. Instead, he said. "You've done well recruit. You are released to your felag. Get some rest. Tell your felag you all will receive a commendation from me later. And you might warn them the king is at his lodge. You might want to prepare in case he decides to arrive here in the future." With a salute he dismissed her.

Lyos' approach saved him from further brooding. "Thane welcome to Boar Akarn." He said. "Any word of Crispin?"

"Not a one my friend. Not a one. I wish I had more to share. I left a contingent at the last sign of the yetann and felag we found. I don't mind telling you Crispin has me worried. He would have sent word by now if he was able." Awrick replied. "Where is your command post? I want a bath and after that, I will want a full report of the happenings here."

*

A shout went out in the camp which caused Herr Vogan to look up from the game of queen's retreat he and Herr Frigg were playing. A man pointed up and north. Turning he looked toward the point indicated by the pointing. Up, on a rise in the land, a large white flag waved. Well, there went his mark. He was only a day off. Baldur the Grey had won the wager. Some would have thought it strange that no one had wagered that Crispin would not return. But no one who knew him would be.

He sent his footman to fetch Vali and his felag of horse. Before Lini got to his feet, Vali and his horsemen rode up. "Well, go fetch them" Vogan smiled as he gave leave. With Crispin found they would soon be back in their barracks and their soft beds. Maybe.

Vogan watched the horsemen disappear up the slope. They should arrive where the flag had waved in a couple of shadows. That is if they did not meet the descending band on their journey down the mountain. At the earliest, he expected to see them again about dusk.

"Shall we finish this game while we wait?" He asked Frigg. Frigg just nodded her head as she waited for Vogan to make his next move. Vogan would be lucky to win this match. Frigg had learned some new tricks since the last time they played.

*

Catherine sat on a log examining the sole of one of the moccasins Drew had loaned her. "Well," she thought, "I'll need to buy Drew a new pair. These are worn to a frazzle. I can see the bottom of my foot through the soles."

"What are you looking at, that put such a frown on your face," Eric asked as he and Jae approached.

"I'm afraid I've ruined Drew's moccasins," Catherine told him.

"I expected that to happen sooner or later when I gave them to you," Drew said from behind her. "I meant to give you these before this, but they kept slipping my mind." He finished as he dropped several pieces of leather in her lap. "I waited too long. Best thing to do now is to find a couple of pieces to slip into the shoe. You see, these were never meant to be worn for extended periods of time. They're for stalking and silent moving in a forest. They did better than I expected. Hopefully, they will last until we can get you a proper pair of boots."

"Thank you, Drew." She said as he stood and gave her an almost smile. Then he walked away.

"Did you see that Jae?" Eric asked. "I think he's in love with her. I've never seen him talk with a woman that long before. You've got some competition" He teased.

Catherine smiled as Jae's ears began to grow red. She liked these young men she found herself surrounded by. They would make good comrades. She looked at Eric and he gave her a big smile and winked. He enjoyed turning Jae's ears red almost as much as Drew did. She hoped the day would come when she would be as comfortable teasing him as his friends were.

Vali pulled up his horse and gave a whistle to gather his felag. He approached the lost felag at a slow walk. Their number had doubled from what he could see. What a motley group they had added. Two young women, one just a slip of a girl. Two pyris males, one of which was securely tied, and walking with them a strange green fellow. A memory flooded into him. It was as if he had ridden into one of his grandpap's stories. He pulled his horse to a stop as he studied this stranger. Who, seeing Vali watching him, smiled and waved. Well, in all the stories his grandpap told, the green man was a benefactor. He nudged his horse ahead a little more before he dismounted. Then he walked over to Crispin and grabbed his arm.

"Where in Hel's realm have you been? I lost a wager; I was sure you would be back two days ago with a yetann on a leash." Vali told him.

Crispin smiled back at his old friend as they gave each other a brief hug. "I had planned on your help with that." He told Vali. "But since you were nowhere to be found when I needed the help, I had to use what was at hand. The læknir and the green man were much rougher on the yetann than you would have been. So, we had to bury them. All we have to show for our trouble is a few pieces of armor. And a story you'll want to hear, I'm sure."

Seeing Catherine standing near he turned and bowed to her "Læknir Catherine, may I introduce you to my good friend, Vali Arinsen."

Vali removed his hat and made a sweeping bow to Catherine. Crispin smiled at this knowing how his friend loved to be dramatic. Catherine grinned and offered her hand entering into the play.

Turning to Crispin Vali asked. "When did you begin traveling with a læknir?"

"Since she helped us defeat the raiding party. She was the missing maiden." Crispin told him.

This brought a curious look to Vali's face and a question was on his lips when Crispin continued. "We're tired and hungry. If you and your men will help us with our baggage, we can begin to make our way to your camp. On the way, we will relate the tail of the læknir and the green man."

In short order, the young men of the horse felag had dismounted and distributed the baggage between the horses. Soon they began to descend to the camp. As they walked down the deer track Crisping began his tale.

It was dusk when the group entered the camp. They were tired and hungry. The hunger was quickly assuaged by the camp's cook, a jolly man who took great pleasure in feeding the hungry. He was Matsveir, the thane's cook. When the thane had headed back to Boar Akarn he had insisted on staying behind. He had a wager on Crispin's return. Besides he was enjoying rediscovering the tricks of cooking on a campaign.

There was also the other reason. Matsveir was sure that the aspen grove was the home of a dryad. Late one evening when they had first arrived, he saw movement in the grove. He had walked only a short distance into the grove when a sense of foreboding overcame him. The trees seemed to close on him. Oh, yes there was a dryad here. And he had been trying to coax her into revealing herself. Nothing he had tried had worked so far, but he felt that the possibility of meeting her would be worth the effort.

He had a special treat planned for tomorrow. He and a young scout had persuaded a hive of wild bees to part with some of their honey. The few stings they had to endure would be worth it. It would be the most amazing breakfast that any army in the field had ever had. If he could pull it off. Thankfully the flour was plentiful. The starter he had carried with him was still potent. The bread would be ready for his grand experiment. If the cinnamon and honey rolls did not impress the dryad, nothing would. You see he planned to deliver the first ones to the dryad as an offering. The fact that he had successfully made enough to feed the two tyge and their guests demonstrated the power of his gift.

*

The camp exploded with excitement as Crispin and his lost felag walked into camp. Crispin appeared to be friends with everyone there. A large older man gave him a bear huge then turned and introduced himself as Herr Vogan. Then a lady, Herr Frigg, took his hand and pulled him into a bend to lay a kiss on his cheek. Several others jostled to greet him. A couple of young archers attempted to kiss his lips, apparently in an effort to win a wager. Neither one was successful as he deftly avoided their lips. Then a grey-haired man named Baldur handed him a small bag of coins. The bag contained a tithe of what he had won. He thanked Crispin for picking this day to arrive. Valmi and Wedi were fed and moved to a tent with a rizi who had been found wandering the nearby forest. Crispin warned those escorting Wedi to keep a close watch. This was one of the ones who tried to attack the group. That aroused questions about what happened. To which Crispin replied. "Find a balladeer and after I have been fed, I might sing the story for you."

It was then that Drew and Jae intercepted the guards trying to hustle Cu lain away. There were some raised voices when someone in the crowd asked who would be forced to sleep with a mortdingya. It looked like a fight might break out when Eric in a quiet voice that seemed to hint a little of death told them. "He's a member of our felag, he'll sleep with us." A man near the back of the group seemed to drift off when he saw where Eric's hand was resting. Herr Vogan quietly called Lini his footman over and sent him off to find the instigator of the conflict along with his superior. He wanted to see both of them at his tent in an hour. Catherine had held tightly to Ceri's hand during all this and bushed away anyone who attempted to find a better place for the young rizi to be.

Somehow in all the hustle and bustle that was occurring as they entered the camp, Catherine and Jae were seated together as they ate. There was not much chance for conversation, not with all the people talking and interrupting to ask questions.

Ceri was already dozing off as they finished eating. Catherine began to wonder what her sleeping arrangements would be, as pyris didn't appear very popular with this group. She started to ask Jae if perhaps they could have a spot in the tent with the felag, when a woman who introduced herself as Rizna, walked over with a young archer named Vaetta. They had a tent ready which they would share with Catherine and Ceri. When they arrived at the tent Rizna brought out a measuring tape and proceeded to take down their height, waist, leg, and chest measurements. She then left the tent. Vaetta pointed out the warm water they had ready. Catherine removed her shirt and washed the dust off her face and body. Vaetta laughed a little as she eased Ceri into her bed, the child was asleep standing. Vaetta gently tucked her in, and then helped Catherine into a nightshirt. A luxury Catherine had almost forgotten. Catherine was asleep before Rizna returned.

CHAPTER 12

Karl stood near the dryad grove. He had not entered it the evening before because the message sent by her mother needed a bit of light to work properly. The only people awake this early besides the watch was the cook and his helpers. The aroma of what they were baking permeated the morning breeze, Karl had been waiting for this first breeze of the morning. A breath of air would aid in his delivering her message.

He wondered how much the cook's efforts would hinder his. As he began to approach the grove, he noticed a movement to his left. There came the cook almost prancing. In his hands was a plater bearing four rolls. It was the baking of these rolls which had infused the air around the camp. Karl wondered how anyone smelling those rolls could still be sleeping. He supposed that part of the silence of the camp during this magic show the cook was preparing was the fact that the breeze was blowing across the camp past the cook's camp kitchen and then into the dryad grove. What was this fellow up too?

He decided to find out and walked over to the cook. "Let's see, what was this fellows name? Oh yes, it was Matsveir. The name coming to mind, Karl said, "Chef Matsveir, what have you produced that bears such an amazing aroma?"

Matsveir stopped, how had he missed seeing this bear of a man? He had noticed the green fellow the night before but had attributed the color of his skin as a trick of the evening light. The same might be said for the morning light as well. But today the fellow was standing much closer. The fact that his attempted miracle appeared to be succeeding had also let him release his focus and observe other things.

"I aspired to be a chef at one time, but fancy food did not serve the army as well as good solid food did. So, I am just a camp cook now. Thank you for the compliment. You can have some of the other rolls. Go over to the boy attending the fire and tell him I have given you leave to take a few." He quickly said this, for he was intent on presenting his creation to the dryad before too many people stirred. "These are for someone else" He finished as he flourished his creation. He had hoped that this quiet morning would encourage the dryad to reveal herself to him. He had wanted to meet a dryad ever since his grandfather told him the tale of being protected by one during one of the battles with the Tyr yetann a century ago. He wasn't going to let anything distract him now. So, he turned away from the green fellow and once more headed toward the grove.

"Are you hoping to impress the dryad with your baking?" The green fellow asked.

That stopped Matsveir. He turned and looked at this fellow interrupting his effort. "What do you know of dryads, stranger?" he asked back.

"Her mother has sent me with a message for her" Karl stated.

That gave Matsveir pause, but only briefly. "My gift to the

dryad will be cold by the time you get done. Let me present these at their best."

"You know the dryad probably can't taste your offering." Karl countered.

"Shows what you know, green man. If one can smell it, one can taste it." Came a raspy voice. The voice seemed to be coming from a hole in the base of a large ancient oak standing just outside of the dryad grove. As they watched a face made of decayed wood peaked out of the hole. "I have appreciated the aroma of this fellow's baking. I prefer the smell of his baking over the stink of men and horse dung. What is it you have there, man? It smells of honey, yeast, wheat, and what is that other odor?" She said as a body made of sticks, twigs, and pieces of decaying wood emerged from the oak tree.

"That's not the most attractive dryad manifestation I have ever seen. I wonder why she picked such an unattractive way of displaying herself." Karl thought.

Matsveir almost took a step back as the dryad stood up to her full height which placed her head just above his own. Her head turned to him and the holes in the piece of wood where eyes should have been seemed to focus on him. How they gave the impression of focusing on him, he could not tell, for they were open holes in the piece of wood that was the dryad's head.

A cough, (Or was that meant to be a laugh?) escaped the dryad. "Not what you had expected man?" Her raspy voice queried.

Gathering his courage Matsveir took a step forward extending the hand holding the plater toward the dryad's manifestation. "I really didn't know what to expect. My grandfather's description seemed to imply a more delicate figure." He tendered.

"Humph," came from the dryad. The sound coming from the grove this time. "I found that this form was much better for dealing with east mountain yetann whenever one wandered through on a pilgrimage west. They seemed to listen to me better when I manifested this way. I can look very wicked in this form when I want to." She said. Being a piece of decaying wood, her face gave no hint of emotion. She appeared to Matsveir formidable just as she was now.

"As for you, green man." She turned her attention to Karl. "My mother's message will be easier understood a day or two after this odorous crowd has left. I am sure that you would not be able to carry my reply to her anytime soon. If you find your way back to mother and pass this way, I will send a message then."

Karl produced a small envelope made of tree bark and handed it to the dryad. She took it and it disappeared into a cavity in the pile of leaves and sticks that made her chest.

She took the plater from Matsveir's hand. She then turned back and entered the hole in the oak tree. Both he and the green man supposed the interview was over and prepared to leave. To say Matsveir was disappointed by the abruptness of the event would be an understatement. Karl thought he looked crestfallen and was determined to try to encourage the man later. After all, he had impressed this dryad enough for her to manifest for him. He was sure she would not have done as much for him.

Then her head once more appeared. She held something in both her hands. She extended her left hand and presented a small leather bag to Karl. "I've spent years collecting this. Don't you dare let anyone know where this came from. I don't need gold hunters traipsing about fouling up the place." She placed the bag in Karl's hand.

She then turned to Matsveir. Holding the other object in one hand she carefully uncovered a small group of seedlings. Karl counted maybe five. They were bare of foliage and had no earth covering their roots. "What is your name man?" She demanded.

Matsveir was looking so intently at the small trees that he was startled by her demand and gave a little jump. Looking up to her face, such as it was, he said "I am Matsveir the cook, my lady." And gave a small bow.

"I have desired to have children of my own just as my mother has children of her own. That I would trust a man with my first effort surprises me. But I see something in you I like." The dryad began. "It will be a challenge, even with your best efforts she may die. Do you know of a place in the foothills or better yet up in mountains that might accept a dryad's presence?"

Matsveir stood gazing at the small dead looking trees. A faraway look came to his face and then he smiled. "I am in need of a vacation, I'm sure the thane will allow me leave for a month or two. My grandfather's farm is in the mountains north of Merki. He still lives there. I send a housekeeper once a month to see to his needs. He no longer farms. He would be delighted to have a dryad near."

"It will be many summers before she will be able to communicate or even have the desire to do so, Matsveir. Twenty, maybe up to a hundred summers perhaps. Your grandfather will never know her." The dryad warned him.

"Just the knowledge that he has given a home to a dryad's child will comfort him, I am sure," Matsveir replied. "How must I care for her? She looks almost dead." He said as he tenderly removed the cluster of little seedlings from the dryad's hand.

"I have made her dormant. She can stay this way for a month possibly two. It would be best to find some good rich soil and a large pot to place her in before a month is over. Water it well then let the soil almost dry completely. She should sprout leaves soon after the second watering. If not let the soil dry a bit more than you did the first time. Too wet could cause her roots to rot. Once she has greened, she needs to be placed in her permanent location before the end of summer. The sooner the better. She would do best if you awoke her before planting where you wish her to grow. Water her well once she is in her new home. That will be all you can do for her. The rest is chance." She gave her instructions, then "Is the farm far away. I have no idea you see. My mother has the stream to carry down some of her thoughts and I the breeze when it flows up the mountain. Never mind. If she awakes from her sleep and is planted and lives, a few years from now you could come and let me know if you can."

"I will dear dryad," Matsveir told her. With his promise, the dryad's manifestation turned and disappeared into the old oak tree.

Overwhelmed by emotion Matsveir stood looking at the tiny fragile child of the dryad. He had hoped to meet her. He had never imagined that she would trust him, a stranger with such a treasure. It was several minutes before the noise of the camp brought him from his revelry. Someone called his name and he turned to return to his duties. The routine was ingrained in him from his many years serving with the thane. He was almost halfway back to his cooking tent when he stopped and looked around until he saw the Green man standing not far from him.

"What am I to do? I can't take her near the fires. I don't have the time now to pack her someplace safe!" He wailed to Karl.

Karl walked over to him and place his hand on the chef's shoulder. "I believe I can help you, friend." He said. "I have a place, a special pocket that will keep her safe until we have to part ways or until you are ready to deal with your charge."

With trembling hands, Matsveir placed the tiny dryad into Karl's outstretched hand. "Let me show you where she will be until you ask for her." He said as he moved his hand over his bare chest and down to his stomach area. There to Matsveir's astonishment, an opening appeared. Carefully Karl placed the tiny dryad into this hidden pocket in his body. "She will sleep there until you are ready to plant her, or we must part ways. Don't fear she will be safe." Concluding their exchange, he tuned the chef around and pushed him gently toward his duties.

His concern for the dryad's child momentarily allayed, he rushed back to the task of feeding the scouts as they came in their shifts to be fed before they finished packing up the camp. When the camp was packed, they would be heading for Boar Akarn and their thane.

*

It was still dark when the smell of fresh baked bread woke Catherine. Last night she and Ceri had been placed under the watchful care of Vaetta and Rizna. It wasn't long until they had Catherine and Ceri securely wrapped in their warm blanket of care. It had been a long time since she had felt this secure.

As she moved to get up from her pallet her hand brushed

something. She examined what she had touched and discovered a pile of folded clothing and what felt like a pair of boots. It was barely light, but she could tell that Ceri had a similar stack next to her bed. She sat up and in the feeble light began to decide what was what. Was this a shirt? No more like a pair of pants.

"You're awake." She heard Vaetta say. "Let me open the tent flap, maybe then you can see well enough to dress."

Vaetta opened the flap and enough light entered for Catherine to dress. How had Rizna managed to fit her so well with the few hurried measurements she had taken last night? It was then that she noticed that Rizna was nowhere in sight. As she turned to ask Vaetta where Rizna had gone so early, Vaetta told her. "Here's Rizna, wake Ceri and get her dressed. She's secured us a place in the front of the line. We'll get some of that bread while it's still hot!"

Talking and laughing they managed to tease Catherine about how nice Jae looked and the way he looked at her enough that Ceri joined in twice while they walked over to the cook's tent. They introduced them to Matsveir and his two chef assistants. Then the smiling cook had piled Catherine and Ceri's plates to overflowing. He even gave each of them, two of what turned out to be the most amazing rolls Catherine had ever eaten, sweet and sticky with a spice she could not identify.

The rest of the morning was spent taking down and folding the tent, packing, and generally getting ready for another hike. Vaetta and Rizna both had disappeared, and Catherine was wondering who her traveling companions would be. She missed the felag who had been down the mountain with her.

The pack she hoisted to her back was small and light. The only things in it were the articles of clothing that the felag had loaned her. Catherine appreciated the new boots Rizna had secured for her. Though she had spent most of her time barefoot in Boar Akarn, she liked having her feet covered while hiking in the wilderness.

Ceri was standing near her a small bundle of clothing all she had to carry. She was nervous and stayed as close to Catherine as she could. When male scouts walked close, she almost clung to Catherine. Catherine tried to assure her, but her experiences with the male pyris gave Ceri a distrust of strange men. And there were over fifty strange males milling about now. Some gathering the tents and other supplies the small army would be carrying on their journey.

As Catherine scanned the area, she saw the green man a small distance away looking about. So, she waved to him. He gave a shout and strolled over to her and Ceri. He extended his hand to Catherine. As they exchanged greetings Ceri, who had been watching the two men picking up the folded tent they had slept in, became aware of Karl's presence and leaped into his arms, much to his and her own surprise. She was suddenly embarrassed by what she had done and began to profusely apologize. Karl laughed and gave her another hug. "I missed you too, Ceri. It warms my soul for such a sweet child as you to want this old green man about." He then settled her arm in his as they stood and talked. He told them of his and Matsveir's encounter with the dryad.

As he finished his story Rizna and Vaetta walked up carrying two extra water bags and much to Ceri's delight two more of the sweet bread rolls. Ceri's roll disappeared almost as soon as it was presented to her. Her fears forgotten with the presence of Karl and the return of the two. Catherine carefully packed her roll into her pack, planning to share it with Ceri later.

It was then that Catherine heard her name called. She turned and saw Crispin and her felag. "Now isn't that funny to think of them as mine?" Intruded into her thoughts. That was nonsense she was sure, but it was a comforting nonsense, nevertheless.

With them walked Cu lain. He was sporting a new set of clothing too. Someone had trimmed his hair into the current style that most of the scoutss were wearing. If this had been the first time, she had seen them together she might have mistaken Cu lain for a long-time member of the felag. There following close behind was the architect of Cu lain's transformation, Elgar. Her felag, her home was complete. That brought an unpleasant thought to mind. Someday soon she would probably be separated from these friends.

She had been beaming only a moment before. What has changed her mood so quickly? Wondered Jae. It had been less than a day and he had missed her presence at their campfire. And then he knew as surely as if she had told him. The thought of their parting had crossed her mind. Well, they had at least three maybe four days before any possibility of that could occur. He decided then not to waste another day worrying about red ears.

"Hello, friends." Crispin began. "It has been decided to split the command. Herr Frigg with ten of her tyge and the felag of horse will travel with us. We will travel light and hope to make it to Boar Akarn in three or four days. The rest of the contingent will follow behind and bring all the heavy baggage. They are going to bypass Boar Akarn. Depending on the weather they could take as long as two or more five-days to arrive at Utroor. That is where they have been stationed. There they will store our baggage."

He paused, then proceeded. "Catherine, you could travel with the slower portion of our forces. And when you get near Boar Akarn you would be escorted there. But I would prefer you to travel with us."

"I would prefer to travel with you as well," Catherine responded. "I have things that need attending to in Boar Akarn."

Ceri hearing in the conversation the possibility of being separated from Catherine wrapped her arms around Catherine's left arm and whispered. "Please, may I stay with you? I won't slow you."

"Herr Frigg sent us to help læknir Catherine and Ceri prepare for the journey." Rizna broke in. "Besides water and trail rations, we brought socks for their boots. They should help prevent their new boots from rubbing wrong."

"A rider has been sent ahead. Herr Vogan wanted to relieve the worry of the king. It seems he arrived at his hunting lodge just after the raid. He may even meet us in Boar Akarn." Crispin relayed. "We'll start in half a shadow."

Crispin turned to Karl and asked. "I need a boon from you, my friend. Would you carry the old seior's chest? I want it with us."

"I can do that." Agreed Karl "The armor will be taken straight to Utroor then? When will Cu lain, and Catherine receive their bounty for it?"

"Soon after a scholar examines that armor with the engravings a value will be set," Crispin told him. "It's too fine a set to be sold to some merchant. Those engravings have some meaning I have not puzzled out."

The path led along the north bank of the Laek Gritter. The babble of the stream joining in the conversations as they traveled down what had once been a deer trail. The couriers and their horses had worn a clear path here, where the valley floor was almost level.

The felag of horse divided and circled the group guarding their path ahead and watching the surrounding country. The two felag of archers walked in front and to the sides leaving Crispin's felag with little to do but talk. Which was fine with Catherine.

Vaetta took special interest in Ceri. Vaetta was raised in Ritsker where there was a large colony of pyris who labored in the city's port. She drew Ceri out by admiring how much her gith were growing. Ceri was soon skipping ahead to be close to Vaetta as she rotated to the front of the travelers.

Time to time one of the other scouts would walk close and ask to be regaled in the story of their battle with the yetann. Eric decided he was the storyteller of the group and soon Catherine hardly recognized the tale. It finally became too much for Drew. He told the story himself in a way that satisfied his dzwerc senses. One of the young women among the Archers, Catherine thought it was Eir, but she wasn't sure, brought out her mandolin, and set a few of Drew's words to music. Someone playing a flute joined in. There was applause when they stopped. And for the first time that she could remember Catherine saw that even a dzwerc could blush when the young woman kissed

Drew on the cheek and told him how she admired the Dzwerc sense of rhythm.

The sun was high in the sky when they stopped for lunch. Catherine and Jae were sitting beside each other watching the trout chase water striders and some bits of trail ration that Jae had tossed into the stream. Their hands were almost touching.

"This would be a grand place to camp. If I had my rod, I'd catch a mess of those trout." Jae told her.

"Aren't these the same fish we ate while traveling down the mountain," Catherine asked.

"Yes, but caught with a rod makes it more sporting. Something about catching them that way seems to make them taste better than when using a net as we did on the mountain. I do prefer them pan cooked rather than boiled as well." Jae responded.

"Is the fishing good where you grew up?" She asked.

So, their conversation wound about them. Neither ready to speak of the parting they were expecting too soon. The connection they had felt since meeting growing. The roots of their lives were entangling much as the roots of the green man and the dryad had on the mountain.

After a short rest, they were on the march again.

*

As they prepared for the night Catherine noticed Ceri walking strangely. So, Catherine sat down and called Ceri over and asked her what was wrong.

"I have a small sore on my left foot," Ceri told her.

Well take off your boots and let me look at it." She was told.

Catherine examined Ceri's left foot and found a small spot on her left heel where a blister had formed and then rubbed raw.

Ceri wiggled her toes and sighed. "Bare feet are so much better for walking." She told Catherine.

"Except when walking in the wilderness where you may step on a sharp rock or stick unawares." Catherine lectured. "And why aren't you wearing the socks you were given?" She asked.

"Oh, they made the boots too tight," Ceri responded.

"That's part of why you wear them. They help keep the boots from slipping on your feet. That's why you have this raw spot. The boot slipped on your heel and caused a blister." Catherine told her. "Now sit still and practice the calling as I taught you."

Sitting facing each other Ceri and then Catherine closed their eyes and called to Ceri's lorki. Ceri made a good effort but it was to Catherine that they responded. Ceri's effort rallied her lorki but it was Catherine that directed them.

A quarter of a shadow passed as they sat there. When Catherine opened her eyes, she noticed several of the band gathered around watching.

Vaetta was first to speak. "What are you doing? Her blister is so much better. I can't believe how much it healed in so short of time."

"I just helped call Ceri's lorki to aid her wound. Don't your læknir call the lorki to help heal you?" Catherine asked.

"Most of our healers use potions and other medicines. I've only known one or two that even spoke of lorki." Rizna said. "I'd like to know more of this."

"I use potions and other medicines too. But If you can call your lorki to assist, healing occurs faster. Each person's relationship with their lorki is unique, but I'll show you what I can." Catherine began.

The rest of the evening was spent helping those who wanted to explore the relationship of their bodies and the lorki.

CHAPTER 13

From Jarta Thorsen's tome "A Short History of Alfheim" fifth volume.

Virkiflyot was originally built to guard the western approaches of Arnarhvall. It now houses the Legur Haskol (Royal Academy). Which has become an almost forgotten term. Virkiflyot is now used instead of the Legur Haskol, much to the disapproval of traditionalists such as myself.

*

They were up and traveling before the sun peaked over the horizon. Jae had traveled ahead with the lead scouts. He was seeking to hone his skills by watching the seasoned scouts.

As they walked along Karl moved in beside Catherine.

"What you did last night was remarkable." He started.

"Oh, dealing with Ceri's little blister wasn't much at all." Catherine deflected.

"No, that's not what I mean. You were amazing as you helped those who listened last night become aware of their lorki. Very few of those around us seem to acknowledge how important our lorki are. Most healers are at the mercy of the strengths or weaknesses of their potions and medicines. At least four of your students rallied their lorki, even if they were barely aware of it. One might even develop into a healer if she continues practicing the simple exercise you taught.' He told her.

They walked silently for a short distance while Catherine considered this. She really didn't think she had done that much. The lorki were so much a part of her life.

As they took a short rest, Karl asked her. "How aware are you of the lorki that surround us, filling our world?"

"I know that the lorki are present in almost all life. But I have only experienced them while practicing healing." Catherine told him.

"Well let me be the instructor. I suspect that my explanation of what I want you to try will be as cryptic as what you talked about last night was to most of those around you. But, since we are stopped for the moment, are you willing to try something new?" Karl asked.

"What do you have in mind?" she asked in return.

"See that hawk flying over the forest?" He inquired. "Have you ever looked through another's eyes?"

"No, I've never heard of such a thing." She told him.

"Try this. Expand your awareness as you do when you would begin a healing exercise. As your awareness broadens think of the hawk. Don't try to force it. The creature will respond if you ask it to loan you its eyes. Make it a request. Relax, shut your eyes, and try." Karl encouraged.

Catherine sat down and closed her eyes. Her breath slowed as she let her awareness expand out into the forest. To her amazement, she found the hawk as it circled above seeking prey. She thought, "May I see what you do?"

Suddenly she was above the trees! The hawk ignored her presence as it rolled over in its flight and dropped down toward a tree. It swooped down and almost hit a tree limb before it did another roll and snagged a squirrel in its talons.

Catherine gasped and opened her eyes. The earth seemed to move around her. She grabbed Karl's arm to steady herself. "That's incredible! I don't know if I could do much of that. My stomach is unsteady from it." She told him.

"Perhaps I should have waited until we saw a vulture or even a heron. They don't make such violent maneuvers. This ability can be useful at times. It would bear to practice it some." Karl smiled as he spoke. "This is a very remarkable young woman." He thought. He wondered how her abilities hadn't brought the accusation of witchcraft in the backwoods hamlet she had lived in. Perhaps her powers were just now developing?

It was mid-morning when the column came to the first camp providing a relay station for the couriers. The felag greeted them and directed them up a hill. They were told that was the best path toward Boar Akarn. The trail following the stream would end up near Utroor. The next relay station would be closer in distance but uphill. It would be best to camp at the next station they were informed. The trail then would wind through the woods before descending to the last relay station. A short distance from there was an abandoned road that would lead them into Boar Akarn. The scouts speculated that perhaps at one time there had been another hamlet at the other end of the road.

Jae was almost out of breath as he topped the hill. The fellows below hadn't been exaggerating when they said it was a climb. On level ground, he would have made it this far without a rest. As it was the party had taken five rests on the way up. The men at the next camp were just a short distance off on what appeared to be the most level spot on this ridge. They waved as they recognized some of the people approaching their camp.

As they arrived at the camp the felag passed out cups of hot tea. They encouraged everyone to settle in. They expected a shower about sundown, so they brought out some tarps and stretched them between a few trees. It was dusk when the short shower passed through the area. After the rains, they ate a light meal and using some ground cloths settled in for the night.

CHAPTER 14

Chapter 5 of Heimr Scholar Durathror's tome "Knowing Your World"

In the region historically known as Alfheim reside the Alliance known as the Free States. The region suffered most during the Hegemony of the Thyr Yetann. They are called the free states for two reasons. First, they are free from the Thyr Yetann Hegemony. Second, all states in the alliance have outlawed slavery, though indentured servitude still persists it is frowned upon. The present free states within the region are Alfheim, Duchy of Jorunn, Idoneal, Kalfa, Northeim, Ringsfjord, Thryheim, Vanaheim, and Vestan.

*

A letter from the queen.

Ari reread the letter his mother had sent him. His mother must have believed some of her more strident letters had been purposely delayed. Because this letter had been addressed and perfumed by a young lady of the court that he had been known to escort during court functions.

After the briefest greeting, she had launched into a tirade about his father's absence from the palace. She related a series of events that his father's presence would have eased and a list of at least three issues that could only be handled by the king. She questioned why his father had not returned. Why he had only answered two of her letters. She ended with a royal command for him to persuade his father to return to the palace and his duties and abandon his great yetann hunt. He folded the letter and placed it in its envelope, with the small envelope addressed to his father by his first name. He walked down the hall to the study where his father was pouring over maps of the region. Old maps, inaccurate maps, the only maps they had of the wilderness that lay north of Alfheim.

"Father, have you been purposely misplacing mother's letters" Ari began. "She seems to think someone in your entourage is keeping some of her letters from you."

His father raised his eyes from the map he was studying, looked at Ari, and said. "Let me see that letter."

"Mother has ordered me to persuade you to return to the court. She tells me that if you still refuse to listen to reason, I am to read what's in this second envelope aloud to you." Ari told him as he handed the letter to his father. "Knowing mother, we'll both be embarrassed by that."

King Awrick chuckled. "Yes, we would." Looking quizzically at Ari he said "Let's say you have persuaded me. How would you propose to discover what has happened to Crispin and his felag? If, I put you in command."

Ari's dark mustache twitched, would his father finally put something under his command? He had tried to get his father to give him command of a border garrison West of Merki two years ago. He had graduated from Virkiflyot two years before with hard earned honors. It seemed that he had to work twice as hard as any other student to make a passing mark. As if the staff took perverted pleasure in thwarting the heir to the throne. He barely made passing marks in any of his courses the first two years. The last three had not been much easier. But by then he had found his stride. With the cohort of friends, he had developed and the extra hours of study he graduated with honors. Yet with all that, when others had been given posts in the army, he had to return home to the palace.

"Son, where did you drift off too?" His father asked.

"Oh, no where important." He replied.

"As I was saying it is too late in the day to start out. But, first light I want you to take a tyge of horse and proceed to Boar Akarn. Have a felag meet us with the prisoner at Utroor. Leave a felag to guard the victim's home. It troubles me to have to do that. I had thought our people were made of better stuff." He fluttered his hand in frustration at the need to guard a victim's house. "Take command of the combined force and go to the last known location. From there you are on your own. Make your own choices." Looking directly into Ari's eyes his father continued. "Take advice from the more experienced officers. It's never a shame to listen to others. Usually, the shame comes from not listening. I will take my remaining guards and return to the palace and your mother."

Decision made he reached out his hand to take the small envelope his son still held in his left hand.

Ari grinned at the prospect of commanding a group of scouts as large as the contingent that had been stationed at Utroor. He handed the envelope to his father, took a small bow as was proper etiquette, turned, and left the room.

The king raised the envelope to his nose. Yes, this indeed was a personal message from the queen. His queen. Opening the envelope carefully so as not to damage it he read "Darling my bed is cold. Come home to warm it."

That brought a smile to his face. Yes, it was time to return to the palace.

*

Hltar was laying his suit out when Ari walked into his room. The old guardsman who functioned as his valet, his bodyguard, and confident always insisted that he dress properly for dinner. Even on a hunt, Hltar insisted that the prince show the proper decorum. He insisted that an officer always had to present himself properly if he expected his men's respect. Hltar was also able to deflect the more ardent ladies who were in pursuit of marrying a prince. The first few times he had intruded on a hoped-for dalliance, Ari had been more than angry. Then came the time Hltar took him on a tour of the hidden passages of the palace. And quite by accident, so Hltar claimed, they overheard a trio of young ladies wagering on who could bed the naive prince and thus force a marriage. That ended the joy of the chase for Ari. At the start of his third year, the prince had much more time to give attention to his classes.

Hltar hadn't noticed Ari standing at the door yet, or he gave no indication that he had. So, Arai cleared his throat. Hltar turned and gave a small bow. "Your attire is ready my prince," Hltar said not missing a beat.

Thank you, Hltar" Ari said. "The king has given me an assignment. Do you think you can have us packed for wilderness travel tonight? We're to leave at dawn."

"My prince, I've had your wilderness gear ready since we heard of the raid." Hltar replied. "after all you are the most logical person to carry the king's concern into the wilds."

This brought a smile to Ari's lips. He was glad once more for following his father's advice on who should be his valet. They spoke of which horses he should take for his mounts as Hltar helped him dress for dinner.

*

Verdandi had outdone herself. It amazed Ari how this woman could take the most basic ingredients and produce a meal as fine or finer than the best chefs in Arnarhvall. Ari would miss her cooking. Though he had heard that Thane Awrick had an equally amazing cook attached to his dirfylk. He would be happy to test that rumor.

They had just finished the fourth course and were waiting for the dessert while sipping their wine when they heard a commotion at the entry of the lodge. Bui walked in escorting a young woman courier. She stopped short in seeing the king stand when she entered.

"Well, do you have any news? Spit it out. I can read the missive later!" king Awrick demanded.

At this, she straightened her spine gave a salute, and in a barely trembling voice said. "Visi Crispin has returned. And I heard that he arrived with his complete felag and the kidnapped woman. My lord."

A gentle look and a smile came to the king's face. He walked over and took the missive from the courier's hand. He then

142

placed his hand on her shoulder. He looked down at the missive again noticing the time and date it was sent. "You made very good time on your ride. What's your name?"

"Fylki Knapdottir, my lord." She looked down at the floor waiting for the king's laugh. She had become use to that, what with her father's play on words in naming her. His name meaning rider. Making her a filly rider's daughter.

"Beinir, take this scout's name down and recommend her for a commendation. I suspect we will come to respect her skills more when we head to Boar Akarn tomorrow. Bui make sure this scout is given a good meal. Find her a place to rest tonight in the lodge. Dyri, send another rider back to Boar Akarn to notify them that we are coming. Frau Fylki can ride with us tomorrow." He finished as he tore open the satchel. He walked over to his chair and sat down

After reading the missive twice he looked up. "Ari, do you suppose your mother will forgive me for not starting to return to the palace right away if I bring Crispin back with me?"

"Well, there goes my first command." Thought Ari as he assured his father that she would.

*

It was one shadow until dusk when they arrived a Boar Akarn. Herr Lyos was drilling his men. He was leading them through exercises that supposedly prepared them for combat with yetann. Crispin reflected as he watched, that not even having been in combat with the yetann seemed to prepare one to engage in it again. The only enemy more difficult to anticipate than the yetann was man, and that was only because you thought you knew your fellow better than a yetann.

Lyos' second drew his attention to the group entering the hamlet. So, he called his men to attention and dismissed them. He saluted Crispin and Herr Frigg as he walked up to them. "It's good to see you well, friend Crispin." He said. Then he sent his second to find the thane.

Orders were given, tents were set up for the scouts and the new arrivals fed. Jae, the rest of the felag with Rizna and Vaetta escorted Catherine and Ceri to what had been Catherine's home. There was a felag guarding the house. They appeared to have been good friends with Jae, Drew, and Eric, what with the familiarity of back slaps and kisses on the cheeks the young men received. Catherine recognized a bit of jealousy in herself at this.

There was a small comfort. As Jae was about to leave, he took her hand. This was the first time he had been bold enough to do so, though Catherine had given him opportunity more than once. He held it for the briefest moment before telling her. "Good night, I'll see you in the morning." He turned and walked away. Just as another scout came to take the felag for a review of their reports, Jae turned to her once more and gave a wave.

Catherine had noticed a tall willowy blonde, who in her opinion had kissed Jae too close to the mouth. She was beautiful. As Jae and the others left the young woman returned to her post guarding the backdoor.

Catherine entered her house with Ceri close behind her. Rizna and Vaetta started to say goodbye when Catherine stopped them and asked if perhaps, they could share her house for the night. They both quickly agreed. Vaetta left to gain permission from Herr Frigg.

After a brief search, Catherine found her tinderbox and lit a candle. With the candle, she found two lamps, and using the candle, lit them. She went to the pantry to retrieve more oil for the lamps. Strangely the pantry was locked and had a board nailed across it. Rizna then left to get extra oil for the lamps from the garrison's store. That left Ceri and Catherine alone.

Taking one lamp Catherine climbed the ladder to the loft which had been her bedroom. The old feather bead was still there. She shook out the sheets to be sure no scorpions or other vermin were hidden within. She then called the exhausted Ceri up. Ceri was soon dressed in one of Catherine's nightshirts. It almost swallowed the child whole. That brought a smile to both their faces. Ceri was asleep soon after she was tucked in. Catherine left her sleeping and descended the ladder.

A cold drink to share with Rizna and Vaetta would be good.

Though she was tired, and her feet ached from the rapid pace of their march she was not yet ready for bed. She almost knocked the tall blonde over when she exited her back door. This brought about an exchange of apologies, then a brief introduction. Asleif was her name. she had a hint of an accent that Catherine could not place. No doubt the young men would find it adorable. They had a bit of polite conversation as Asleif walked her over to the springhouse. She insisted on taking the lantern from Catherine and looking inside the small stone building that had served to keep cool what she and the widow had wanted cool. There inside Catherine found the last two bottles of elderberry wine the widow had made. Catherine had been saving them for some unknown reason. Tonight would be a good night to use them. Looking about the small building she found nothing else she would care to worry with. The butter, even in the spring house, would have turned rancid after all this time. The beer was older than Catherine. She had tried it once when she was younger. It was worse than the cheapest swill that Bjorn served. Catherine suspected later that the widow had kept it just so whoever took from her larder without her permission would be properly awarded. There was a ham hanging from a rafter. It didn't look too moldy, but she and her friends had already eaten. Let the next owner of this house decide if they would risk an old ham.

She returned to the house, hardly exchanging words with Asleif. And while she waited for her friends to return Catherine found some mugs for their drink.

Later the three sat and talked about the army. What life in it was like. Catherine questioned them about the absence of healers in the dirfylk. Catherine thought that at least a felag of læknir should be attached to each dirfylk. Better yet two læknir for every tyge. The others agreed with her but finding trained læknir that would willingly endure the hardships of the military was hard. Even harder during this time of relative peace. In the cities, a popular læknir could earn as much as a wealthy merchant. This was troubling to Catherine who took her healer's oath very seriously.

They talked and laughed till the bottles were empty and the oil running low. Rizna and Vaetta lay their pallets in the large greeting room and lay down to sleep. Morning would come sooner than any of them would like.

Catherine climbed into her room. There on the floor in a makeshift pallet lay Ceri. Apparently, the featherbed mattress was too soft for her. Catherine climbed in and after waking several times, finally made herself a pallet with the comforter next to Ceri. She then drifted off to a sound sleep.

CHAPTER 15

In Boar Akarn

Something was tapping on wood. "Are you awake yet?" called a soft voice. As the clouds of sleep dissipated Catherine recognized the voice of Vaetta calling her to wake up. She opened her eyes. It was just beginning to grow light.

"Good morning Vaetta" She greeted her friend.

"I thought you might want to get up early enough to bath and put on a fresh set of clothing before the men arrive," Vaetta told her. "Rizna has water heating. We found a large tub that looked the right size for bathing."

"Oh, thank you both. That would be so nice." Catherine responded.

"We also thought we and Ceri might get a bath if we all hurry." Smiled Vaetta.

"So, you might if I get moving." Laughed Catherine.

Ceri had just finished her turn in the warm water when there was a rap on the front door. Her hair was wet, and the strange garb Catherine called a dress was settling on her. The outfit had been one of Catherine's when she was twelve or so summers and it was a loose fit on Ceri's sparser frame.

Catherine was wearing what had been her favorite outfit. The dress was green and red with the widow's careful embroidery work setting off the neck and hem. It had fitted her perfectly when the widow had gifted it to her on her fifteenth summer. Now it was a tighter fit than she liked. She remembered how beautiful she felt in it the first time she wore it. Now she thought a loose shirt and a pair of pants suited her better.

Rizna waved for Catherine to remain seated as she sat her cup of tea down and stood. She then walked from the kitchen to the greeting room and opened the front door. Crispin, the felag, the Konkur called Cu lain and the green fellow were standing there. She gave a polite bow and told them. "She's in the kitchen wanting to know why her pantry is nailed shut?"

That brought a smile to Jae and Drew while Crispin put on a more serious face. As they entered the kitchen Catherine stood and greeted them.

"I had the pantry nailed shut to protect a box the tinker had tried to steal. I thought that the extra protection a few nails gave would save a busted lock. You must admit the lock on that pantry wouldn't be much protection from a determined thief." Crispin gave a wry smile as he explained his actions.

"We brought tools to open it with and I have the key in my pocket." He continued. "By the way how well did you know tinker Asvald? He seemed to know exactly what he wanted to steal."

Her smile left Catherine's face at the mention of the tinker. "I only met him once. When he first came through Boar Akarn. He had a donkey that was lame. It wasn't much a small bruise on one foot made the poor thing limp. It just took a little rest to make the creature right." She told him.

"When was that?" Crispin asked.

"Several years back." She said, then it dawned on her. "Why you know it was the summer after the widow Sturlasda died. I found him walking around the house. It was when I asked what he wanted he told me of his donkey. He had to go fetch the beast. He didn't return with it until the next day."

"I found out information from Herr Lyos and the felag I left that the tinker was working with the raiders," Crispin told her.

They talked about the whys and wherefores of this for a time until Vaetta broke into the conversation. "Well open the pantry. Let's see what he was trying to steal. Maybe it will tell us something about why Catherine was kidnapped."

With that Jae and Eric produced a couple of pry bars and

began to pull the nails from the board. Each one made a horrid screeching sound. Ceri covered her ears while the others winced. As Eric and Jae worked on the last two nails Drew stepped forward and took the board just before it fell.

Crispin produced the key and opened the pantry. He then reached in and picked up an ornate wooden box. The box was made of strips of different woods inlaid with figures of different animals made of what looked like mother of pearl. He handed the box to Catherine.

The box she held in her hands looked familiar. Was it? Yes, it was her father's puzzle box. She moved her hands over the box. Turning it over she heard something moving inside. She carefully examined it from all angles before deciding where the top of the box was. She walked over to the kitchen table and sat the box down. Now, if after all these years she could remember how to work the puzzle. Pushing and trying to slide various pieces of the interlocking wood that made the puzzle box didn't seem to do anything.

Then she remembered. She placed her left thumb on a particular piece at the particular place she remembered. Then on the other side of the box, she was able to slide a piece over just a little. After moving her right hand to another place and placing her forefinger over an inlaid piece shaped like a bird, she was able with her left hand to slide another piece over, exposing a button. Sliding that piece back into place she then slid a piece on the lid that hadn't moved before. She placed her finger on another inlay shaped like a dragon. Then while holding her finger over the dragon she once again exposed the button. Pushing the button, she heard a click and a piece of wood popped out forming a small handle which she then turned to the left and the lid opened.

Inside the box was an envelope with her name on it. Under the envelope lay a pearl ring and a necklace with a pearl in an ornate setting forming the pendant. The chain of the necklace had no break or jump rings all the links appeared solid. How the pendant was placed on the chain was a mystery.

She sat down on a nearby kitchen chair and examined the envelope. On the back of the envelope was a seal that she did not recognize keeping the envelope from opening. She started to remove the seal when it grew warm at her touch, which gave her pause. Wax seals should not grow warm at the briefest touch.

"Do you see that?" Jae queried. "The wax is melting."

As they watched the wax continue to melt the flaps of the envelope slowly began to open. At last, the flaps opened enough to expose a message. It read, "Dearest daughter, Greetings on your sixteenth summer."

Catherine sat with her hands on her lap. "The widow died at the end of my fifteenth summer. She never told. She must have been planning on surprising me with this."

The wax was still soft when she touched it again, but it did not melt at her touch this time. She gingerly opened the flaps and removed several folded pages of fine paper. When she touched the paper, it shimmered for the briefest moment. So brief that if she alone had seen it, she would have thought it was her imagination. But Jae, Drew, Crispin, Eric, and Ceri all saw the same thing. She unfolded the letter exposing a short paragraph that ended with her father's signature. She flipped through the other pages, but they appeared blank.

Her father had written. "My dear Catherine. Known in our heart as our daughter Sivea A'celun. Your mother and I had planned to be presenting these artifacts to you together. Unfortunately, circumstances have not allowed either of us to share this happy time. At this time in your life, your abilities and gifts are maturing as you have been discovering under the widow's care. The ring and necklace are especially attuned to you. You alone will awaken their properties.

Place the ring on your right hand first then wait until it attunes to you. You will know when this happens. Next place the chain over your head and around your neck. Place the pendant next to your skin. You will feel it warm and then cool. After this please read this message again.

With love dear child

Your father, Aderyn A'dylan, or as you have known me Snorri Viorson."

Catherine read the message again. She then picked up the ring and carefully looked it over.

"What does the letter say?" Eric asked.

Catherine began to give a brief answer to Eric's question when Crispin interrupted. "Catherine may want to keep this private." Turning to Catherine he said. "Forgive me but I was able to read a part of your letter. If I were you, I would do this in private. There may be things you do not want to share. We can secure the house for you. Come, search the house and stand at the doors. Let Catherine have her privacy."

At this Rizna whispered something into Vaetta's ear. In response, Vaetta touched Ceri's arm and motioned her to follow them. Ceri was glad she did when they asked her to climb the stairs and gather any other of Catherine's old dresses, she had given Ceri. They had a friend who was accomplished in alterations. She would be glad to fit the dresses to Ceri and make them truly hers. Hearing this Ceri rushed upstairs picked out the three Catherine had given and a couple of others that were too small for Catherine but with patterns, Ceri liked and left with the two women.

As the others started to leave the room, Catherine said. "I'm not sure I want to be alone."

"You should only have someone who you trust without doubt. You have known us for less than two five-days. While I am sure Ceri has complete loyalty to you, she is a child and may speak of things she shouldn't by accident. We are your friends and we will only be a call away. Let us make sure the house and later you can share what you want with whoever you choose." Crispin told her.

She reluctantly agreed. She waited alone till she heard Crispin's call "Secure." Then she slipped the ring over her finger. As it slipped on it appeared to be a size too large for her finger but as it reached its intended resting place it became warm and seemed to adjust to a perfect fit. Not so loose as to slip off by accident, and not so tight as to be hard to remove. It cooled and her lorki which had been agitated as the ring slipped onto her finger once more became calm.

She held the ring on her finger up to the light coming into the kitchen window. Upon examination, she was sure that what appeared to be a pearl was not one. With the light playing over it the pearl appeared to have a depth she had never seen in the freshwater ones she had traded her treatments for in the past. Thinking of this she went to the closet where Crispin had stored the box and removed a small tin. Sitting down again she opened it and removed the largest pearl of her collection. Comparing the two it was obvious that the one on her ring was not a pearl but something entirely different. What she could not say.

In some way, the ring felt as if it always belonged on her finger. It had come home. Catherine removed the necklace from the box and carefully slipped it over her head. Then she tucked the pendant into her dress where it would touch her skin and waited.

She didn't have long to wait. Soon the pendant against her chest grew warm almost too warm. She was about to remove it when it began to cool. It seemed to cool faster than it had warmed. She felt energy touch her then after feeling a slight drain of energy all was once more, quiet and balanced. She searched her lorki and all appeared well. So, she picked up her Fathers letter and began to read it again. Only this time strange letters seemed to float over the paper. For a moment they were unreadable, then they settled into her father's familiar script. The letter now read.

"Sivea, my darling daughter you have your mother's eyes and my red hair. We are among the last of the Sihiratia. We were the crafters of the gods. Our libraries hold tales of our exploits, at least the books that can still be read. We have dwindled in numbers since the gods abandoned Ymir. They abandoned all the Sihiratia as well. In the end, we too were just tools to them as were the Vanir. The Vanir were not as dependent on the gods as we were. They were better adapted to this world. Some of their number had been the gods hunting companions. From the Vanir came many of the races of man we know today.

For over five hundred summers the Sihiratia have been governed by the council of the hundred. The Nokug Saja. Supposedly our council was led by elders, those wiser and more experienced. If your mother's and my experiences dealing with them are any evidence that is no longer true. The council today is made up of wicked men who not only enslave the other beings of Ymir but enslave their own people. They hide from sight and siphon wealth from those who suppose them, benefactors. Beware of them.

For now, you are well hidden with widow Sturlasda. A wise and kind woman. She has hidden from the council for longer than I have been alive. She helped your mother and I escape the council when we were discovered in Valdres. And she took you with her to safety in Alfheim when I no longer could remain hidden in Kalfa.

She can help you learn to use these small gifts your mother and I have to give. We had planned to gift you with an artifact that would match your natural talents. Sadly, we discovered that the artifacts we had allowed the council to trace us. We found no way of disabling the signal they sent through the ley lines. We did find a way to mask them.

We are hoping that the council will destroy itself with the infighting we witnessed when we were captive to them. If not, do not attempt to follow the clues we have left for the three artifacts that are your heritage. Dare not attempt to find them alone. Only with powerful allies will you be able to gather the artifacts we have hidden.

They fancy themselves huldra. Hidden from outsiders and justice. In truth, they are the last of a wicked band of thieves. I pray for their demise.

The other pages of this missive are keyed to open on your eighteenth and twentieth birthdays. It is my hope that your mother and I can join you before then. I have not lost hope. Now that I know you are safe with widow Sturlasda I will endeavor to lead our enemies on a chase. I have one broken artifact that I will allow to signal them as soon as I have secured passage on a ship.

As for our gifts. The ring is a vel opna, it will allow you to access the abilities of many artifacts. The ring will also develop a green glow when an artifact is dangerous. In bright light that will be hard to see. The necklace is a vel eiga, it will increase your vigor and allow you to extend the time you can use your lorki before you become fatigued. I pray they serve you well.

With my deepest love, Your father."

*

While Catherine and the others were discussing the implications of her father's letter, Karl excused himself. He needed a walk in the sun he told them. That was not a lie, for indeed he did need a walk, and the more sun the better his green body would feel. The sun, the breeze, and the ley lines would speed the healing of his wounds. Wounds the severity of he had not revealed to his new friends. He did suspect that Catherine knew more of them than her respect for his privacy would allow her to intrude with.

More than that he needed to search his memories, such as they were. A quiet walk would give him time to sort through the haze that was his memories. Those who had conspired to kidnap Catherine appeared to be the last remnants of enemies that tried to destroy the dryad. Still dangerous but only a shadow of what they had been. The loss of Catherine's father from their number had to be a blow. He appeared to be one of the few who could repair and attune the ancient artifacts.

What was apparent in Karl's thoughts was that Catherine's kidnapping may have been designed to be a distraction from an attempt to steal an artifact they believed she had. Bringing her back into their control would have been desired but if her father had managed to secure artifacts that allowed him to attune and repair other artifacts well, that would be a prize indeed. They were wrong of course. What Catherine had now would have disappointed them. Not only were they unusable to anyone but

Catherine, they were not the powerful tools Karl believed they were searching for.

He was sitting in the sun musing on these thoughts that would not completely connect when something brought him back to awareness.

"What an odd fellow you are!" A child's voice disturbed the afternoon's silence. Turning toward where the sound came from, the green man began "I believe I am." Then he stopped. There before him was a boy of about 10 summers he would venture. There was something about his eyes, were they green or blue? Was that red? The child coughed and shut his eyes. "Sorry, sometimes I forget." Then, the green man was looking into ordinary brown eyes. "Would you like skipping some rocks with me? The mill pond is just the place" Pointing a little to the left where a millpond sat with its still surface beckoning. "I've gathered a pile of nice flat rocks. They should skip just fine. They are only waiting for me to find someone to play with." A shy smile played across the boy's lips.

Karl stood. "Seeing that I have never attempted that before, you will have need of teaching me. But it does sound like a pleasant sport to learn."

That brought a wide grin to the boy's face. He skipped away toward the miller's pond with Karl following behind. For all appearances an ordinary boy reveling in finding a new playmate.

They spent the better part of a shadow with the boy teaching Karl the finer points of rock skipping. The boy seemed quite satisfied with himself when under his instruction Karl gave ten skips to a stone. Of course, the boy's skills were more refined with him attaining fifteen skips with most of his throws. He clapped his hands once when he managed twenty.

He then turned toward the green man a serious expression occupying his face. It made him look much older, an ancientness seemed present in that look. When Karl noticed the change come over the boy's face, he knelt to face him. He bought himself as much to the boy's level as he could. It was at this point he began to have an inkling of who he was dealing with.

"The girl began to disturb the leys two summers ago." The boy began. "I thought little of it seeing that finding a single person with such weak evidence would be almost impossible. Then an old friend appeared within the patterns of ley and lorki and the two patterns seemed entwined. The old friend faded away as I was observing, and the girl's pattern became clearer. I thought that my friend would not have hidden without good reason and from the patterns she had also hidden the girl."

He paused a moment. "We, you, the dryad, and I have ancient foes. The dryad might consider me one of hers."

He hesitated and dropped his eyes to the ground. "I was once more naive than I am now. I traveled with a man to find a dryad. I had never met one and I always loved adventure. I was tricked and didn't discover that until it was too late." He looked up at Karl with tears in his eyes. I would have stopped him if I had known in time. He sent me to the stream to fetch some trout for dinner. The dryad had not spoken to us as I was told she would. I think she knew he was one of our enemies. He had a device that he planted in her midst. Near where we were camped."

He stopped to wipe his eyes. "I should be old enough not to cry by this time you would think."

He looked up into Karl's sober face trying to discern if he might need to run. "I can know so much and see so many things. If I can ask the right questions the correct way, I can find out almost anything." He said. "I didn't ask the right questions before I started up the mountain to the dryad. And the journey was so distracting."

"As I neared our camping spot, I saw the device. My companion on the journey was nowhere in sight at first. Then I saw him higher up on the mountain. You were running down the hill from the west and everything went black.

"I awoke days later. A crater was where the dryad had been. You and the man were gone. I nursed the remaining aspens and did what I could to contain the poison. While I was nursing her remnants, I realized that the man who claimed to be a scholar and friend had attempted to kill all three of us at once. He almost succeeded.”

“So, you were there?” Karl asked. “You see I don’t remember any of that. I wonder if the dryad does. That explains why I killed the man in Niflheim.”

The boy nodded his head in agreement.

“Do you think she is still angry with me?” he asked.

“I don’t believe she knows to be angry with you. And I very much doubt she would be. She seems wiser and kinder than that.” Karl told him. “That was long ago, and we have today to worry about. Do you think our enemies have any more such devices?”

“No, I traced the thing back to where he found it. It was the last of the cache of the false Thor. He sought to destroy the lorki and according to his message cleanse Ymir, so the gods could return. Seeing that the gods who were, either fled or died in Asgard, long before the false Thor came and placed his artifacts where he could deceive others into using them. It is doubtful that allowing the gods to return was his real motive.”

“I sensed one of his artifacts close by where I found you and the dryad’s patterns intermixing with the girls. It faded from sight not long after it had blossomed brightly.”

“I believe it will never blossom again.” Karl interrupted. “It is planted where no one will ever find it.”

“Do you think the dryad will let me visit her?” The child changed the subject once more.

So much like a typical child of ten or so summers, Karl thought.

Tugging on Karl’s arm the boy pleaded. “Ask her when you see her again. Ask her if I can come visit? Please. I will know the answer when she gives it. If it is no, I will respect it. I’m not as narcissistic as some believe.”

Karl thought he saw tears forming in the boy’s eyes once more. “Child, I will ask when I see her again. But I need to neuter our enemies before I can return to her. I want to see her again much more than you.”

That caused the child to focus on Karl once again. “Yes, I believe that is true." He said as he tilted his head in thought.

"I have been able to gather evidence that the cabal seeking the artifacts and the girl have only two people who can use the device they found her with. And fools that they are, they have made it, so it takes both together to use it. The leaders distrust each other so much, you see. It is my hope one dies before they train another."

"I don't travel so far south any longer. You see I was a slave once. I do not relish the thought of being trapped in that again. Even with my talents escape was difficult." The boy told Karl.

"I have been encouraging the path Alfheim and the other free states have taken. It is my hope that we can bring the end of slavery to all Midgard." The thought brought a smile to the boy's face.

"I haven't forgotten your concern, friend Karl. I believe it is safe for you to return to the dryad as soon as you wish. The enemy's intrusion into your life was an accident on their part. They would be terrified to know they have alerted the green man and the dryad to their presence.

I think I would prefer you delay your return to her. The girl has found some friends, but your presence would give her more security. Someday she might be a needed ally" the child told him.

"Her name is Catherine. I think you know that. Maybe you should meet her if you will be guarding her." Karl interrupted.

"Oh, I'm not going to guard her. That's why I want you to remain. I have a journey to Gandvik I must make. I believe I will meet Catherine at a later date. Wish her good journey please." The boy told him.

"See unlike some thought long ago I have a few manners." With that, the boy shook Karl's hand and walked away.

"So, this is the Child." Karl thought. He's not quite what the stories in my memories would make of him. But, what to make of him Karl was unsure.

CHAPTER 16

Catherine, Rizna, and Vaetta were sitting on the front porch being entertained by Ceri. She was so excited by the way the three newly altered dresses fit. She was changing from one to another in quick secession. No sooner had she displayed how well one fit than she rushed back into the house to try on another. When she had finally slowed down it all started again when the cobbler delivered the two pairs of boots Catherine had ordered the day before.

They were exceptional work the best Catherine had ever seen from cobbler Stigveil. The day before she had been haggling about the specifics of the two pairs she wanted. He was firm on his asking price, two pence and a katl which she had no trouble with. It was the material and style of the boots they could not agree on. She wanted boots that could stand along wilderness walk. He thought a daintier more feminine boot would better suit her and some flimsy half made sandal was all her rizi servant needed. She was about to give up and wait until they arrived in a larger town to acquire the footwear, she knew they needed when Crispin walked up and asked what was happening. Stigveil winched when she expressed her opinion. She was turning to leave when Crispin asked in a quiet voice. "Cobbler, do you know the king's standard?" To which Stigveil acknowledged he did. "These are your options. If the boots are ready tomorrow by second shadow and are acceptable to Læknir Catherine. I will pay three pence to you. If they are not up to the Læknir's expectations, they are hers at your expense." When Stigveil started to protest Crispin held up his hand. "We are not negotiating my friend. You can accept my terms or forfeit the sale. We will look elsewhere for our needs. Before you answer listen to your final option. If they are delivered on time and meet what I consider the minimum within the king's standard, you will be paid a skalt for the pair. Is this agreeable?"

A calculating look passed over Stigveil's face as he considered the offer. A skalt was twenty times the pence he would receive from any other buyer. He would be pressed to finish such fine worked boots and if they did not please the girl, he would gain nothing. He knew what he could do. He was at one time well known for his boots. That was before his trouble in Skalafell. Could he find the skills once more to make boots to the king's standard?

"Aye, I accept the challenge," Stigveil said.

"Do you have the measurements you need?" Crispin inquired.

Stigveil nodded his affirmation and began to look thought his stock of leather.

Now she and Ceri were wearing them and they were amazing. Nice looking with beautiful stitching and the fit was perfect. They were more comfortable than she had thought Drew's moccasins were when she had first put them on. Well, old Stigveil earned his three pence. And if they met Crispin's expectations, well maybe they were worth what Crispin had offered.

A half shadow later Crispin and Elgar walked over. Catherine offered them some tea. Which Crispin declined, and Elgar accepted.

As Elgar took the mug from Catherine's hand Crispin asked Ceri to let him see her new boots. To which she raised the hem of her dress slightly and slowly turned around. It took a bit of persuasion before Ceri took her new boots off and handed them to Crispin to inspect. He ran his hand inside and out and pulled on each seam before he tossed them to Elgar and requested Catherine's. He examined Catherine's more closely if that was possible. After Elgar handed Ceri's back to her he tossed Catherine's to him. As Elgar examined that pair of boots. Crispin turned looked at the women and informed them. "Prepare for an invasion. A rider arrived half a shadow ago informing us that the

King will be arriving soon. Rizna and Vaetta please help Catherine and Ceri prepare for the event. And Catherine an event it will be. Whenever the King appears it is an event, no matter how hard he works for it not to be. Well Elgar, what do you think?"

Elgar looked up from his examination of Catherine's boots and smiled. "Reminds me of some work I saw in Skalafell long ago. Very fine." He then handed Catherine's boots back to her, leaned against the porch post, and sipped his tea.

Crispin started to turn. Then he stopped and told them, "Expect a twenty of horse to arrive within a shadow. They will, in all likelihood, place the king's pavilion in that lot in front of your house. Elgar will remain here to see that they don't overreach their assignment and try to move you from your house. After all Catherine, the king will want to see you after the excitement of his arrival settles."

Crispin then walked toward Stigveil's stall.

*

It was half a shadow until noon. Catherine was glad for the large front porch on the widow's house. All the felag, Cu lain, Karl with Rizna, and Vaetta were gathered on it. Ceri bustled about serving tea with pieces of bread and cheese. They all listened as Karl told of his encounter with the Child.

"So, if I understand, what you learned from this demigod agrees with and adds to what we learned from the letter Catherine's father left her. Somehow widow Sturlasda was able to hide Catherine and herself from the huldra." Elgar spoke slowly mulling the information about in his mind. "And you, Catherine have no idea how she did it?" Catherine shook her head no. "So, there is no way that you know to hide from, what did the boy say? Do I understand that somehow Catherine, the artifacts, and maybe others disturb the leys and the lorki to produce some sort of pattern that the Child and some sort of device can detect?"

"That's the way I understood him" Karl responded.

"Do you think the widow might have something in her books that might help?" Jae turned to Catherine and asked. Jae and Catherine were standing together leaning against the porch rail.

This gave Catherine a comfortable feeling. It was becoming much too comfortable. She knew that it would make their separation that much more painful when the time came.

"There is nothing like that in her three journals or her ancient tome on the uses of common herbs," Catherine told him.

"Have you looked at them since you got your ring? It made a huge difference in what you could read in your father's letter." Jae probed.

At this thought, Cu lain excitably broke in. "Frau Catherine! Do you suppose your ring would open the grasblett's book? "

They were silently considering all this when a twenty of horse stormed into the hamlet. After the horsemen brought their mounts to a stop two officers circled the village and settling on a spot started barking orders to the men. Quickly the twenty dismounted and unloaded the pack animals. Crispin had been correct on the location that had been chosen for the king's pavilion. Soon it and several other tents were rising in the vacant area.

The officers circled the lot once and then rode over to the group on the porch. They were just beginning to order the group to move to another location when an older scout walked up and grabbed Crisping by the hand. "Visi Crispin I was so glad to hear of your return. As I told my felag if anyone could lead a felag against a horde of yetann and return with the felag intact it was you!"

"Good to see you again old friend. So, when did you begin riding with the king's guard?" Crispin asked.

"Oh, I don't remember for sure maybe a couple of years back." The man told Crispin. "I've best be off to tend to my assignment."

As he turned to walk away, Crispin slapped him on the back, leaned close, and whispered. "Nice of you to save your officers' embarrassment, Carl."

The older officer cleared his throat. "My apologies visi Crispin. I did not recognize you. I have never had the honor to meet you before. I am Albiorix and this is my second Herr Aki."

They both dismounted, and Crispin walked over to them and shook their hands. He then introduced them to each of the group on the porch saving Catherine and Karl for last.

"This is læknir Catherine the owner of the house." Then he turned and said. "This is Karl Greenman. Together they helped my felag defeat the yetann raiders. Be sure you let your men know that their honor is the king's."

"We understand." Herr Albiorix said. "We do have duties we must attend to if the pavilion is to be ready when the king arrives. If you will excuse me, we will be about them." At this, he and his second saluted Crispin, gave a respectful nod to both Catherine and Karl. Then led their horses away.

Crispin turned to Elgar and said. "I think that we must hide Catherine the way we hide the king. What do you think?"

This made the others wonder what he was talking about.

Before anyone could question how they were to hide Catherine, Crispin turned to Cu lain. "Time for you to change. What you have looks fine, but I know you've worn it for several days. Not your fault no one has bothered to supply another. Besides that, you are wearing the king's uniform and you need something different for now. I have taken the responsibility of having another set of clothing tailored for you. I hope you don't mind."

Cu lain looked a bit confused by this. He had bathed in the cold stream at least twice; he didn't think he smelled that much yet. And would it offend the king so much to have a konkur wearing his uniform?

Before he could say anything, Crispin went on. "Jae run to the quartermaster and request Fra Angian to give you the clothing I requested. It will be ready if I know that woman at all." When Crispin saw Jae hesitate as he stole a glance at Catherine, Crispin added. "Well kiss the læknir on the cheek and be off you need to bathe and change as well."

Drew's mouth twisted into a smile but before he could speak Crispin turned to the rest of the felag and ordered. "Off with you all, time to prepare for the king's arrival."

The others rushed off the porch. Jae was starting to follow

when he felt a tug on his sleeve. He looked over and saw Catherine presenting her right cheek to him, so despite his embarrassment, he leaned over, and much to Catherine's surprise kissed her briefly on the lips. Before she could recover, he had leapt over the porch rail and raced off on his assigned errand.

Vaetta suppressed a giggle, then she and Rizna excused themselves, for they too needed to prepare for the king's arrival.

"Well off to the millpond, I suppose." Cu lain sighed.

"Hold on a moment," Catherine told him. "Ceri is the stove still hot?"

"Yes, it is?" Ceri replied.

"Karl, would you fetch some buckets of water from the well. Please?" Catharine looked over to him. He nodded his assent. Then he went in and grabbed the two buckets that were stacked in the corner of the kitchen.

"Cu lain, there is a tub hanging in the back outside wall. Fetch it if you want a hot bath. You don't have time to argue."

Cu lain could tell that arguing would bear only sorrow, so he went to fetch the tub.

Cu lain was in the tub when Jae reappeared with Cu lain's new set of clothing. He handed to clothing to Ceri and before Catherine could move raced off to where his felag was camped.

Ceri carried the outfit into the greeting room and unfolded it on the small table by the window.

The outfit was made of deer leather bleached almost white. Frills ran down the back of the arms of the shirt and the collar was made with, to Catherine's eye, peculiar folds in it. The pants matched with frills running down the outside seam of each leg. A white belt and almost white boots lay in the bundle of clothing.

Ceri's eyes were wide with wonder. "I didn't know. Oh, how I would be beaten at home for looking such a one in the eyes as I have done to trum Cu lain." Her voice trembled at the thought.

"What is a trum?" Catherine asked her.

A noble, a chief, a rizi of the higher ranks." Ceri told her.

"Well, I know for a fact that though Cu lain is noble of spirit and action he is not a trum. He's proud to be called jarl. So, if you feel the need to add an honorific to his name use jarl." She told Ceri. Which lead to a discussion of what an honorific was.

"I do see what Crispin has done. Don't you, Ceri?" Catherine asked. Ceri shook her head no.

"He is raising Cu lain's status. I believe he wants to bring Cu lain to the king's college. And though, from what I heard, the king would accept a man on his own merits, some of the nobles are not so kind. If the nobles who travel with the king perceive Cu lain as a noble it will make approving of whatever future Crispin has in mind for Cu lain easier for the king to approve." Catherine explained. The explanation made Ceri's head spin. The world she knew had much different politics.

Karl ambled up to the door and knocked on it. Ceri ran and opened the door and ushered him in. Catherine then showed him the outfit. It was while she was displaying it, she noticed that Karl no longer wore the yetann kilt. So, she stopped and lay down Cu lain's new clothing. She stepped back from him and walked partly around him. "What have we here?" she inquired.

"Oh, this. It was the dryad's suggestion. While we journeyed down the Laek Gritter I have been growing it. I'm glad it had grown enough. I have in mind something of what Crispin has for Cu lain. Putting my best foot forward as it were. It never hurts to impress a king or the nobles with him." Karl explained.

"Where's my clothing?" Came a plaintive call for the kitchen. "I handed out what I had at your insistence and now there is nothing here for me to wear!"

Catherine handed Karl Cu lain's new clothing and directed him to the kitchen door while she and Ceri exited onto the porch to avoid bringing any more embarrassment to Cu lain.

*

Awrick dismounted his horse and handed the reins to his horse master, Gudvaer. The man always insisted on personally tending to his king's mount. The hamlet of Boar Akarn was just over the hill from here. He did not want to arrive too soon and embarrass the men preparing the pavilion. He had once in the first year of his reign. He had been in a rush to some function he didn't remember the purpose of, but he did remember the results. The embarrassment the commander of the advance twenty had felt led to his resignation and nothing would change the man's mind. He had been too good a man to lose that way. Herr Albiourix was another good man. As eager as he was to see Crispin and hear the tale firsthand, they could take a break, eat a light lunch and arrive after the noon meal. There was plenty of time. He could wait. And the delay let him consider the unpleasant duties he would have. Since he would be there the fate of elder Oysten would be in his hands.

Ari handed his father a water bag. His father tended to forget his water when on a hunt or in this case the end of one. It would be good to see uncle Crispin again. Though whether Crispin was really his uncle he did not know. He did know how valued he was to his father, the king.

They ate their trail rations cold much to the distress of some of the nobles riding with them. The better part of a shadow passed before they mounted their steads and journeyed on to Boar Akarn.

*

It was a full shadow past noon when Ceri called their attention to a large band riding into the hamlet from the southwest. She was sure the man riding at the front of the group, flanked by two other horsemen was the king. His noble bearing, the fine workmanship of his tack and saddle. The silver on the saddle sparkled in the sun. He pointed off in a couple directions and two felag of horse broke off from the group each heading toward one of the two points he had indicated. This was the man in charge.

Catherine was not so sure. Something about hiding the king. In the group of riders were several men who were dressed in hunting outfits. Some more ornate than others but nothing that stood out. There was one younger man, a rather handsome one in Catherine's estimation. His hair was in a long flaxen braid down his back. He also was the only one in the group without a full beard. He wore a dapper mustache the same color as his hair with the ends curled up. Was this prince Ari? If so, the man riding next to him with similar facial features must be the king. His hair was a touch lighter than the prince's, what might be the first evidence of it beginning to gray. His full beard was neatly trimmed, his hair was cut short, hanging just over his ears.

She recognized Alvi Geirson. It was his wild beard that first alerted her to his presence. Last summer he had been through Boar Akarn on a hunt for wild boar. He had found one and it had found him. The wound was not serious and was easily treated. He had been gracious, but it was obvious to Catherine that he was anxious to get back to his personal physician despite her assurances that the wound was minor and would heal within a five-day. To trust a girl of sixteen summers would not have been easy no matter how competent she seemed.

The others in the group were unknown to her. Most looked tired and rather grim after their early morning ride.

The prince, Vaetta had confirmed who he was, nudged the man next to him, and pointed toward the group on the porch apparently recognizing Crispin. He said a few words to the rider in front of him. Then orders were given. Two felag of horse left the formation and rode east past the pavilion and the porch. They took up station there. Another group rode south passing the house on the west and disappearing behind it. Catherine assumed they would be guarding the back of the house. After that, the prince and the king advanced together toward the porch before dismounting a short distance away. They both dropped their reigns and advanced on foot. As they came toward the group on the porch, a man rode up to the two horses dismounted, and after gathering the reins lead the horses away.

Crispin was on his feet when they had begun to ride forward. As they dismounted, he strolled to them. The king embraced Crispin and gave him a brief kiss on the cheek as they parted. The prince shook Crispin's hand and then Crispin led them to his friends on the porch.

As they were introduced to the king, the nobles scattered to their tents to refresh themselves. A guard of four felag maintained a presence but the rest of the troops scattered to set up their camps.

"There will be a banquet this evening you are all expected to attend." King Awrick told them with a smile. "Crispin, please attend me in the pavilion. I want to hear firsthand what I read in your reports. There are many details I want clarification on." The king started to leave then turned back. "Please stay near. I may be calling you each to the pavilion as I want to hear your stories as well. I hope you won't mind too badly my calling on you throughout the afternoon." With that, the king, prince, and Crispin walked over to the pavilion.

As it happened Catherine, Ceri and Cu lain had a boring afternoon. Rizna and Vaetta were soon called back to their felag. They had to attend their duties. And the king did not call for them at all. This didn't seem to bother Karl. He sat down in the sunniest spot he could find next to the small stream escaping from the spring house. There with his feet immersed in the water, he appeared to sleep.

Catherine spent part of the afternoon searching through the widow's journals looking for clues on how she had hidden them both from being detected by the huldra and the Child. She found nothing there. No magical pages, no explanations. All that was there were records of patients. She found nothing else. That is until she was almost to the end of the widow's last journal when there was a passage commenting on how the lorki seemed to be eager to listen to the young lady who was living with her. Unlike all the entries about her patients no name was mentioned, but Catherine knew it was her who was being discussed. That placed the end of this journal nearly eight summers ago. Did the widow quit journaling after Catherine arrived or was there a missing journal that covered the last eight years?

She picked up the tome on herbs once more, but it was still the dull old book it had been when she was a child. She saw where she and the widow had placed notes on most of the descriptions and uses of the herbs. Correcting and adding to the entries. But there was no magical information to be found there.

About three shadows past noon Ceri had made them each a cup of tea. It was after they had finished the tea, that Catherine noticed Ceri yawning. She smiled at her and told her she might as well take a short nap. "I'll wake you if anything happens," Catherine told her. Ceri was glad to ascend the ladder to their room. Where she lay down under the open window for a nap. That left Catherine sitting alone. She read her father's letter once more. Then folded the pages together and placed them in her puzzle box. She locked it and placed it on a shelf in the pantry. She made herself another cup of tea and spent the rest of the afternoon thinking about Jae's quick kiss.

Ceri came down the ladder about a shadow from dusk, her hair a tangled mess. She fussed and moaned trying to comb it out until Catherine sat her down on a kitchen chair and proceeded to brush it out. It was while Catherine was finishing brushing the tangles out, that there came a knock on the greeting room door. That knock roused Cu lain from the nap he would deny taking. He jumped up from the overstuffed chair he had been sitting in, almost drawing his sword. He put on a sheepish grin when he finally realized where he was and saw Crispin peeking through the door's window. He then walked over and opened the door for Crispin and Elgar. They were standing there grinning.

"The king sends his greetings læknir Catherine," Crispin told her when she appeared at the kitchen door. "He desires your presence along with fra Ceri and jarl Cu lain." Looking around he inquired about the location of Karl. When Catherine told them she last saw him sitting outback, they sent Cu lain out the back door to rouse him. It was time for them to join the king in the pavilion.

As they approached the king's pavilion Catherine wondered how such a large structure was able to be carried through the wilderness by only a twenty of riders and their pack horses. How had they managed to assemble it and the other tents that they had carried before the king's arrival? They had arrived before the king, true. But it amazed her that they were able to assemble the whole complex of tents in less than two shadows.

The pavilion itself looked to be thirty feet on each side. Each corner had a circular pinnacle. The material stretched on the sides between the pinnacles and across the top making the roof was made of alternating dark green, blue, and light green stripes. Atop each pinnacle's spire flew flags bearing the same colors.

A flagpole was mounted in front of the entry into the pavilion. It flew the flag of Alfheim. The flag's field was rectangular. A broad band of blue meandered like a river from the top right to the bottom left of the field. The field above was a dark green and the field below was a lighter green. The blue band symbolized the rivers that joined the kingdom together. The dark green symbolized the great expanse of forest that covered much of Alfheim. And the lighter green symbolized the fields of Eastern Alfheim where the grains that fed Alfheim and much of the world were grown.

As they neared the pavilion Crispin asked to take Catherine's arm. When Ceri questioned the why of it, Crispin explained that at a function like this, ladies should be properly escorted. Wanting to be a proper part of the splendor Ceri took Elgar's arm just as Catherine had Crispin's.

When they drew near to the pavilion two scouts in fancy dress uniforms opened the flaps that functioned as doors for the large tent. Ceri's eyes grew wide as they walked in. She had never seen anything like this. She later related how it seemed magical that something so grand and beautiful could appear in such a backwoods place.

They only had a moment to take in the interior of the pavilion. The center was open to the sky and across the opening, ropes stretched bearing specially constructed lanterns. Each lantern had a polished circle of metal to direct the light down. The light was aimed so that each table and those sitting at those tables would be lit when it grew dark. Three rectangular tables sat in the structure.

Seated at the table on their left with Thane Awrick sat the various noblemen who were accompanying the king. At the table on the right sat a mixed group, Eric and Drew sat on the right side on the end nearest the king, Asleif and Jae sat on the left side. On the end furthest from the king sat the three remaining village elders. The elders all bore troubled faces. The attention of the king made them uneasy. Two chairs at the table were empty. One on the end nearest the king and one to the left next to Asleif. At the center of the table directly in front of them sat the king and to his right sat the prince. Both were wearing simple gold circlets.

With everyone already seated Catherine was worried that they had arrived late. But as she later learned this was exactly as the king had planned.

The group came to a stop in front of a serious looking older man. Behind him stood two guards facing each other holding lances that crossed between them preventing passage. This man, who Catherine later learned was Beinir the king's secretary, held out his hand in expectation. What he expected Catherine could not tell. But a small card appeared in Crispin's hand which he handed to the man. The man turned and walked past the guards who had raised their lances at his approach. In a voice that carried across the room called, "Presenting the visi Crispin and the læknir Catherine."

At that announcement, Crispin and Catherine followed Beinir as he slowly walked across the open area in front of the king's table. He brought them to the right side of the center table. The man pulled out the chair on the king's left and seated Catherine there. Crispin took the seat at the left end of the table.

As Crispin and Catherine were being escorted Elgar leaned over to Culain and whispered. "This is all a show, my friend. The king wants it to be apparent the respect he has for you and Catherine. Ceri and I will be next and then you will be walked across to your seat. Walk slow with your head high. You look rather grand in your new clothes."

The lances opened and closed and Beinir held out his hand for another card, which Elgar handed him. He turned and walked through past the guards and announced. "Presenting jarl Elgar and Fra Ceri." Once again, he slowly walked across this time to the table where the felag was sitting.

The lances once more were blocking the entry as Cu lain stood there feeling alone. The guard on his left turned his face to him but his face was empty of expression. The other guard softly cleared his throat which caused the first guard's head to snap once more to face his opposite.

The lances opened and Beinir was standing in front of Cu lain. Realizing that he had no card to present to the man Cu lain gave a weak smile as he looked into the man's face. The man smiled back and gave a wink. He held out his hand as he had previously and before Cu lain could react, he made a motion with his hand and a card appeared in it. He walked forward and announced. "Presenting the jarl Cu lain Hultia."

Cu lain's eyes blinked back tears when he heard the honorific hultia, guardian. He thought only he and the dryad knew. It had to be Catherine she was the only other person who could know. As the man started to walk toward the king's table Cu lain straightened his back and as elegantly as he knew how followed. He would do his læknir proud.

He had expected to be escorted to the table with the felag instead he found himself seated at the prince's right hand. As he settled in his seat the prince gave a nod of acknowledgment.

Beinir walked across the open space. The lances opened. As Beinir walked through the gap he gave Karl a nod and produced another card. He then turned and announced. "Presenting jarl Karl Greenman."

Cu lain was feeling very uncomfortable as he watched the man escort Karl across the room. He knew how to act in the wilderness. Which had surprised him as most of his life he had lived in the city. He knew what his new friends expected. Here, even in the fine clothing, he had been provided he felt out of place. He was determined to do his best. He heard Catherine laugh at the far end of the table. He wished he was sitting closer to her. The woman, who, while he helped rescue her, had rescued him.

He heard a voice speak to him, but he didn't understand the words. He looked up from studying his hands and turned to where the voice had come from. The prince had said something.

"I'm so sorry, I didn't hear what you said." He told the prince.

The prince smiled. "Call me Ari. I said relax. I know how over-whelming this all can be. And I started attending these shows while still a child. I can hardly imagine how my father deals with it. Look at him, able to tell a joke in the midst of all this. It was just last year I was able to deliver a toast to the new year without stumbling over my words."

"Your father is the king; all others must bow to his authority." Cu lain replied.

The prince leaned close, so Cu lain could hear him "That's what I thought at one time. Since then I've learned that gaining voluntary obedience is a very complicated dance. My father told me that you can force compliance while you or a trusted agent is watching. But it is best if people obey because they desire the outcome of that obedience.". After Karl had been seated on Cu lain's right, a musical group began to play. The songs and cords were unfamiliar to Cu lain.

A flute started into the next song soon joined by the two smaller stringed instruments. A small drum beat out a rhythm and as the food began to be carried out the large stringed instru-ment began to play.

A bowl of soup was placed in front of him. He wisely waited until he saw the prince begin to eat. He noticed that the prince did not take a bite until his father had sampled the soup. For the rest of the meal, he watched the prince so as not to embarrass himself in such unfamiliar surroundings.

CHAPTER 17

From Larea Visiput's "Etytha Kendt Verden" (Study; the Known World).

The Kentta is a large expanse of grasslands. The rolling hills are occupied by large herds of bison and other herbivorous beasts. The herds have developed migration patterns that to the uninitiated appear as chaotic as the Great Migrations were. In the past, those patterns were used by the Great Yetann of the west or as they are also called the Plains Yetann.

The grasslands of Kentta

An ancient fortress stands on a hill in the grasslands of Kentta. The last citadel of the Sihiratia, Tsitadel Tumamae. The once smooth walls still gave no handhold with which to climb. The walls appeared as if they had been carved from a single stone. They stood fifty feet high. The single entry stood on the south side over ten feet above ground level. At one time access was gained by a bridge that would extend across to the hill opposite the opening. Sadly, that bridge was only known because it is mentioned in one of the few functioning ancient books. Entry was now gained with the aid of a ladder that the guards lowered once the correct password was given. The only other openings were high on the two towers that still stood. A third tower had once stood to the east overlooking the vast grassland. It was taught by the Nokug Saja that that tower collapsed when the gods destroyed Bifrost. This was a convenient lie. It was intended to hide an ancient betrayal. The story also attempted to conceal that they no longer possessed the power to destroy or build as they once had.

The shorter of the remaining towers stood over the entry. Once a terrible weapon graced it. Now, ballista provided defense.

The center tower stood over one hundred feet high. It was round and what might be windows circled its upper story. They were the only visible openings in this tower. The roof appeared to be made of a dark green material. A remnant of rope hung from the spire in the center of the roof. If your eyes were exceptional you might detect inset handholds in the wall that led from one of the openings to the roof.

In this tower, two men were working over a strange device.

Arukais and Nuteka gingerly moved their hands over the controls of the Larte Otsing, the ancient device they used to search for artifacts and people. They were watching a dim image that was cast in the air in front of them. Once the windows were open to the air and light. Now the image cast by the device was so dim that heavy curtains had to cover the windows, so it could be seen.

Their vigil had started before dawn when they woke the device. Once long before the memories of any living person, the Larte Otsing was attended constantly. Overnight vigils were not uncommon, but now it would not operate at all when it was dark. Worse its' reserves had to be filled before each use. The filling usually took three five-days, and if it had been cloudy maybe four. After all that preparation only one day of service was then obtained. They had found that cleaning the roof helped speed the process.

Bird dung and dust had been cleared from the roof two weeks ago. Only two slaves lost their lives this time. They were among the new trainees. The four older slaves who had been performing this duty were much more cautious. They insisted on following all the safety protocols that had been relearned over the last hundred years. No amount of threats could make them hurry. What saved them from the council's wrath was the fact that so few of them were left to serve. Until the ranks of the cleaners were once more filled, they would be safe.

As the Larte Otsing came awake a sphere appeared above it. It slowly turned revealing a view of Ymir. Thousands of ley lines wigged and twisted across the world. Then slowly a pattern of tiny hexagons appeared. Once the mountains and rivers were visible, the two had begun their work. First, they stilled the rotation of the globe until Midgard was centered in their view.

From long and necessary habit, they brought the area surrounding Tsitadel Tumamae before them. They then studied the interplay of the leys and the lorki of the area. Identifying allies and those not quite enemies. Each found where their allies were stationed, and they closely examined the area for approaching enemies. No attack had been directed at Tsitadel for centuries, but caution pumped through their veins. Each was a member of one of the two factions that controlled the Nokug Saja. Their alliance gave the two groups control of the Sihiratia. By their agreement, the Larte Otsing could only be operated when a searcher from each faction was present. Over fifty summers past the last search was trusted to a lone searcher. Now it was attuned to the two chosen from the factions and the device would no longer function unless both were present.

Nuteka had been trained by the now dead Saethur. Rumor had it that he died peacefully in his sleep. That would have been an injustice. Nuteka suspected that he had been poisoned, but what poison was so powerful that Saethur's lorki had not defeated it? However, the man died not long after the Larte Otsing had been attuned to Nuteka.

It was three shadows in the morning before they were able to bring the area of the council's interest into view. The area surrounding Boar Akarn. Unknown to them Boar Akarn appeared on their display almost 10 days journey from where it actually presided.

Together they watched the flow and patterns revealed by the Larte Otsing. They reviewed the patterns for the last four fivedays, never questioning how that was possible when they believed that the device, they used had been dormant.

They found the traces of the agents they had dispatched.

They watched as the signals designating two of them faded away. That meant that they either were dead or had been separated from the artifacts they wore around their necks. Those artifacts had been attuned to each agent and gave out a signal that the Larte Otsing used to identify each agent. They had no power to assist those who carried them. They were poorly made replicas of devices that at one time aided the Sihiratia. Now their only function was to allow the watchers to discover their whereabouts.

After much searching, they found the pattern that marked Catherine. It was so faint they might have missed it. If the artifact around the neck of Seioknar Prysivolar had not been close by, they would have.

They were amazed when the signature of some ancient artifact flared brilliantly in the north of Alfheim. Pausing the display, they carefully mapped where the signal had come from, not realizing that the instrument they relied on was so out of adjustment that the area they marked was in the high mountains of the northern Dragon's Spine. Nowhere near its actual location.

They were amazed once more when the artifact's signal disappeared. Not even a trace of it remained. That indicated its destruction or equally hard to believe it's burial deep in the earth.

A mark appeared on the display when Catherine placed the ring on her finger. The pattern it presented was the one they recognized as locating the maiden who the Nokug Saja wanted to possess. Only this time it was brighter. They paused the display and discussed what the increased strength of her pattern might mean. Then after marking the location on a map in the log, they were required to keep, they moved time forward and all vestige of the girl's location was gone. They reviewed what had occurred several times. Then they moved time forward until they reached the hour they stood in, dusk.

Both were almost exhausted from the long day of studying the display of the Larte Otsing. Both feared the judgment of the council. From what the device had indicated the hunt had been unsuccessful. The resources devoted to it wasted. The device the council desired more than the girl lost to them.

They had a brief meal, their second of the day. They began to search the old journals for clues to the meaning of what they saw. Perhaps they could identify the artifact that had briefly blossomed to life. Maybe discover how the girl disappeared. The pattern that identified her was unique to her and once recognized, even as faint as it was, it had been easy to find. For that to vanish would take more magic than they had witnessed in their lives.

Something troubled Arukais as he searched the old journals. The oldest he had access to was from over one hundred years past. As he compared the map of the area they were concentrating on, with a map in the old journal, he found the placement of the hamlet of Boar Akarn to be different, significantly different. He called out for Nuteka to join him. As they studied the differences, Nuteka suddenly got up and ran over to the shelves holding the journals he brought back two from different decades. The location of all the identified towns shifted over time. The towns seemed to drift north, then east, then southwest.

Each promised the other to hide this disturbing news until they had time to decipher its meaning. Each knew the other's promise was false. Each reported their findings to their faction as soon as they left the room.

The slave Tohk puttered about the room. Picking up the journals scattered about by the searchers. Carefully he placed each journal into its proper location. He dusted as he went through this process, taking his time making sure each journal was in its exact location. It would not do to be beaten for a misplaced volume. The last journal he replaced was the one with the searcher's newest entry. He paused, leaving the journal where it lay, he walked over to the stairwell and listened. He walked down it a few paces and extinguished two of the lanterns part way down. Then he returned to the journal and opened it.

The slave Tohk was chosen because he was unable to read. But the agent Nirk could. He smiled to himself. If the fools who thought they controlled the Nokug Saja, only knew. Carefully he read through their newest entry. Having attended to the needs of the searchers while they were on their search, he knew they had not entered everything they had discussed. It was a shame he did not have access to their private journals. They had carefully read each other's personal journals then left the Larte Otsing. What they entered in their journals after they were in their private quarters was unknowable. What they sent to the factions they served hopefully Kilpik would intercept before sending it on.

With his eidetic memory, Nirk did not bother to write down what he had read. He then returned the journal to its place on the shelf. After once more listening at the stairwell, he turned to the Larte Otsing and appeared to dust it. Slowly the last image the searchers had viewed began to form. He had discovered that this would happen when he first began to serve at Tsitadel Tumamae. That first time he had been afraid that the searchers would return and discover him operating the device. That would have ended the life of Tohk the slave and the career of Nirk the spy.

Now he knew that the two searchers would not return until a few days before the next use of the device. How they had missed that the device was always on was a mystery. That the image it cast would not appear until the proper sequence of movements had been performed appeared to be an ancient security precaution. But, once performed the image would return with a mere touch for several hours. It was true that over the course of a day the image would fade until no longer visible. Which it was doing now.

Nirk walked around the room extinguishing all but one of the lanterns scattered about the room. Then he carefully ran the images of the last day over the display. So, they either did not notice or what was more likely, did not share that whatever had hidden the girl's pattern also hid some anomalies that must have been patterns of some unknown persons of power. Throughout his enslavement here, Nirk had learned a lot about what the images of the Larte Otsing meant. The slaves living in Tsitadel Tumamae were in constant fear because they believed that their masters could locate and observe each one of them. This may have been true at one time, but not now. Now with the image so faded even people with power were hard to find.

Nirk walked over to the desk and removed a small roll of paper from a hidden pocket. Using the quill, the searchers had so conveniently left for him, he wrote out his report. He left out the information about the girl fading from sight. That he wanted to deliver personally. There was no telling how many hands his missive might pass through and that information could identify where the messages originated.

What he did write would be the final coffin nail of the control the factions exercised over the Nokug Saja. They had wasted an immense amount of resources on this quest. All for nothing. No powerful artifact and no girl. The value of either to the business of the Nokug Saja had been questionable. It was time for the men who could grow the business to take control. It was time to abandon the myth of the glory of the Sihiratia. It would not be a bloodless coup. Nirk would see to that. When the signal came the last of the searchers would die and the resources wasted on this crumbling fortress would be channeled to more productive uses.

Carefully, he tightly rolled his message, before slipping it into a small wooden tube. That slipped into a slightly larger metal cylinder. He cleaned the quill before returning it to its proper location. Then he picked up the lit lantern. He walked around the room opening the curtains that had darkened the room during the day. He passed by the small closet where he hid the bow. Stringing it took only a moment. As he walked to the west side of the tower, he threaded the metal cylinder onto an arrow's shaft. In the distance, now hidden by the darkness was a small grove of trees that marked a spring. He blocked the light from the lantern for a moment then lifted it and swung it back and forth slowly. When a light blinked in reply, it gave him notice that not only was his contact on location but also where to aim the bow. Taking aim at where the light had been, he shot the arrow over the fortress' wall. His duties completed, the slave Tohk descended the stairs and soon was asleep in his assigned bed among the other slaves.

CHAPTER 18

A flock of red topknots fluttered through the cherry tree scavenging the last of the ripe fruit. The small birds with their red crests in constant motion had been some of her favorites when she was a child. Their arrival had meant the spring had truly come. Their crests jumping up and down made one think that they were signaling each other. They might be for all Catherine could tell. Before she had been abducted, she was planning on harvesting those cherries for preserves and pies. Now those plans, like so many others she had made, were dashed. The desires and needs of others outside of Boar Akarn were calling her. Not that she was making any plans, yet. This morning she was weighing the different opportunities that had appeared before her.

She could stay here, perhaps. Elder Isleif had approached her last night while they were at the king's banquet. That only he approached her meant that not everyone would welcome her staying. They, like her, might harbor fears that her presence would invite more raids. Elder Ani Askelson, now that elder

Oysten was disgraced, was the prominent elder and influenced the most people. If he made her staying difficult, she might not be able to act as the village healer. He had opposed her taking the widow's place after she had died. If he had his way she would have been evicted from the house. It was her aiding in the delivery of a healthy child to Fra Trena after a difficult pregnancy that had swayed the village for her, preserving her home then. But memories were short, and she could sense the uneasiness in the villagers, even the few she counted as friends.

Her conversation with the dryad had awoken other options. Including returning to the dryad and hiding there. Something Catherine was not inclined to do. She had thought to join the king's army and use her skills as a healer among the scouts. A choice the dryad supported. Or she could set up a practice in one of the larger cities of Alfheim or one of the other free states. Another suggestion from the dryad. Still yet the dryad teased, she could marry and settle into a quiet life. As if a quiet life was possible if she was still being hunted.

Last night the king and prince suggested two possible directions for her life. Both required attending Virkiflyot, the king's college. She could attend the military academy there and receive supplemental training in the healing arts. Then join the army. The prince laughed when the king suggested that. "Father," He told the king. "You've missed the stories told by Crispin's felag about what this læknir can do. She would be more qualified to teach."

"Then she should attend the medical college and obtain an appointment as a king's læknir. Practice the required two years and teach." King Awrick suggested. That was a much more likely suggestion the prince agreed.

Crispin had walked up as they were speaking. "I believe the king would be better served by thinking of Catherine as Seior Catherine or to be closer to the truth, Seioknar Catherine." He spoke in a quiet voice as if he didn't want his voice carrying past the four of them standing there.

Catherine felt her cheeks warm and began to protest. But before she could deny what Crispin had said he held up his hand. "Læknir Catherine I do no propose any of us call you seioknar. I'm just informing the king of something you know or at least should suspect. You are more than a læknir."

He smiled at the king and bowed his head toward him. "As your majesty is aware, the best plans require accurate information. May I suggest that planning Catherine's future wait for another day?"

The king looked at her then, reappraising his assumptions. "Forgive me seior Catherine for my unfounded assumptions."

"Please, your highness Catherine or læknir Catherine, not seior" Catherine pleaded. Today in the bright light of morning she still was unsure of how Crispin had assessed her abilities.

The prince and king had occupied almost all her time at the banquet. She had barely even talked to Jae or the others of the felag. Elgar had gathered them, Cu lain and Ceri not long after the elders of the village had departed the king's presence.

It was not a shadow later that the nobles had excused themselves leaving only Crispin, Karl, and her with the king and prince. That is when they briefly discussed the seior's wood plank and the possibility that it might work for her now that she had her ring. The king had to be persuaded not to have the chest brought to him immediately. It was Beinir who pointed out that Ni'o had risen and Mani's crescent was about to set. Seeing that the king would need to rise early the next day and attend to an unpleasant task. He told the king. "You will be more able to decide a verdict that would not haunt you later if you have had adequate sleep."

The king slapped Beinir on the back and thanked him for informing him of the time, pleasantly surprising Catherine. She thought, "Maybe this is why he is called Just."

She found her mind wandering to a kiss. A kiss that was too quick to suit her. If she was going to be kissed, she wanted a proper one. Jae's quick kiss, the day before made her determined to receive a proper one soon. Hopefully, before the next day was out. The thought made her smile.

She descended the ladder to the kitchen. Where she found the stack of clean clothing widow Njord had washed for her. She was too young a widow. Her husband was the one who died during the raid. She appeared to be among the few that did not blame Catherine. They had a friendly relationship before, though; Catherine would not call them friends. Njord was always busy with her cooking and gardening. They had spent a little time before the birth of her son discussing what to expect during childbirth with the widow Sturlasda. Catherine had assisted in that birth. That would make her son five summers this year. Oh, how he must miss his father. Much to her objections, Catherine had paid her the mark she had found in the widow Sturlasda purse shortly after her death. She had hidden it with her freshwater pearls. She had forgotten about it until she had looked through those pearls shortly after receiving her ring. Perhaps that coin would support the new widow through the next difficult year.

She found the clothing she wanted. The shirt and pants she had received when they had joined the detachment. The new boots would match them nicely. She then sat a pan of water on the stove. The wood box next to the stove was empty, so she walked out the back door to fetch more. That is when she noticed the woman sitting on the back-porch stoop. She stood when Catherine came out of the door. She introduced herself as Herta, and she was with the felag that had been assigned to guard her home while she slept. Catherine began to apologize to Herta for having to lose sleep because of her. Herta smiled waving off the apology "I'm glad for the duty. You can't imagine how boring garrison duty is. I didn't join to sleep, I joined to fight. And though this isn't fighting, it's better than the barracks in Goa Vollar."

Catherine returned to the kitchen and started the fire. Soon the water on the stove was hot enough to use. After pulling the curtain across the kitchen window she stripped off her nightshirt and bathed. She washed her hair as well. Happy that its shortness made it so easy to care for.

She was dressed before she woke Ceri. Leaving Ceri in the kitchen to bathe and dress, Catherine entered the greeting room. She paced the floor while she waited for Ceri to finish. Would Crispin send Jae to fetch her or the whole felag?

Njord and her son were coming over and spending the day with Ceri. At her insistence, she would help clean the house. Then help Ceri learn to stitch. She planned to leave her son Eikin with Ceri for part of the morning, so she could pick vegetables from her garden. Then she planned to cook lunch for Karl and Cu lain. In this way, she would not only keep herself busy but also keep Ceri and Eikin occupied. Both had voiced the opinion that they were helping care for the other.

Catherine's day promised to be busy. After the morning session, she was expected to attend the king for the noon meal. Then she would be attempting to use Prysivolar's wood plank. How she was supposed to accomplish that, was beyond her imagination.

Ceri called out that she was finished and that she was starting the porridge. Would Catherine like some of the dried currants added? Catherine gave her assent. She then opened the greeting room window, stuck her head out it, and greeted the scout standing on her front porch. Then she walked to the kitchen door throwing it wide and opened the kitchen window. That allowed the morning breeze to blow through the house.

A thought occurred to her; "Maybe she could do better for Njord than just that measly mark?" If the king agreed, she would have a larger household traveling with her. After all, for the present, she was paying for everything with the king's credit. She hoped Crispin was right and the bounty she would receive from the spoils would give her several years' expenses.

*

Jae was up and walking the camp long before dawn. He woke thinking about kissing Catherine. Had he been too bold? She had teased him into it. If she hadn't presented her cheek to him, her lips would not have been so near. He thought about how much nicer a longer kiss would be. As brief as it was, he had thought then that she had kissed back. This morning he wasn't so sure. Would he get a chance to speak with her today? The night before he had barely been able to greet her. The king and prince had occupied her time. Many of the women in the ranks thought the prince dashing, even some of the men thought him handsome. Did Catherine?

He avoided the camp guard. The places they were watching and the places they were guarding. He did so without appearing to be avoiding them. He had approached several and greeted them. The best way to avoid a guard's scrutiny was to not avoid them. At least not so they noticed.

He found himself near Catherine's house. There were two felags guarding it. One at the house surrounding it. They were spaced around it, so they could see each other and each of the possible ways into the house. The other patrolling around the area. Jae was sure that if he started to walk up to the door he would be challenged before being allowed to pass. But, after gaining the door, what then? The house was dark. A guard approached, and he greeted her. He had not met her before, but she knew who he was. He was one of Crispin's felag, after all. The ones who had rescued the læknir and defeated the yetann. The notoriety embarrassed him. Crispin assured him that it would fade in time. The guard told him not to worry over the læknir's safety, they had her well-guarded.

Jae thanked her for her assurances even though he knew Catherine would be safe. He could sense the interwoven blanket of protection surrounding her. Then it struck him, what had been bothering him since yesterday. He leaned against a tree and shut his eyes. Relaxing and reaching out with his senses until he found the green man, then he found Catherine. Their presence, the patterns that he recognized as theirs. He had known where Catherine and the green man had been almost from the moment, he met them. The sense of where they were in the wilderness had been so strong that when he had been sent out scouting, he could find where they were without tracking. He didn't understand how he knew where they were, he just knew he did. And unlike the reaching out his grandfather had taught him; it had not taken the same concentration the same reaching. Until recently. He had been so busy, and there was so much to do, he hadn't thought of it. Then his and Catherine's lips met and there she was visible not only to his eyes but also in what his grandfather called sjón, the inner sight of the vanir. Something had obscured their presence to that inner sight. He wasn't sure what to make of it. Was it some danger or maybe? Yes, that might be it. The obscuring of their presence had not occurred until after Catherine had put on her ring and necklace.

He had wanted an excuse to visit Catherine, but this wasn't the time. This was something to bring before Crispin, and later Karl and Catherine. He still hadn't figured out how to gain another kiss, the longer one he hoped for. With the new mystery disturbing those thoughts he walked away in search of Crispin.

*

Ari was up early, just before dawn, the day promised to be very busy. The king's court would take most of the day. He suspected the king was keeping several advisors from their breakfasts. He was proved correct when he found his father sitting in the main pavilion surrounded by Gaut Bjornson, Varin Arfastsen. Thane Awrick and Thane Dyri. The best advisors available for now.

Finding that answer will take time, my lord." Thane Dyri answered. "I would recommend Thane Awrick for the job. That is if you didn't already have other plans for him."

Thane Awrick looked from one to the other wondering what plans the king might have for him.

Prince Ari thought he knew what the plans had been. He couldn't be sure, but in past conversations, he had overheard, a plan to organize a landskap between Alfheim and the etunazi coast with the adjoining hill country had been discussed. So, he thought he knew. Especially now that they knew the raiders had originated from that coast. If he were offered a wager, he would bet that Akarn Landskap would not be the only new administration area the king created this year.

"Awrick," the king asked. "would you mind taking the duties of lanstor for a short time?"

Thane Awrick considered the king's request. "Are you planning on announcing the new landskap today?"

"This could only be temporary. We will leave you and your dirfylk to start. When the Hilmar Vorth meets at the start of the next ninety, I will endeavor to have a new landskap organized. Until then you will be in command

After a bit of consideration, he answered. "As you command my lord."

*

Beinir and Sihtric once more walked through the king's pavilion. It no longer looked cheerful like it had the night before. The lighter colors had been replaced with darker ones. The banners and party decorations were gone. It was no longer open to the sky. The cloth across the opening dulled the light giving the room a sober cast. The right and left alcoves were lined by dark green curtains. Where the king's table had been sat a dais with alone chair waiting for the king. A table and chair sat to the left of that. This is where Beinir would transcribe the proceedings. Between the king's seat and the rest of the room, a thick rope hung. A podium sat forward of the rope and to the right of the king. This was for those who were addressing the throne. Whether it was for testimony or with requests and complaints to stand. A felag of guards would stand along each wall ready. At last satisfied the pavilion was ready, they walked out the back of the pavilion and notified Thane Dyri. This set the proceeding in motion.

*

Catherine was almost finished with her porridge when Njord arrived. She was much earlier than Catherine had expected. Eikin was in tears as she carried him into the kitchen her mending sack dragging the ground. The evidence of tears was still clearly visible on her face. Ceri ran over and fussed over the sobbing boy. He buried his head on his mother's shoulder and began to wail. That started Ceri's eyes to tear up. She took the

189

mending sack from Njord and walked it into the greeting room. There she found a chair and began to sob overcome by the boy's grief. Eikin had always been so cheerful and active. She never remembered crying for her own sadness, in the world, she grew up in showing your grief was frowned upon. So, she added tears for her own grief and a few for having found a safe place to grieve.

Catherine pulled a chair out from under the table for Njord. Eikin had stopped crying by the time his mother was seated. Catherine was able to coax him into a chair of his own with a bowl of porridge and currants. Catherine knew that the cream she had poured over the porridge was from a cow that once belonged to Njord and her husband. All the cattle had been sold while Catherine was in captivity. Catherine was more than happy to leave this village that has so little mercy as to take advantage of a newly grieving widow. There were very few people in this village she would miss.

"Njord, what is troubling you?" Catherine asked. It took very little persuasion before the events of this morning began to unfold. It was still dark, and she had been sitting in her favorite chair, the one Arukas had made for her while she was with child, thinking of him and drinking her first cup of tea for the day. Then her landlord Dan Grissen had knocked on her door. She had not answered it soon enough to suit him, so he pounded harder, waking Eikin. She had wrapped a shawl around her shoulders and stepped out to find out what the man wanted. It seems like he had found out she had come into some coin and was there to demand the rent. Her husband, Arukas, had always paid twice yearly. She was sure Arukas had just paid him the month before his death. Now jarl Grissen was at her door demanding a year's rent. And more than that he thought she should pay double a whole mark. How he had decided on that amount Njord could not say, but she found it strange since that was what Catherine had just given her the day before. Jarl Grissen had pointed his finger at her face and wagged it about telling her she needed to jump to it and bring him the coin. That was when Eikin had stepped between her and him and gave jarl Grissen a little push.

Grissen then had slapped Eikin in the face. Eikin had let out a wail his pride hurt more than his face, though at the time there was a large red mark across his little cheek. She had thought the hateful man was going to try to force his way in when a woman's voice called from the road.

"What's the trouble here? Man! Is that your child?"

Jarl Grissen had turned around and started to dress down the woman who had dared interrupt him. He quickly changed his tone when he noticed she was one of Thane Awrick's scouts and she had her hand on the hilt of her sword.

"I'll come back later for the rent." he had told her and started to leave when the scout walked up and asked his name. He balked at telling her. So, she called out to one of her felag to come over. They both explained that the king frowned on children being hit especially when the child was not theirs. They then ordered him to avoid this part of the hamlet. He was told that if they found he had approached this area again that they would be personally affronted and would have a coin toss to see who would challenge him first. At that, jarl Grissen quickly walked away. They then confirmed the man's name with her. They left her with assurances that jarl Grissen would not trouble her again while they were about. They then called over two other scouts and asked them to pass around the foul man's name and description.

Spent from the story she let out a sob. "Here," she said "is your mark. Keep it. That man will never have it. If Eikin and I must live in the streets, I'll not pay him another farthing. And if he touches me or my child, I'll, I'll" She leaned against Catherine and sobbed.

The thought she had entertained earlier this morning solidified. "Njord, move your things here. You can have the room the widow used" she told her.

Njord looked up at her. Not sure she had heard right. "I heard that you would be moving away. The elders are already arguing over who will gain the rent from this house." She told Catherine.

"I'd like to see them try," Catherine responded. "The king's secretary Beinir has assured me that this house is mine. That the king will have his seal placed on the house until I decide what I want to do with it. If you want, you can stay here. You could be my caretaker. Thane Awrick has told me that he was informed that the king wanted more patrols through the region. So, at least for a few years, the presence of the king's law will weigh on the actions of village elders. You would be safe to stay if you want"

Catherine paused before she told Njord. "I would like you and Eikin to join Ceri and me on our journey. I don't know where we'll end up but I for one feel the need to leave this village behind."

Njord's eyes widened; she had never considered the possibility of leaving. She had never been adventurous. That's when a knock on the front door interrupted them. Catherine quickly told her. "Don't hurry your decision. You have at least a day before the king will leave. For the present, two felag are going to stay."

She was hoping that her felag, especially Jae, had come to fetch her. She was a little disappointed when Rizna and Vaetta walked through the kitchen door. It was time to attend the king's court

CHAPTER 19

About Fourth shadow

Halfdan was fidgeting in his seat while they waited for the proceedings to begin. It was already growing warm in the pavilion. Two rolls of five chairs each sat on the east side. The planned witnesses in the Olsten hearing would sit there until called. Crispin had walked over and greeted Catherine while she was being escorted to her seat by the solider who had met her at the entry. Then he had taken his seat once more. Sitting in the roll with him was Herr Lyos, Arnor, Brita, and Asleif. Three of the scouts who had been stationed at Boar Akarn while Crispin had been searching for the raiders and Catherine. Halfdan was the only witness from the hamlet present when Catherine entered. A half shadow before the court convened, Runa and Frida, the wife and daughter of the elder Oysten were seated. It was a quarter shadow later that Biorn the tavern keeper was escorted to his seat complaining about the business he was losing because of this. From what he said, the hamlet was busier than usual on a first day. People from at least four of the other nearby hamlets had journeyed to Boar Akarn. The presence of the king in such a backwater place was uncommon and exciting. Biorn thought there were over two hundred additional people in town besides the scouts.

Jae, Drew and Eric stood in the back of the pavilion watching the crowd. The pavilion was packed full. Twenty or so people were milling about outside unable to enter the pavilion. Few in the crowd realized that besides Jae and his friends another felag was scattered throughout. The ten men standing at the sides of the pavilion in their dress uniforms were not the only ones who would help keep order if the need arose. Eric had already caught a pickpocket while they approached the pavilion. That man would face the judgment of Thane Awrick the next day.

Thane Awrick and Thane Dyri took their places. Beinir was seated and ready. Two guards then escorted Oysten in. Jarl Alvi Geirson walked beside him. When he appeared Thane Awrick and Thane Dyri simultaneously announced "Be still, prepare for the king's court." When this did not seem to catch the crowd's attention, they drew their swords and struck them together. This produced a ringing sound that silenced the crowd. Once more they announced, "Prepare for the king's court." The room was now almost silent. Jarl Alvi speaking in a voice that carried through the crowd said. "I am jarl Alvi Geirson, I stand as Vathalit."

Turning to Oysten he said, "As your Vathalit, I inform you that you are about to appear before the king's court under the charges of treason and accessory to murder." Oysten's expression became more dejected. Alvi continued. "You can choose to face a lower court first. If you face the king's court today there will be no appeal. Facing a lower court would give you a chance at appealing the sentence, but there is no appeal from the king's judgment.

Oysten nodded his head in assent. "I have chosen the king's court."

Jarl Alvi placed his hand on Oysten's shoulder and looked him in the eye. "If you have any questions or need help understanding what is happening, look to me. If I don't respond say my name. I will help." He told him. Then he stepped back to the right facing the crowd. He then gave a nod to Thane Dyri.

Thane Dyri announced. "The king's court is now in session. Face forward and acknowledge your king!"

The king walked in and stood facing the crowd. Some kneeled, some only bobbed their heads in acknowledgment of their king. King Awrick then stepped onto the dais and took his seat. The room was silent for the first time that day. But it was only a moment before the whispering once more began.

Thane Dyri stepped forward and said "Jarl Oysten Korisson today you stand before your king accused of treason and accessory to murder. Are you ready to be judged?"

Oysten whispered, "Yes, my lord."

"Why," King Awrick asked, "did you conspire with tinker Asvald to kidnap laeknir Catherine Snorridot?"

Oysten shook his head. Then he looked at the king. "I did not conspire with the tinker to do anything. He and I were business partners of sorts. I helped arrange lodging for him when he was in the area and he sold my hams at other villages on his route. He ran a route from Goa Vollar to Hlifsleid. He stopped at several of the smaller hamlets as well."

He was interrupted by someone in the audience. "We never saw no tinker in Hlifsleid!" A guard grabbed the man's arm and started to escort him out. When Thane Awrick commanded. "The king desires that this man come forward as a witness. So, he was marched up to the witness stand where he stood shifting his weight from one foot to another. Looking nervously about. He had not meant to draw attention to himself.

"Your name?" The king asked.

"Eldon Baldwensen, my lord," he answered.

"If you know this man and he is Eldon Baldwensen of Hlifsleid raise your hand." Thane Dyri commanded. Ten hands were raised in response. Followed a bit later by a couple more. Thane Dyri counted the hands as two scouts passed through the crowd gathering names. Satisfied he turned to the king and told him "The witness has been attested to.

"So, Jarl Eldon what do you know of the matter?" The king asked.

"The only tinker through Hlifsleid in the last two years was a fellow named Copper. He told us his hair had once been red and so the name." Eldon told the king. "He walked with a limp from a broken leg that was not properly set. It had a bend in it just above the ankle. He had a mule. I heard tinker Asvald had dark hair and carried everything on his back. Tinker copper let his mule carry all his gear and him too at times." He finished.

"Oysten, how do you answer that?" the king queried.

"I can't my lord. I only saw him here. I never traveled with him. All I knew was what he told me. He gave me a good profit on the hams I sold him."

"You deny conspiring with him?"

"Yes, my lord." Answered Oysten.

Thane Dyri then spoke to Eldon thanking him for his testimony and dismissing him from the witness stand. He turned to the crowd and said "If you have evidence to present, please speak to one of the guards and he will bring your name forward. Otherwise remain quiet. We have other witnesses to hear"

The next two shadows were spent hearing testimony. It had grown quite warm so the side panels of the pavilion and the openings in the peaks of the pinnacles had been opened releasing some of the heat from inside.

It was half a shadow pass noon when Beinir stood and walked over to the king. He handed the king a note. He then returned to his seat.

King Awrick glanced at the note and motioned with his hand toward Thane Dyri. He walked up to the king. After a moment's conversation Thane Dyri faced the crowd and announced. "The court is now in recess. Find some drink and food. Return here in two shadows and hear the king's verdict."

Rumors were circulating. The speculation ran wild. Someone started a story that an invasion from the north was coming. The raiders, so the tale went, were an advanced guard preparing the way for an invasion from an unknown yet ann kingdom hidden to the northeast of Alfheim. Some believed that the king planned to abandon the hamlet. Many believed the fact that Catherine had lived here made it a target for other attacks. They also believed that the king would not want to invest royal funds to protect such a backwater place.

*

The king, prince Ari and the two thanes sat around the table eating a light lunch. That is if you could call anything that Matsveir prepared light.

"What do you make of Crispin's story?" Thane Awrick asked.

The king shrugged his shoulders. "I heard stories when I was younger that I viewed as pure myth. Have you read Crispin's report? That artifact they discovered on the mountain was straight out of what I had considered myths and nightmares."

"I'm curious" prince Ari interrupted. "Did anyone ever find out the names of the ships that dropped off the raiders?"

The king laid down his fork, before answering. "I don't know if anyone has asked that question. It's possible that the Konkur Cu lain or the Rizi child Ceri might remember it they were asked. They both were drugged at the time they were landed, but they might know something that would help. We need to enlarge our guest list for tonight to include them."

CHAPTER 20

From Larea Visiput's "Etytha Kendt Verden" (Study; the Known World).

The Elfra is the river of Alfheim. The river is navigable almost its entire length. The only interruption is the Rif which separates the lower Elfra from the upper. The upper Elfra soon divides between two primary tributaries the Vestelfra (west Elfra) and the Auselfra (East Elfra).

*

The Lodda Hytte in Eyrrborg was a disreputable looking place. The roof covering the wooden walk in the front of the building sagged. The walk creaked and groaned with each passing step seeming to threaten giving way. The inside was not much better. There was a stain spreading across the ceiling, whether the leak in the roof had been repaired was anyone's guess. Not that many of the patrons of the tavern would have noticed. Not only were they unconcerned with the condition of the ceiling above them, the room was dark and smoky, the only light came in through the open door and the two windows covered with a light cloth. It served the local rivermen. It was filled with those who worked the barges that carried the goods and travelers up and down the Auselfra. Even though Asvald was the only vanir in the tavern he felt secure here. This was not a place he expected to be searched for the missing tinker. Even if they searched the place he wouldn't be suspected. They were looking for a dark dynoi with black hair, not a fair-skinned blond vanir.

His head and skin had itched for days after he had washed the dyes out of his hair and skin. He had doubted that anything would be able to accomplish what the ancient's chemical mixtures had accomplished. He had applied the dye to his hair daily fearing that the growth of his hair would betray him. Whatever had been used on his skin to darken it to the olive hues of the dynoi worked differently, he had been assured the color would last until after his mission was accomplished. He had been dark-skinned now for two months this time and would have remained so for another two if he hadn't had the special mixture to apply to his skin. He had looked sunburned for days after his bath in the cold Laek Gritter.

He recalled his escape from Boar Akarn. He ran almost the whole night. He smiled; they would never expect a dynoi to travel as far in the dark as he had been able too. He silently thanked Loki for his vanir ancestry. The wench serving the tables must have mistaken his smile as a request for more mead. She approached him and sat a fresh mug in front of him. She then held out her hand for the farthing he now owed. He hadn't planned on spending another farthing from his meager purse, but the tavern was crowded and there were other patrons standing about looking for a place to sit. A farthing was a small payment for a place to sit and plan his next move.

He had made a show of purchasing a place on the next barge heading downriver. He was still trying to decide if he would take it or walk cross country to the lower Elfra and take a less expected route to flee the king's searching men. That is when a self-styled bard seated himself on the stool that stood on a raised platform on the back wall of the tavern. He strummed a few chords after he had tuned his lute. At first, Asvald tried not to listen to the off-key ballad. It was then that the word yetann caught his attention! How had the news of the raid and the destruction of the hunting party traveled so far? Up until this moment, he hadn't known what had happened to the raiders. He had assumed that they would arrive at their departure point as planned. But, if half of what the balladeer sang was true, they had been defeated by a felag of trainees and a wisp of a girl. Then came the line about the grey-eyed tinker. Thankfully they had also called him a dark dynoi. He had no way of disguising his eye color and if the fisherman who had floated him down the Laek Gritter was questioned he might remember the dark stain in the water and the sunburned vanir. He had commented about both as he helped Asvald climb into his flat-bottom boat. Cross country it was then.

Asvald, who now called himself Vind Passat, downed half the fresh mug. Then he walked out of the tavern and went in search of stables. Perhaps he could afford a horse for this stage of his journey. He could sell it for passage down the river to Gandvik when he arrived at a village along the lower Elfra.

*

The woman was alone in the dimly lit corridor deep in the bowls of Tsitadel Tumamae. It was the quickest way between the slave quarters and the master's quarters, but it was a foolish place for her to be alone. Tohk timed their passing to his advantage. They passed each other at a door to an unused storage room. Before she could pass him, he roughly grabbed her, pulled her close, and forced a kiss. Then he unlatched the door and shoved her in. She screamed as she fell to the floor. He looked both ways down the corridor before he stepped into the room. He slid the bolt, locking the door.

"Well, did you entertain anyone with the show?" She asked as she sat disheveled on the floor.

"I don't think anyone was around." He answered.

"No one was. I was sure of that." Kilpik said as she stood and dusted off her dress. "Try being less dramatic next time. If I sense anyone around let me make the show."

"I thought you liked it rough," Nirk told her.

"This is business, not pleasure." She responded. "I'll seek my own pleasure when I'm free of this place."

Nirk nodded his head in acceptance. He had not planned on any pleasure while here. He was testing her. If she had offered, he would have taken. But he knew indulging in pleasure dulled the sense of danger that kept him alert.

The next twenty minutes were spent comparing the notes

Kilpik had transcribed from Arukais and Nuteka private journals. As he had thought they entered other observations in their personal journals than they had shared. What they wrote there, filled in what Nirk had ascertained, had in fact corrected some things he had thought he saw. He took the offered paper and writing instrument, an ancient artifact that wrote on the parchment in letters that disappeared until touched a second time by it or another instrument like it. Kilpik had been given this treasure so she could smuggle information out. Nirk wrote his observations out and then let her read them. He read over her shoulder as she added things, he would not have been able to see. Then they touched the instrument to the paper and all they had wrote disappeared.

Their business finished, she tore her blouse and removed her lower undergarment, tearing it before she dropped it to the floor. He unbolted the door and stuck his head out. Gave the hall a perusal and then walked away leaving Kilpik to find her way back to her quarters. He suspected that Kilpik was the personal servant of one or both operators of the Larte Otsing. Who she was when not the slave Kilpik, he did not know. Did not want to know. Just as he did not reveal Nirk to her. To her, he was the slave Tohk. The leer of a successful conquest came over Tohk face as he strode to his assigned task that had been so pleasantly interrupted.

CHAPTER 21

From Larea Visiput's "Etytha Kendt Verden" (Study; the Known World).

The Rif is a series of cataracts that separate the lower Elfra from the upper Elfra. Traveling over the Rif the river drops dramatically. Barges can be moved with great difficulty up and down through the rushing water. Most cargos are unloaded and transported by wagon between the ports of Arnarhvall, on the upper Elfra and Ritsker, on the lower Elfra.

A bright encounter

It was as if Karl dreamed as he chased his memories. Each promising lead traced until it ended. Each memory of her carefully stored away cataloged and cross-referenced. It seemed for the time being he was more a librarian of her memories than a lover of a woman. That brought vividly to mind the memory, or was it a dream? It was at least partly memory. He had found a brief memory of that dance hidden in him. Trying to remember the kiss brought another alive of kissing her. Then another memory intruded of another woman and a brief affair as they traveled between stars. Now was that a real memory or some almost forgotten dream. Had he traveled between stars? It took an effort to direct his thoughts away from that series of memories. What did it matter? What mattered was remembering the woman he loved. Who was now a dryad. She is "The Dryad". Myths and stories about her circulated in his thoughts until he once more focused on finding her in his memories, the real her. He knew he dare not return until he found her name. Her real name in his memories.

It was while chasing memories of her he came across a vivid image of them holding each other close under the stars of Midgard. He heard her speak. "Daniel, I love you" His eyes opened. It was now mid-morning, approaching noon. He had been chasing her memory all night. And by accident, he now knew his real name. Daniel, Daniel Alvis. There had been jokes shared about how his last name fit the theme of Midgard. Now, where did that memory come from? He pulled himself back from that rabbit hole. That would bring him no nearer to what he wanted, needed.

Should he uproot himself and go to the king's court? No, he would only be a distraction to the proceedings. He stretched tendrils of roots out of his feet as they dangled in the water. He then ran his mind through the routine that would refresh and add detail to his kilt. It was while thinking that through, that a memory of the first time she had teased him into wearing a kilt surfaced. "Esmerelda," He had said. "I would look so foolish!"

"Oh, but you do have such handsome legs, my dear." She had responded. So, to please her, he had worn it. Those many years ago.

He thought through that memory over and over. Esmerelda. She was Esmerelda!

He was overcome with joy. A bud shot out of his growing kilt and burst into bloom. He looked at it and chuckled. Well, he could pick it later and throw it away. No one need be the wiser.

His thoughts were so focused he almost didn't notice the child walking up to him. Blond hair, blue eyes, she was of the vanir who lived among the daonna majority in Alfheim. She was the only one in the group of children he had met while entering the hamlet, who had not to run away after they had asked. "Are you the green man?" Which in reply he had said. "Yes, I am." As the others ran away. She had smiled and said "So, nice to me you, jarl." as she curtsied. She then turned and skipped away.

He focused his awareness on her. She was about to touch him when he twisted his body around and faced her. She stepped back then, startled by his sudden movement.

"I thought you asleep and that I needed to wake you." She told him.

He smiled down at her. Even sitting he was taller than she was. She must be only six or seven summers. "I was just waking up. Nice to see you again." He greeted her.

"My parents have sent me to invite you to lunch. If you can come. Papa says you're much too busy and important to eat lunch with a family of poor farmers. Brother laughed when I insisted that we should invite you anyway." A serious look came upon her face as she related her story.

"I hope your mother does not have lunch already prepared. It will take some time for me to be able to come. I must bring in my roots before I can. See," He told her as he pointed and at his wiggling toes with their tendrils of roots waving in the stream's water.

She giggled at that. "No, jarl green man. She sent me early. She told me to ask as soon as I could. Perhaps we would be the first of the day to invite you. She was the only one of the family, besides me, who thought you would come.

"And I will come, child. Run and tell your mother so. Also, tell her I won't need much so do not prepare a lunch much larger than the family will eat. I would hate for some of your food to be wasted." He responded.

She didn't seem to hear him. Her eyes were focused on the flower growing from his hip. "That's so pretty! All the frills, red and yellow. Does it smell nice?" She asked.

He laughed aloud as he picked the flower. "Smell for yourself," he told her as he handed it to her.

She brought it to her nose and looking up at him smiled. "It smells very nice."

"What is your name?" He asked her. "I'm sure you're tired of me calling you child and I tire of people calling me green man. My name is Karl, so you know."

"I'm Bjor because papa says I'm his bright spot on cloudy days. Pleased to meet you, Karl." She said as she extended her hand to shake his now that they were doing proper introductions.

"I'm equally glad to meet you, Bjor." He said as they shook hands. "It will take me half a shadow to get up. So, as I asked you, please run home and let your parents know I am coming. Then about the time your lunch is ready come back here and show me the way to your home."

"I will." She tossed over her shoulder as she ran off toward her home.

*

Catherine caught the fragrance of Njord's cooking as she walked up to her front door. "Where's everyone?" She asked as she walked into the kitchen.

Njord laughed. "Cu lain made the mistake of offering to gather some watercress to add to the greens for lunch. Eikin insisted on helping. I think they have been playing in the water since then. I should see if I can call them in. The food is ready."

Cu lain had squatted down to show Eikin the watercress growing in the stream that began in Catherine's spring house. The boy wasn't sure how he felt about the peppery flavor of the plant. But he was enjoying splashing in the stream.

Cu lain suggested to Eikin that they walk downstream a little and find a patch of yellow sorrels. The boy jumped up eagerly abandoning his attempt at catching some of the small fish that lived in the stream. He loved the sour taste of that plant.

Cu lain hoped the sorrel's adventure would give Eikin time to dry a little before his mother called them to lunch.

Eikin started waving so Cu lain turned to see Njord waving to them from the back porch of the house. Lunch must be ready.

*

Matsveir had looked everywhere he could think of. It felt like he had walked all over the hamlet twice. What started as a warm loaf of bread was now cold. Where had that green fellow disappeared too? He had seen him twice. Both times he was so busy that he hadn't been able to go to him. He had the baby dryad that had been entrusted to Matsveir.

There he was! Holding the hand of a little girl as she skipped

205

down the road. They stopped beside a small building, a hovel. A woman opened the door and greeted the green fellow and then ushered him inside.

Matsveir wasn't sure what to do. Hope to catch him some other time? Or, yes, knock on the door and talk to him now. He was deeply concerned for the little dryad. She was, after all, his responsibility.

It looked to him that the hovel had been there for a long time. The logs it was made of were settling into each other. The bottom row was decaying into the ground and the roof cried for new shingles. It bowed like a swayback horse.

Karl, that was his name, had stooped and barely squeezed through the door. Matsveir hesitated. He took a deep breath and knocked, fearing that the rotten leather hinges would give way with his blows.

A boy of about ten summers opened the door. Karl had settled on the floor and the girl was leaning on his shoulder, obviously intent on acquiring Karl's lap for her seat. A man, her father Matsveir supposed, was telling her. "Sit on your own chair, as you've been taught is proper when we have a guest."

Seeing Matsveir at the door the man and woman stood.

"Good to see you, friend" Karl called out. "I was planning on hunting you down after sharing this meal with these new friends. Do I smell some of your fresh bread?"

"Jarl Threski, please, invite my friend, Matsveir in. I'm sure he will share his bread with us. Especially if you share your wife's excellent smelling rabbit stew." He interjected.

Karl didn't stand as he began the introductions. If he stood, he would have had to stoop. And Bjor had just gotten comfortable on his lap. "Jarl Threski, fra Troth, this is my friend Matsveir, chef for thane Awrick. Jarl Matsveir, let me introduce you to jarl Threski and fra Troth in whose house we are."

The introductions over it didn't take long before the couple had persuaded Matsveir to stay and share the stew. The room was filled with the smell. It took a lot of effort not to start asking questions about what was in this stew. There was a fragrance of some spice he did not recognize. He sat in the offered chair and unwrapped the loaf of bread he was carrying. If he had known he would be sharing a meal with a family, he would have brought two. From a pocket of his apron, he was almost always wearing one, he pulled out his sheaved bread knife. As the good woman of the house dipped out another bowl of stew from the pot steaming on the fire, he sliced off wide pieces. He handed an end piece to the child called Bjor after she had expressed her love of crust.

As Matsveir asked for a little more stew, he could resist no longer. "Fra Troth, would you kindly share how you made this wonderful stew? There is some spice I do not recognize. I must have its name. I want to surprise Thane Awrick with a new flavor before I take leave and travel to see my father."

"There's nothing special in it," Troth told him. "Just, two rabbits, some new potatoes, carrots, wild garlic, onions," She hesitated. "I did use some of the dried leaves of the old tree behind the house. That's something my granny Greta taught me. It thickens the stew and adds some flavor to it. I don't have a name for the tree. In the spring we look for saplings of trees like it and dig the roots to make a tonic. Granny called it a tonic tree."

Matsveir and Troth began a long discussion on this spice. How she dried the leaves, how much she used in a pot. Did it go well with beef? She didn't know but it did with venison.

Bjor, her belly full, had fallen asleep on Karl's lap before they were finished. Threski had sent Klifra out to bring back a twig with leaves to show Matsveir what the tree looked like. Then he pulled a crock filled with the spice out from an old cabinet and gave it to Matsveir. Matsveir pulled a pence from his pocket which Threski refused. It was time to gather and dry more he explained. Moreover, Matsveir was a guest. That was that. He would not take even a farthing.

"I'll send someone back with your crock in the morning," Matsveir told him, as he let the fragrance of this new spice waft over him "I will remember this kindness."

Troth picked Bjor up from Karl's lap and tucked her into the shelf on the side of the house that was her bed. Klifra wanted to leave. After all, the guests were leaving, and he needed to set his rabbit snares.

That's when Matsveir remembered why he had been searching for Karl. "Karl, you have something you should give me." He said before he started out the door.

Karl laughed "So I do." He moved his hands over his belly and produced the young dryad. "Is this what you want?" He asked.

"Yes! How is she doing? Is she still alive?" Matsveir asked.

Klifra's ears perked up. She? In the dim light of his house, it looked like the green man was holding a pile of dead twigs. "What's that?" he asked.

Karl lifted the dryad up, so he could see. "It's a dryad child ready for planting." He told the boy.

"Are you planting it here?" Klifra asked.

"No." Matsveir replied. "I'm planting her on my father's farm north of Merki."

"You'll need to plant her in some sort of pot soon," Karl told him. "I can feel her need for water and sun. She wants to start growing."

"Oh, I don't have anything ready. I was hoping to pass through Goa Vollar before I planted her." Matsveir moaned.

"I believe we can help." Troth interrupted. "Dear husband, fill that old leaky bucket with some of the soil you prepared for fra Cnutdot." As Threski went to fetch the bucket of soil she continued. "The soil he's fetching is wonderful for plants. It's made from the hay and dung from an old barn. It's well-rotted, Threski mixes a little sand and clay with it. I'm amazed at what fra Cnutdot can grow from it."

Threski appeared with an old rusty bucket full of soil. Karl could sense the tiny life that thrived in what appeared as ordinary dirt. This would make a good start for the tiny dryad.

"Water her where you don't mind water spilling out. The old bucket is leaky. Leakier since that so-called tinker repaired it." Threski said.

"I'm even more in your debt, friends," Matsveir told them as he hurried out the door eager to plant the dryad.

They all followed Matsveir out the door. Klifra to go set his snares. The parents to say their final goodbyes to their distinguished guests. Seeing the people leaving the king's pavilion Karl told the couple "I'm afraid that we have caused you to miss the king's court."

Threski looked solemn as he told Karl. "We didn't plan to attend. Whatever the king rules will not change our circumstance." He held out his hand. "Goodbye friend Karl, you are always welcome in our home." They shook hands and Karl drifted toward Catherine's house.

*

The shadow had passed, and the crowd grew silent as they watched their king once more enter the pavilion. Thane Awrick called them to order as the king stood looking at the prisoner.

Thane Dyri commanded the prisoner. "Receive the sentence of your king."

His legs had a tremble to them as he gradually raised his eyes to face his king.

"Prisoner Oysten Korisson," The king began, purposely avoiding any honorific. "It is my decision that you are not guilty of treason.

We do find you bear some responsibility in the murder of Arukas Haukson the cowherd. Being the chief elder of this hamlet, you failed in your duty to protect your fellow citizens."

"Here is our sentence." The king paused. "You are removed from being an elder of this village. You cannot serve as one again for a year. You are also fined a mark." King Awrick continued. "That mark is awarded to the widow of Arukas Haukson."

The king returned to his seat.

Thane Dyri then announced. "The king's court has now concluded the issue of Oysten Korisson's misconduct."

As the crowd began to mill about Thane Dyri once more

spoke. "The king has granted a brief althing. Those who desire to voice their concerns to the king will be granted a hearing. The king will allow a shadow to pass while he listens to you." He paused then continued. "All citizens are welcome to attend."

The elders milled about talking with each other. The people who had begun to leave stopped. They wanted to hear everything discussed during the althing. Rumors were already circulating. The speculation was running wild. Someone started a story that an invasion from the north was coming. The raiders, so the tale went, were an advanced guard preparing the way for an invasion from an unknown yetann kingdom hidden to the northeast of Alfheim. Some believed that the king planned to abandon the hamlet. Many believed the fact that Catherine had lived here made it a target for other attacks. They also believed that the king would not want to invest royal funds to protect such a backwater place.

"Will jarl Dan Grissen please come forward. The king wishes to speak with you." Thane Dyri called out.

Dan hesitantly walked to the stand. He wasn't sure what had brought him to the attention of the king. He was sure that it was attention he did not want.

"Jarl Grissen," The king began, "I understand that you sold the cattle of widow Njord?"

"Ah," Dan said. "She was in such distress. I thought she would not be able to care for the cattle."

"How much did she receive for her cattle?" The king interrupted.

Dan stood silent. Before he thought up a good answer. The king spoke again.

"Was it yesterday that you demanded rent from her?"

"That was a misunderstanding my lord." Dan stuttered out.

"Did you strike her child?" The king queried.

"Has Njord made a complainant?" Dan asked.

"Not her or her friends." The king answered. "But We have those in our service who keep us informed."

Dread washed over Dan. He did not like where this was going.

"We have been informed that there were three cows and a calf sold. The cow with the calf was giving milk and the other two are with calf. Is that correct?"

Dan nodded his head.

"Speak up, jarl Grisson" thane Dyri commanded.

"That is so," Dan spoke up.

We have inquired on the value of cattle in this area." The king said. "We have been informed that a cow is valued at a silver skat and a calf usually sells at half that. Did you receive less than those amounts?" The king asked.

"No, my lord," Dan answered. He feared to suggest that he received less. It appeared that the king would know the truth.

"As we see it, you owe the widow four and a half skalt for the cattle." The king paused before he continued. "It concerns us when a child is assaulted. Therefore, for the distress of the child and his mother, we assess a fine of three and a half skalt. That brings the total you owe widow Njord to a mark. You will pay four skalt today and the remaining four skalt by the second ninety, which is the twenty-second of Barnadur. You are dismissed," the king concluded.

As Dan Grisson walked away the king announced "It is our judgment that any debts that may be standing against the estate of jarl Arukas Haukson are void and canceled. If any dispute this, bring it before the courts."

"We will now hear the voice of the people." The king said as he took this seat.

"Line up before the witness stand in an orderly fashion." Thane Dyri told them. "The king will hear you for the next shadow. Those who are requesting a judgment or settlement of disagreements within the community please come forward first. Those whose concerns are for the village and the surrounding areas will be heard and then the king's response will be heard."

After more than two shadows passed the king stood and addressed the people. "We have heard your concerns and fears. It is our belief that this was an isolated incident and not likely to occur again." He held up his hand as a murmur began in the crowd. "We have made Thane Awrick lanstor for the surrounding area. He and his dirfylk will be stationed here in Boar Akarn. The administration and security of this region will be his task until the Hilmar Vorth meets. A final decision will be made then. Until then thane Awrick will be my voice. Go in peace to your homes. Know We have heard you."

As people dispersed. The king and Beinir walked out the back of the pavilion in what appeared to be a deep discussion. Scouts moved around the room, rearranging it to suit the next purpose of the king.

*

Catherine was eager to get home and tell Njord about the king's judgment. Two marks would not replace her husband, but it would relieve the stress of not knowing how she and her son would eat. If, as it appeared to Catherine, she decided to stay in Boar Akarn, Catherine intended to convince her to stay at her house. It would need a caretaker, after all.

From the smells emitting for the kitchen, Njord was preparing a stew for supper.

Catherine took a deep breath and began telling Njord of the king's judgment. Njord sat down and let the tears flow. A short time later, she dried her face.

CHAPTER 22

Lindae Vordottin's gift

Drew and Eric were being no help at all. Jae was in a fix. Two days ago, when he tried to get the hamlet's seamstress to mend a pair of his pants, his effort had been wasted. She had informed him that it was beyond repair and that she was much too busy to make him a new set. Two changes of scouting uniforms were all he had with him. Which shirt was the cleanest was impossible to say. He was sure his mother had sent him a new set. But that was in faraway Virkiflyot. He would have been fine with one pair of pants until they returned to Arnarhvall, except that tonight he might get a chance to walk Catherine home. At least that was his plan.

"You have time to launder the shirt you're not wearing," Elgar informed him. "Toss me your extra pair of pants and I'll do what I can to refresh them with a dusting and an airing out. I tell you, though, she won't be bothered by your dress. She's a practical woman, she is."

"That's the problem. I don't have an extra pair." He said in frustration. "What I have on is the only pair of pants I have."

"You could wear a kilt like the green man." Drew teased.

Resigned to his fate, he gathered the shirt. It would either be dry or almost by the time the king expected them.

A shadow came across their tent flap. "Is anyone there?" Queried a voice that Jae seemed to have heard before.

He opened the flap and standing there was the old seamstress. She was as short as Drew stooped over as she was. She appeared almost out of breath. So, Jae offered her one of their chairs. She responded with. "We don't have time for a sitting, young fellow. I found something I had forgotten I had. Here, strip down and try these on. I've somewhere else I need to be. So, be quick about it." She demanded as she handed him a paper wrapped bundle.

Seeing Jae hesitate, she shook her head and turned to exit the tent. "Don't take too long. Get them on so I can see what I need to do to fit them to you. The pants may be a bit short. We had another fellow picked at the time." She told him as she walked out.

He was out of money. Well, any real amount. He still had a few coins for mead or beer at the tavern. He even could have paid for the mending he had requested. But this outfit. Well, he had watched nobles at parties in less elegant costumes. He had tried to tell her that he couldn't pay her. But she acted like she didn't hear him. There was a light green inner shirt. It was loose and soft. She pulled on some strings and adjusted the over shirt until it fit like it was made for him.

Drew hooted when he first saw it. The shirt boasted loose, billowy sleeves and tightened cuffs, a design favored in the court of Kalfa thirty years ago. The dark green material of the overshirt was accented with lighter greens and yellows. The slashed sleeves revealed intricate arcane designs of red and gold on the inner sleeve. The green brocade paneled pants had open slashes revealing the same red and gold designs as the shirt. The only problem with the pants was that they were too short. "I hadn't expected a tall vanir when I was making this." The old woman explained while she filled their tent with her chatter. It mainly consisted of local gossip. She also shared memories of her children and grandchildren. She made Jae stand on a rickety chair as she stitched on a lace ruffle around the bottom of the legs of the pants.

After Jae thought the fitting was over, she insisted he wear a sword. She picked out the yetann dagger Eric had collected on the mountain. She attached it to a red and green belt covered with more arcane symbols stitched with yellow and gold threads. He would stand out that was sure. She then fastened a large ornate pin to the belt. "That will have to do." She told them. Then she fixed her eyes on him. "Look at me. You are to be læknir Catherine's escort. I think she will be pleased by that. Don't be late." She turned to the broadly grinning Elgar. "See that he is on time and don't let any military nonsense interfere. As I said I have elsewhere I need to be." With that, she walked out of the tent and was soon lost in the maze of the camp.

*

Catherine, with Njord and Ceri's help, was trying to decide what to wear this evening. With all the excitement surrounding the king's rulings. Catherine had forgotten to clean the one dress she thought suitable for the evening's events. Tonight, she would be trying to use Prysivolar's book. The king, the prince, and several of the noble's would be present. She at least wanted to look the part of a wise læknir. Though it appeared that the king was expecting a seior. She ended up settling on her new travel clothes.

Njord seemed to enjoy the thought that they would scandalize the village. It might even distract the gossip about her. The gossip was she was already accepting courters, not much a month after her husband's death. A few of the single village men had happened by with offers to help. That after the king's gifting her with two marks. Even jarl Grisson had come over with an apology and to him, a generous offer, on the rent or purchase of her old home. She had enjoyed the look on his face when she turned him down. She was content to be the caretaker of Catherine's home.

As she was brushing the dirt off her new boots someone knocked on the back door to her kitchen. Ceri jumped up and raced to open the door, expecting Cu lain and Eikin to be there. Eikin knocking would have been a surprise since the door was not latched, he would have rushed in. She opened the door to discover a pair of sparkling grey eyes that were surrounded by smile lines looking at her at the same level as her eyes were. Most people's eyes, except for children's eyes, made her look up if she wanted to see them.

The old woman smiled at her. "So, you're the child læknir

215

Catherine has taken in." Looking over to Catherine she continued. "She's prettier than I was told." Turning to Ceri she said. "Would you help this old fra bring in the packages, child?"

Ceri nodded her head and took the packages from the old woman's arms. The woman then toddled in smiling. "Lay them on the table for me, please." She requested.

"Fra Vordottin, what a pleasant surprise!" Catherine told her. It was a surprise. The circle of women fra Vordottin counted as friends had, for the most part, been avoiding Catherine since her return.

"I've always asked you to call me Lindae, now haven't I?" She said as she patted Catherine's hand. "I know there many who are offended by such familiarity. But it always bought me joy to hear you call my name when you were a child begging for a few of my cookies. I never told you, did I? That I baked those cookies for you. Laeknir Sturlasda frowned at my attempts to spoil you. She told me to scatter my baking around all the children. She was right, if I had done as I wanted the others would have resented you. There I go prattling on. Well, open the packages. I've been working on this for some time. And it isn't quite ready. The bottom will need hemming. I wasn't sure how tall you had grown. After all, I haven't made you anything since you started sewing your own." She grew quiet and gave a small smile as she motioned with her hands for Catherine to open the paper wrapped packages.

"I know, I know this is a surprise. I would have brought them sooner but there was still work to be done." She brushed Catherine's hand from the package Catherine was picking up and handed her a smaller one. In that one was a gorgeous light green chemise. It felt like the silk that the yetann had been wearing under their armor. How Fra Lindae was able to achieve the bright green color she could not tell.

"Put it on. Put it on, let's see how it fits. There are only us women here." Fra Lindae commanded. So, with Njord and Ceri's eager help she stripped off what she had on and slipped into the chemise. It billowed and then settled on her. It came a hand and a half above her knees. A perfect fit.

The old woman handed her the next package. When Catherine tore open that package a beautiful emerald green full floor length dress was revealed. The inner fabric was two-sided cotton. The two-sided front piece was designed to hold the abdomen inside and enhance the chest. Lindae demonstrated as she adjusted the various cords and straps to fit it to Catherine, much to Catherine's embarrassment. She insisted that the front piece be adjusted for a more modest appearance. The old woman acquiesced adjusting the front to suit Catherine's taste. As she finished, she told Catherine. "Remember how well it adjusts to display your figure, you never know when you may want to distract a male. And those make a fine distraction."

"Or attraction" Giggled Njord.

The next package contained a forest green outer dress made to cover what Catherine now realized was an inner one. It had a nice 'V' cut from which the pretty inner piece peeked out. The sleeves marched up to the elbow for a secure fit and moved forward to the higher arm which had slashed sleeves. The slashed sleeves revealed a red satin inner sleeve. Lindae adjusted the flexible pieces to fit Catherine's arms. Just above the elbow before the sleeve billowed out intricate arcane designs of red and gold decorated a band around her arm. The same arcane symbols ran down both sides of the V opening.

Catherine held that dress up examining it. "This is a Seior's dress, not a læknir's, Frau Lindae? Why, Where did you get that idea, and why now?" she asked.

Frau Lindae paused. She looked at Catherine and sat in a nearby chair. "Læknir Sturlasda and I started preparing these for your sixteenth birthday shortly after your fourteenth summer. I asked her the same questions. She told me that you were more than a læknir. She took my hand and told me that she planned to move after your sixteenth summer. You would need different training. The dress was to prepare you for that. Unfortunately, she died before your fifteenth summer. When your sixteenth summer arrived. I thought that the dress would only add to your trouble. As it was, we were barely able to keep you in your home. Without the intervention of Fra Trena, we may not have been able to stop elder Ani from chasing you from your house. I was afraid that some of the villagers would have been frightened by the prospect of a sorceress living in their midst, so I kept them hidden.

You're leaving us. This is the only chance that I have of delivering læknir Sturlasda and my gifts.

The clothing wasn't the only thing I hid." She finished as she pointed to the finial small package on the table.

Catherine tore off the paper exposing a journal. It was widow Sturlasda's missing journal. Next to it lay the ring and a matching necklace that she had worn. Catherine now recognized them as a vel opna and a vel eiga. Catherine had believed that they had been buried with the widow.

"I took and hid them the day læknir Sturlasda died. Small personal valuables seem to disappear when a death occurs. I had to make sure that no one but you would receive the læknir's last journal and jewelry. As plain as they are, she sat great value on them." Fra Lindae finished as a tear dropped from her eye.

*

Drew and Eric decided to join Jae on his walk to Catherine's house. They wanted to watch the reactions of the people who saw Jae in his new suit. Elgar decided to follow as well. They were less likely to get into a fight if he was around. If he was being honest, he too wanted to see the peoples' reaction. What would they make of the outfit that looked much like what his father wore when Elgar was a youngster? Fashion had changed since then. Even the styles wore by the nobles were simpler and more utilitarian than they had been in his father's time.

The calls and the jokes didn't distract Jae, he was on a mission. Though his ears turned red several times he didn't let their baiting take him from the path to Catherine's. He just hoped she would see this new set of clothing as a compliment, not a joke.

Cu lain was on the front porch waiting for them. He wore his white uniform. "They kicked me out of the house half a shadow ago. Some old lady brought new clothing for Catherine and she had to be fitted. I had hoped you would arrive earlier. Karl left to attend to something." He told them. "Njord commanded me to guard the front door. She had put Eikin to bed after the old woman showed up."

Jae inquired about what the old woman looked like. From Cu lain's description she sounded like the same woman who gifted him his new suit. It sounded to him that his prospects of impressing Catherine were growing.

It was a short time later, while Drew was wishing for a cold beer or even a warm mead, Njord opened the door and ushered them into the greeting room. She arranged them in a semicircle about the kitchen door and called to Ceri. "They're ready."

Ceri danced out the kitchen door opening it wide. Standing in the light stood Catherine in the clothing that Jae's suit was made to complement. He remembered the image of a great sorcerous in a children's storybook he had read long ago. Her dress appeared to him more wonderous than the image in that old storybook. Catherine was real and looked, to him, as elegant as a queen. He bowed low to her and then stepped forward and took the arm she offered him as he approached her.

This was some fantasy dream. Catherine thought. The dress was more ornate and formal than she had ever worn. Before her stood Jae decked in an outfit that she might have ridiculed a month ago. But now, knowing what effort widow Sturlasda and Frau Lindae had invested in these outfits, she felt privileged. There was Jae in an outfit meant to match hers. Who was the young man they meant to force to escort her then? Seeing Jae approach drove that thought away.

Several people stopped to stare as she and her felag promenaded to the king's pavilion.

CHAPTER 23

Dining with the king

Alvi Geirsson, Ljot Jartasen, and Varin Arfastsen were huddled in a corner of the pavilion with Seior Lyos Alvisen the Galduryafi (Magic advisor), he had arrived a shadow before dark. They had been in their huddle before Seior Lys had arrived. Not even the masterpieces Matsveir had presented as appetizers stopped their absorption with whatever they were arguing about. Prince Ari couldn't follow any of their arguments. Too many obscure terms to suit him.

The arrival of Catherine interrupted them. And that not for long. When Beinir announced her, everyone looked to see the maiden who after the meal would attempt to use the wooden plank that Konkur Cu lain had insisted was the old grasblett's source of knowledge.

There she stood in the full regalia of a master seioknar of old. Standing slightly behind her was the Einheri (guarding champion). Even king Awrick rose to his feet. A scene from some musical play his father had sponsored long ago jumped into his head. The music had been horrid, but the dramatic entrance of the sorcerous was still vivid in his mind. He walked over to Catherine. She started to curtsey, but he took her hand and raising it to his lips kissing it. "I believe," he said, "this evening is looking very promising.

Many of the early conversations centered on her new dress with side remarks on Jae's new suit. Seior Lyos examined the arcane symbols. He carefully explained what many of them meant and their intended function. At times it was a very dull discourse, especially since they were mere decorations meant to impress, but with no real function.

Ljot commented on her and Jae's matching pins. Did they have a function he wondered? Catherine had no idea. She could not sense any energy in the pins, not like what was in the artifacts they had found on the mountain. Even the replica worn by the grasblatt on the mountain has some energy about it. But, not these pins. Karl agreed that the two pins did not exhibit any sign of being active artifacts.

The discussion of the arcane markings dwindled as the four scholars once more took up the subject that had engrossed them earlier.

Catherine was seated between the king and prince Ari. She would have preferred to be sitting next to Jae, but when the king offers you a seat, well that's where you sit. Prince Ari interrupted her taking a bite of the venison with an offhand comment. "Your hair color has changed since we first met. It's not as bright a red. It's more auburn now than yesterday. How is that possible?"

Jae had noticed the same thing. It seemed Catherine's hair had changed overnight. From the fiery red of the mountain to a much tamer color. What had changed? Did something on the mountain, yetann piss, the hot spring water, or the dryad, change the color? It still should have taken days or even two five-days before the color started to change as the hair grew out. That's the way the henna worked that some of the women he knew used.

Crispin looked over. He hadn't paid particular attention to Catherine's hair. But now that the prince mentioned it. The color was darkening. "What have you done with your hair, Catherine he asked.

This confused Catherine. She hadn't used a mirror since she used those two on the mountain. The only mirror in her house was widow Sturlasda's old scrying mirror. It was so old you could barely make out an image on its dull surface. As far as she knew she hadn't done anything that would have affected her hair color. She wouldn't have. She had decided she liked the fiery color, best to give warning to those who might mistake her for some meek maiden. She looked over to Crispin. He was expecting some response.

"Nothing, as far as I know, I have done nothing." She told him. What was she doing differently since her return to Boar Akarn? She thought about it. Her old routines were a shamble. Well, she had started doing the meditation exercises, that the widow Sturlasda had taught her. There was nothing in that that would affect a person's hair color. Was there? She let her mind drift away and silently went through the mediation routine. Something, yes something was there. Each part of the routine was set to accomplish something. She had always thought the widow intended it to dampen her fiery nature, calm her so she could deal with difficult patients. As she examined each piece of it there were a couple of exercises that seemed to be for something else. Was this set of exercises meant to obscure her presence? If so that gave her the answer to Jae's observation of her and Karl fading from his perception. That it could obscure another person's presence made her wonder if the widow had been the one hiding them. Who else's perception was it clouding? And these three lines of meditation what did they do? Could those little exercises be changing her hair color? The only way to find out would be to stop using them during her meditation. What part did what was difficult to perceive, and it would take a conscious effort to leave out the few lines she intended to. But she could try.

As she came back to the present, she noticed Crisping, the prince, and Jae looking at her. She laughed. "Have I been gone long?" That brought smiles to their faces.

"I suppose that you will share your thoughts in time. "Crispin said.

*

It was shortly after this that jarl Alvi, who was sitting next to Ceri, began to question Ceri about the ship that had dropped the raiders off on the coast. His gruff voice frightened Ceri. She grew very quiet and seemed to shrink as she was quizzed about the ship.

Noticing this Cu lain spoke up. "You should know that we both were drugged before we boarded that ship. I can say that it looked like a merchant knorr. Like the ones I had watched in the harbor of Tawnia when I was a child.

Prysivolar and I boarded a sloop in Tawnia which dropped us at a port somewhere. I was seasick from that voyage and had been drugged to suppress it. He and I boarded the knorr shortly before the pyris did. I do remember a figure carved into the forecastle of the ship. It was a woman with a veil dancing or skipping. There were some words written above her, but I can't read. That's the most I can tell you."

Ceri said something. She said it so quietly that it went unnoticed by most at the table. Except for Jae who was sitting next to her, no one understood a word of it. He leaned over and whispered to her. "It's safe to juggle eggs here." That brought a small smile to her face. "If you will give a moment of quiet to this young lady, I believe she wants to tell us something." He said while he looked to the king.

King Awrick clapped his hands. That silenced the room. "I'm sorry Ceri. You came dancing in here expecting a party and all you've received was lectures by grumpy old men. I wouldn't blame you if you wanted to leave. Please don't. Matsveir will be angry with us if you leave before dessert."

"I know the name of the ship," Ceri whispered.

Ceri, you'll need to speak a little louder unless you want jarl Jae to tell us what you say. And that would be fine as well." He told her.

Ceri closed her eyes. She took a deep breath to calm herself, as her friend Catherine had taught her. "The name of the ship was the Dancing Bride. At least that's what the crew called her when they teased the other female with us. They said they wanted to help make her dance like a bride."

They were silent for a moment. "Thank you Ceri, I believe that will help us," Awrick told her.

Alvi spent a moment running a pencil over his napkin. "I wonder," He asked as he held up what he had drawn If the woman looked something like this?" The drawing was of a woman dancing, he had drawn the dress as black as the pencil would allow.

Ceri nodded her head, "Yes my lord, it was similar but different." Then Cu lain added. "The dress was white on the ship. Maybe it had been painted white."

"Well, I had wondered what happened to her. I had invested in a ship named the Merry Widow. She was lost at sea several summers ago. Some believed she was lost in some storm. It appears to me that she was captured by pirates and now reappears with a new name." Alvi explained.

"Beinir, I believe that is the information we need. Please add that to the letter we've prepared for King Jomath. Then let me read over it one more time before we send it on to Gandvik. Maybe we can catch that ship there." King Awrick called. Then he turned to the huddled scholars. "That's enough discussion for this evening. If you must continue, do so after the meal, or you can leave now." Something in the king's tone gave those men pause. "Shouldn't we have music?" he asked his valet Sihtric. A trio with stringed instruments began playing a relaxing melody.

The music brought a brighter mood to the meal. Ceri forgot her shyness when Matsveir brought out dessert. A cake with three layers, blue on the bottom, red in the middle, and green at the top. He insisted that they had to try a piece of each layer. For each had a different flavor. Matsveir chuckled as Ceri tried each flavor, switching from one to another unable to decide which she liked best. He and Ceri left together to see if he had any of the sweet frosting left. She insisted that Cu lain come with them to help carry the bounty home. She wanted to share some of the cake and frosting with Eikin in the morning. She knew if she placed some in Cu lain's care it would be there in the morning. He reluctantly followed her and Matsveir out, knowing that he had to return for Catherine's attempt to use Prysivolar's book. He was thankful when he saw Eric and Drew standing near the entrance of the king's pavilion as he started to escort Ceri home. They gladly agreed to take Ceri home especially since that meant they could have a piece of Matsveir's cake. He watched as they started off, then returned to the pavilion.

*

King Awrick examined the unusual piece of wood. Truthfully it looked somewhat like a short plank of dark wood that had been highly polished. But it had no grain. Even ebony had a grain to it. He handed it to Catherine.

She turned it over and opened the flap of cloth that covered one side of it. Momentarily the cloth seemed to cling to the surface of the plank. She folded the cloth over the opposite side. Nothing happened. "Cu lain, did the old seior use some magic word to wake it?" prince Ari asked.

"Cu lain shook his head no before he answered, "I never heard one if he did. When he used his book sometimes, he would speak in another language, but only after it was awake. What little I heard was in daonna. If he caught me watching, he would chase me away."

As Cu lain spoke Catherine examined the wood plank. This was the first time she had the opportunity to really look at it. On one of the sides, there was a small indentation. As she positioned her right hand to hold it by that side the band of her ring slipped into the grove. As it did the face of the plank lit up. A line of strange markings moved across its polished surface. Then a spot of glowed blue at the end of the line of markings. Then another line moved across and the spot glowed again. The fifth line prince Ari recognized as a line of letters from archaic Vanir. The sixth looked like some ancient dzwerc Jae had seen. It was the fifteenth line that was in daonna. Catherine touched to glowing spot at the end of that line.

A strange mechanical voice announced "Accepted. What is the subject of your current research?" A pattern of daonna letters sprang across the bottom edge of the plank. There was a long rectangular space outlined on the right of the display with the word space in it.

225

Catherine carefully touched the letters to spell. "What subjects are available" When she finished, she touched the circle on the left with the word enter in it. A list floated up the screen in smaller print. There were ten lines of subjects and the sentence "Touch here for additional options.

The list was. Medical treatments in liquid form. Plants with medical attributes. Recognizing wild plants. The effects of drugs on animals and men. The biology of the yetann. The biology of etunazi. Biological functions of the pyris. Biology of vanir descendants. Methods of medical treatment. Nude portraits of different female body types.

"Can you respond to my voice?" Catherine asked.

The mechanical voice responded "At this time in a very limited way. After some time, I can learn to respond more effectively."

Catherine touched the glowing spot next to "Plants with medical attributes."

A set of plant pictures appeared. Two rolls of five pictures. They did not appear to be paintings but the actual plant. Catherine's finger slipped as she started to touch the picture of the mugwort. When it did another set of ten pictures slid across the plank.

The king held out his hand and asked. "May I see the artifact?" The plank went dark as soon as Catherine's hand left its surface. He placed his ring in the grove with no response. He then borrowed Catherine's, placing it on his little finger. The plank sat awkwardly in his grasp as he slid the ring into the grove. Still no response. King Awrick handed the plank back to Catherine and returned her ring. "It appears that it only responds to a person with a ring matched to them." He observed.

The remainder of the evening was spent asking questions of the device. It soon became apparent to all that the longer it was in Catherine's hands the more it favored her questions. By late in the evening it was only responding to her.

It was soon after Catherine stifled a yawn that the king suggested it was time to retire. When everyone agreed, Seior Lyos

Alvisen the Galduryafi (Magic advisor) stepped forward and took the plank from Catherine's hands.

"And what do you think you're doing?" Ari asked. This drew the king's attention.

"Yes, Lyos, what are you doing?" He demanded.

A confused look passed over the man's face. "Why I'm taking this artifact into safekeeping. It will be stored in the king's archive with the hundred or so others we have there."

"Hand it back to Seioknar Catherine. It will do more good in her hands than that hundred in our archives." The king told him.

Seior Lyos handed the artifact back to Catherine with an apology. "I beg your pardon, Seioknar Catherine. It is a habit I have acquired. I should have known better. This is the only one I ever saw working." Then with a twinkle in his eye, he asked. "Does my lord really think that artifacts should be in the possession of those that can use them?"

"Not just anyone. A trusted citizen of Alfheim. If they can use them and they have a legitimate claim." King Awrick responded.

"And Seioknar Catherine is a trusted Citizen?" He asked.

"Of course!" Ari said in a tightly controlled voice. He was beginning to wonder if old Lyos as daft as some of the rumors made him.

A look of pure mischief crossed the old fellows face. "I know it is late, but I so happen to have a few artifacts on me. Seior Catherine, would you care to examine them perhaps?" He cocked his head at her in anticipation.

He then pulled several artifacts from his pockets. A small ornate hammer with a leather wristband attached, then what appeared to be a wood shaft just over a hand's breadth in length with a pointed crystal attached to one end on the other end was a small hole, next to it he laid a ring with a matching crystal then a sword hilt with an emerald set where the blade should have been and last a large crystalline egg-shaped object. Each object had obscure and ornate symbols covering them.

Thoughts of sleep fled as they gazed on the collection. Ari

picked up the small hammer. "The symbols are a form of high Vanir. Ljot, come here! Do I read this right does it say Mjolnir here?"

Seior Lyos waited patiently as Ljot and Ari picked up one then another, naming each as they did. Mjolnir, Gungnir, Freyr's blade. A puzzled look passed over their faces when they examined the last object. The symbols read krakki lindorm khallir. Which they translated as either "caller of lindorm's child or child calling lindorm". The other names they knew. They had no idea what this last object was.

"I know what they are labeled. If you had waited, I would have told you. I brought these hoping the king would allow Seioknar Catherine to examine them. I hope at least one responds to her. The one labeled Gungnir is the only one that has a matching ring. Imagine an army with only one of these weapons! Now lay them down and let Seioknar Catherine examine them." He told them. "But first." Seior Lyos clapped his hands and a group of burly men staggered in carrying a large boulder. If you will, my lady please only point the weapons at that." He told her as he pointed at the rock.

Sadly, the only one that responded to Catherine's touch was Gungnir. She had removed her ring and slid the ring that matched it onto her finger. When she picked up what they now recognized as a miniature spear nothing happened. But when Jae suggested that she try it with her ring, a faint glow appeared when she held it. When she touched the indent where her fingertip lay light burst forth and formed letters on the boulder then it gradually went dark.

"That's ancient high vanir" Prince Ari observed. Then he sounded out what had appeared "onogur leyfa vel". Between Ari and Ljot they puzzled out the words to mean something along the lines of insufficient device authority.

"Not authorized?" Catherine suggested. "I believe it says that I'm not authorized to use this device. I wonder how one authorizes a person for an artifact?"

No one had a suggestion of how to accomplish that. So, it was decided that it would be best to retire for the night and pursue that investigation after they arrived at the king's college. There they would have additional scholars to help.

Jae asked. "I wonder if it just takes time to authorize to a person. Your ring didn't immediately respond to you and it was made for you. What if it just takes time?"

Seior Lyos stopped and picked up the Gungnir and its opna vel. He knitted his brow. "Now that's a thought. It might hold true for some artifacts. There are stories about families who pass down active artifacts through the family. Sadly, I've only heard rumors. I've never been able to trace any down." He mulled it over in his head and scrunched his face up in concentration. Then he smiled. "Prince Ari, didn't you win the javelin event your second year at Virkiflyot?"

Ari shrugged his shoulders. "Yes, so?"

Seior Lyos didn't appear to hear him as he rummaged through his pockets. He pulled out a copper chain and strung it through the hole at the base of Gungnir. Then using a small pliers, he happened to be carrying, he closed the chain making a loop large enough to fit over Ari's head. He handed Ari Gungnir and its ring. "Wear these, at least until we get back to Arnarhvall. Let's see what happens."

Ari knew better than to argue with the seior and slid the ring onto his right hand. Then he placed the chain around his neck. The ring was loose on his finger. He would have to tighten it with some string when he got the chance. At Catherine's direction, he slid Gungnir under his shirt. "You may feel warmth from them when they align. I did."

As Seior Lyos was packing away the remaining objects Ari picked up the egg to examine it closer. When he did a faint glow appeared. "Look at this he called out." He passed it to his father and the glow faded. The king handed it to Catherine, nothing happened. But when she handed it back to Ari it began to glow again.

"Any idea why it glows when I hold it?" Ari asked Seior Lyos. Lyos just shook his head no. Ari then handed it back to him to pack away. When we get back to Arnarhvall perhaps some of the scholars there can help explain it." Lyos said as he packed it away for the journey back.

CHAPTER 24

From learned Alphere's first year lectures on required knowledge of a warrior.

The major astrological objects in Ymir's night sky are Asgard which is always in the same location in the sky and the moons Y'dalir (also known as Mani) and Ni'o.

Under Y'dalir's Smile

She didn't know how Jae had done it, but here they were. The two of them walking together. Supposedly he was escorting her home. The only problem with that supposition was that he had taken her out the wrong direction. They had left the complex of tents where the king's pavilion was on the side opposite her house. He did seem a bit distracted, but she doubted that what had occurred in the pavilion was what distracted him. He, like her, had been amazed by Prysivolar's wood plank speaking to them. She could feel its weight in the bag she had hung on her shoulder. It still astounded her that the king had entrusted this treasure trove of knowledge to her. Even if it was true that she was the only person any of them knew who could get a response from it.

They had turned left when they had exited the complex. Not right which would have taken them past the pub and the other buildings and homes of the hamlet. Even so, they were not alone. Every few feet they passed a guard on patrol. What would you expect when the king was just a few feet away? The only thing separating the king from those who might want to harm him was the thin cloth of the tents and the guards surrounding him.

Jae was looking up as he spoke. Something about this phase of

the moon being called Y'dalir's smile. He was handsome and so
sober. How he had worked up the bravado to kiss her in front of
his friends yesterday she didn't know. She also didn't know if he
had been thinking of kissing her again. She had been. He turned
and faced her bending just a little, enough she judged. She raised
to her tiptoes and lightly kissed his lips. Yes, it was as pleasant as
the first time.

Jae had been wondering how he was going to accomplish
what she had just managed. He had managed to get her alone.
Well, as alone as they could be, seeing that there were over
a hundred other scouts roaming about. That didn't seem to
bother her, and he decided, it wouldn't bother him either. So,
after the initial shock at her boldness passed, while she was still
standing close, he took her chin in his right hand raising her face
toward him. He bent lower and kissed her again. He wasn't sure
how long had passed when their lips parted. He was glad it was
dark, so she couldn't see how red he knew his ears were. She
smiled up at him "What took you so long? She asked.

He had no answer to that, so he bent down again. She wrapped
her arms around his neck, and they kissed. His arms were
around her waist when that kiss had run its course. They held
each other for a moment. Then they both became embarrassed
by the intimacy. They stepped apart just as they heard the foot-
steps of an approaching guard.

They walked hand and hand, not sure what to say, back to the
front door of her house. They parted after another kiss. It passed
Catherine's thoughts to pull him inside and take him to her bed.
Sadly, she knew that could not happen. Not only was Ceri sleeping up in her bedroom, but Njord and Eikin were in the widow's
room. Besides how long had they known each other? Little over
two five-days!

It was late. Best to go to sleep, for tomorrow would be busy.
The king and his entourage would be leaving tomorrow, and she
and her friends with him. As she climbed into her bed she wondered if she would be able to sleep at all. The excitement of the
trip and the thoughts of the kisses wrestled together for a time

before she drifted off to a dream filled slumber. Dreams of new sights and kisses.

CHAPTER 25

A light rain began to fall as the king's pavilion and all the other tents were in the process of being taken down and packed away. That's the reason why Njord and Catherine found themselves playing host to the king and his entourage.

All hope Catherine had of seeing Jae this morning fled when Cu lain returned with Eikin. They had been out hoping to expend some of the boys' seemingly endless energy. As Cu lain opened the door a folded piece of paper dropped from the door. It had Catherine's name on it. He handed it to her as soon as he saw her. Jae had left it. It told her that he had assigned scouting duties and would not see her this morning. She hoped they would see each other on the way to Utroor.

King Awrick, prince Ari, Gaut Bjornson, and Thane Awrick sat in the greeting room discussing the details of governing a landskap. Matsveir paced the kitchen floor worried over the young dryad in the bucket on the back porch. She was sitting in the rain. "Just where she needs to be, before her journey." Karl had told him before he walked out into the rain himself. Matsveir still worried that she might drown.

Between Matsveir and Eikin all Catherine and Njord were able to prepare was some tea. Which only they sat and drank. Everyone else was much too busy to take the time to relax before traveling to Utroor.

Catherine had packed the night before. Her clothing and her puzzle box were stuffed into a large chest. It was ready to be loaded on to the wagon when it appeared. She was glad she had decided to wear her wilderness clothing. The journey would be miserable as it was. But less than if she had worn her new dress. Not only would it quickly soak through, but it probably would have been left in ruins. Ceri had a backpack full of all she possessed, the five altered dresses from Catherine and a pair of shoes frau Lindae had found for her.

In what they were wearing they could walk or mount a horse and at least be above the mud. Catherine hoped the rain quit before they began their journey. But it was impossible to predict the weather this time of year.

*

The felag had left at dawn. They were together again. They had been training together in this felag since starting at Virkiflyot. Arnor, as usual, was the point. They had been assigned with another felag to be the first scouts ahead of the king's party. Another two felags would follow just ahead of the king. A felag of horse would travel on either side. A third felag of horse was across the laek gritter scouting that area, just in case.

"Well, what happened last night?" Eric pressed Jae. Though Jae's ears reddened he ignored Eric.

Eric persisted which drew Arnor's attention. "We've been given the honor of scouting ahead of the king. This is a real mission. It's the first real assignment we've had together. Possibly the last. Besides, everyone knows they kissed last night. Epli told me they kissed for a long time." He tossed that tidbit behind him as he turned to continue through the forest.

Jae's ears reddened more. Then he turned upslope to see what lay beyond the low hill they were passing.

Asleif pretended not to have heard. A lump formed in her throat. "That tart!" she thought. Knowing the judgment unfair. Still saying it helped. Even if it was said only to herself.

They spread out on the slope of the hill west of the trail. Scattered up and down the slope, they made sure they always had at least two others in sight.

They found the tracks of a wolf pack. A badger that didn't care to have them in the neighborhood and let Eric know about it. They found nothing that would cause concern for the king's safety. The only other tracks they found were their own.

The early morning rain had caught them as it raced up the slope toward Boar Akarn. It did not surprise them to find the ford over the stream they had stepped over on the way up two wide to jump across. So, taking off their boots and socks they put on their moccasins and waded across.

"I suppose they will widen this into a road and build a bridge here," Drew observed. "Seeing how this area is now a landskap this trail will see more travel."

They arrived at where the king's party would camp for the night. They circled the area and came across the other felag doing the same. Vaetta was the point of this felag. She winked at Jae, "I hear you had a pleasant evening last night." Eric and Drew chuckled a little at that. Then they shared what they had noticed.

Jae had managed to secure enough of the roast Matsveir had prepared the night before to share. That with the bread Vaetta had liberated made them a fine lunch.

Egil brought up what they were all curious about, the artifacts. After some persuasion, Jae described the objects. Haaken got excited at the mention of the miniature Freyr's sword Jae had handled. His family had an object much like it only its gem was a ruby. Family stories told of the great, great grandmother losing its ring down the well. He wondered if it might be worth descending into the well and trying to retrieve it. The sun broke through the clouds reminding them of their duties.

Jae's felag headed down the trail and Vaetta's back up the trail. Both planning to again circle the camping area. Making double sure of the king's safety.

CHAPTER 26

A box canyon northwest of Boar Akarn

If you followed the abandoned road as it wound north of Boar Akarn you would find a cliff lined box canyon. Something began to stir there, Lindorm had been summoned. Her egg had called. How long had she slept? Much too long from the condition of her wings. Immediate flight would not be possible, and she was hungry. Thankfully her nest lay atop a coal seam. That would have to do for now. Coal and later young trees would feed her for now. She needed to repair the damage that sleeping so long had allowed.

Her precious egg was moving away from her lair. That was troubling. The summoner knew that his possession of her egg demanded battle. Why would she be summoned, and her challenger then run away?

She remembered being defeated. Too many times to count. Of the thousands of battles, she was only able to retrieve her egg a dozen times. The gods cheated. They always did. Her memories were not complete. How had she been defeated? What ploys did they use to defeat her? How had she won?

Her routine had been to keep the warrior alive and demand a ransom. Then she slept, only to awake to meet another challenger who had her egg. It seemed that shortly after she demanded the ransom that she fell asleep. Before her egg could hatch. Would it hatch? That was the ingrained hope that drove her. If she could keep it long enough it must hatch! After she possessed her egg she hungered for gold. An inner urge drove her. Did she need gold to hatch the egg? If she had gold would she be able to produce another egg? She would need to be much more cunning. This time she would kill the bearer of her egg. Killing the challenger perhaps would keep her from sleeping and losing her egg again. That is if she could overcome the routine that seemed to govern her actions.

Lindorm flexed her wings scattering the leaves and soil that covered her. There were some parts of the wings where barely a framework remained. She opened her mouth and scooped in a mouth full of coal. Nasty tasting stuff. But it would serve her need. She moved out into the full sun and spread her wings wide. After another mouth full of that distasteful black nourishment, she rested and began the long work to rebuild herself. It could take over a year before she would be able to hunt. She would need some metal. Would she be able to find a source close by? How long before she could pursue her egg? She surveyed her damaged state. It might be the next summer before she could begin. Or longer, that possibility troubled her, but she would find her egg. She knew the direction it had moved. How far the challenger would dare take it she did not know. But she knew the revenge she would wreak on her journey to retrieve it.

*

It was a pleasant morning as Jae and Catherine walked together their hands almost touching. With so many people watching they were not able to figure out how much affection they could display without offending the other. They had been able to share a brief kiss the night before. Too brief a kiss for either of them, but the best they could do.

Jae figured that if they kissed as much as he wanted too, they would never make it to Arnarhvall. He had obligations to the king. How to become Catherine's life partner and meet his obligations at the same time, he could not fathom. Would she even want that? They had not had an opportunity to discuss their future. The back of his hand touched hers and she turned and smiled at him. Her green eyes danced at his touch. So, he took her hand in his. Deciding to live fully in this day.

As they followed behind the couple Eric punched Drew in

the arm and laughed. Drew gave a tight-lipped smile. He liked Catherine. More than he would admit even to himself. But what would a romance between her and Jae portend for the adventures they had planned. After their four years of service to the crown, they would have the skills to adventure across Midgard. What would happen to those plans? He supposed he would just have to make the best of it. It was possible that having Catherine had made the adventures start sooner. Who would have thought they would battle yetann with the aid of a dryad and the green man? Perhaps that was the high point of their adventures, but he thought not.

King Awrick and his entourage rode behind those who were walking. When they traveled in a mixed group like this the king tended to take the rear. It left less mess for the walkers to walk through. Less mud and less dung. He had followed a parade of horse walking once. Only once. His father had laughed at his ruined boots, before slapping him on the back. He had expected a lecture on caring for his new clothing. Instead, he got praise for rising to the challenge. His father told him he had done well to ignore the obvious insult that the governor of Merki had intended. "The people of Merki had been walking behind such parades for a long time." He told him. "Just next time ask for your horse."

Awrick's walk that day had an unintended result. The next Merki Althing resulted in the man who tried to insult him being rejected as their governor. The people had requested the prince to govern. The city his father had feared he would lose was knit closer by Awrick walking through the horse dung. Governing Merki opened Awrick's eyes to the challenges his father faced. It was after three years of serving as governor that the king had requested the return of his son. Merki still held a special place in Awrick's thoughts.

Ari road beside his father watching the young couple hold hands. They had a freedom he did not have. He tried not to be envious of them. They would face their own challenges. He knew that he couldn't just hold a young lady's hand without the gossip spreading through the land. He hoped when the time to choose a bride came, he would be as blessed as his father and mother who genuinely cared for each other. He knew couples who presented a pleasant display but in private wouldn't even eat together.

He reached down and adjusted the ring he was wearing. It seemed to move where it wanted to sit then. Last night he had thought it a bit loose. He soon forgot about the ring as he enjoyed the ride. The sun was bright and warm. They were leaving the almost wilderness and entering the almost settled lands. It would be about two five-days and he would be home. Best make the best of the time with his father. He believed his father intended for him to gain some hands-on training soon. What exactly his father planned had not yet been revealed. He suspected his mother would need to approve before his father would tell him.

He had graduated from Virkiflyot last year. He knew people expected him to earn his place. He was ready to do just that. His mother had suggested sending him to her father in Kalfa for a couple of years to become acquainted with her father and his court. Ari had dreaded that. He had spent his fifteenth summer with his grandfather. It had been pleasant enough. He had espe-cially enjoyed fishing in the ocean. Yet the court in Kalfa seemed too stiff and formal. The young ladies his grandfather tried to interest him in were nothing like his mother. All seemed to want a title more than a partner. At fifteen summers Ari had decided that if he could not find a partner he would not marry. Celibate or a mistress but no wife he could not trust.

Crispin rode up with a dozen trout breaking Ari's reverie. That was just as well. Daydreaming about a wife would not make one appear. Fresh trout now that brought back memories of times when he and a few friends joined Uncle Crispin on trips to some high mountain stream. That's where he learned to fish and to love his land.

It was early for lunch but in less than a shadow they came across Elgar and the fire he had ready for the trout. So, His father and he dismounted and sat around the fire with Elgar and Crispin while the others went on ahead. A felag of horse stayed with them of course. Sad for them, as they only had their trail rations.

It was while the trout were being consumed that a second felag of horse appeared to escort them back to the group traveling to Utroor. That was when the king told those who had watched them eat that they were free of all duties for a five-day. Just be sure to be back at the garrison in Goa Vollar on time. Crispin gave them his two poles and told them where he had caught the trout. Then the four of them, with their escort, slowly rode toward Utroor.

CHAPTER 27

The palace in Arnarhvall

The garden was warm in the early morning sun as Frida watched her daughter's unarmed combat training. Many in the court were appalled that the king's daughter was receiving this training. Thankfully Awrick was in full agreement with her. Their daughter should be given every opportunity their sons were. Be as prepared as her sons for the challenges ahead. Each of them had started their combat training during their twelfth summer. Hilde was doing very well for her third session.

What concerned Frida was that there was very little lorki training available. Not for either her son's or daughter. Most of what was taught at the college was little more than magic. There were several of the scholars there that she respected, but most of the ones who seemed best to know lorki lore were relegated to cataloging and sorting stories and artifacts. It was evident to her that things were changing. There had been ten artifacts discovered this spring. That was more than had been found during the rest of Awrick's reign.

She reread her husband's letter telling her that he would be delayed again. She wasn't as perturbed as she wanted to be. After all, Crispin was still alive. By some miracle not only he returned, but all the men he had disappeared with chasing those yetann raiders were also still alive. He hadn't lost a single one. She started to read Crispin's report that her husband had included with his last letter. The one she reserved for reading when she was alone. "He could be so..." She smiled. Yes, he could. She looked forward to having him home. After all these years together, he still warmed her soul.

The fairy tales her grandmother told seemed to come alive as she read this report. The green man had come down the mountain with them. Not only that, But the Dryad was somewhere up that mountain. Two other dryads were in that area too.

What caught her attention was the kidnap victim, the young woman was more than a grasblatt. She was a genuine læknir. From what Crispin wrote, she was even more than that, Crispin suggested that she was a seior.

Queen Frida had studied every book available, when she had noticed her younger children showing the lorki signs her grandmother had taught her, those long years ago. She believed that Ari also was so gifted. She had been so young when he was born. The tragic death of Awrick's father had thrust them into the tumult that being the king and queen entailed. She could be forgiven not noticing the signs then. They had been so involved in stabilizing the nation. Thankfully King Bergus had already turned much of the day to day concerns of the kingdom to Awrick.

Now there was this young woman who defeated a yetann with her lorki. Being this powerful already meant that as she matured, if the books Frida had read were even close to being correct, she could develop into a Seioknar. There had not been a real Seioknar since old Haaken died. That was five years ago. His students still practiced his lore but none of them seemed practically gifted in teaching lorki lore. Their other problem was they were all old men who believed that women were only able to be læknir. Frida had no way of proving it, but she suspected many of the women læknir could do more than practice the healing arts.

Now the college would have to deal with a woman Seioknar. She smiled she hoped they would be up to the challenge. Even if the Seiors of the college balked, her very presence would help solidify the equality of women in Alfheim, hopefully in all the free states. In most of Midgard, women lived precariously. The free states were just a breath away from bride prices. She suspected in some of the backwaters of the realm dowries were still expected.

From what Crispin had written this "Catherine" had taught lorki lore to a rizi girl and a konkur. Then she proceeded to teach the felag with him how to detect poisons with just their breath. Perhaps she could be persuaded to sit with her children and impart some of her wisdom to them. A woman could hope.

Hilde ran up to her mother and demonstrated a new move she had learned. "Do you think I can surprise Ari with this when he gets back?" She asked. Brightly planning to take her older brother down.

"You can try." Frida laughed. "Don't be disappointed if he already knows that move."

"But he won't expect me to know it. Will he?" Grinned Hilde as she ran off for her riding lesson.

*

As Karl journeyed with the king's party, he sometimes drifted out into the forest exploring the area. He had been in this area before; it was vaguely familiar. Enough so that he knew that the course of the Laek Gritter had moved closer to the hills on its north side. Most of the memories were as insubstantial as shadows. But there was a place that stood out. It was where the trail that passed for a road was squeezed tight against a rocky bluff. There was an overhang barely big enough for two people to fit. He knew the place. A memory flooded his mind. He remembered hiding there, holding her as she cried. The effects of the treatment she had received were just beginning to show. It was before he turned green. Then the memory ended as arbitrarily as it had begun. He blinked and realized that Drew had said something to him. He turned to the direction of the voice. "I'm sorry, I didn't hear what you said."

With an earnest look Drew replied. "You looked as if you had left us. As if you were miles away. I asked, where are you?"

"Not miles, years, years away," Karl said as he started down the trail again.

*

The Kattyri (cat's paw, spymaster) read once more the reports. Perhaps he had missed something. Singa had boarded a sloop of a known slaver and agent of the huldra. He had not reappeared yet. The council had expected him to appear in Tawnia. This he had not done. The one ney snack of information Singa had been able to convey to the Kattyri was cryptic but it indicated that he was joining some sort of raiding party. Apparently, it represented a major investment of the huldra. The expedition was in search of some sort of treasure. Possibly an ancient and powerful artifact that was still active. Singa's trail ended at a pirate den somewhere on the greater dragon's claw isle.

It appeared to him that the party Singa had joined went north. What they wanted north was a mystery. One he would be hard pressed to solve. Handicapped as he was. He had managed to gain access to information in all the courts of the Slette Yetann. He had even managed to infiltrate many of the mountain and forest yetann kingdoms. He had informants in the courts of Torion, Reistara, and Vior. Yet he had not been able to gain access to reliable informants in the free states, and that is where the expedition had appeared to go.

Singa would get word back to him if there was any way to do so. There was nothing more he could do. He hoped his liege lord would understand.

CHAPTER 28

The sky was just beginning to hint at the dawn. Matsveir and his helpers had been up preparing a "light" breakfast. If you considered eggs, ham, bacon, flatbread, hot cereal drowned in butter and the odds and ends of fruit he had managed to acquire, light.

Jae and Catherine had managed to find themselves alone. They kissed and held each other. With so many people to possibly interrupt them, their hands didn't roam as they wanted to. As the light increased and before the breakfast bell was sounded, Jae expressed his concern for their future. How he could not make the promises he wanted too. Catherine, with a slow lingering kiss, interrupted him. "I know." she then said. "Where our paths are headed is uncertain. We have today. We'll face tomorrow when it comes. Keep talking to me. We can find a way."

As was his nature the worry lodged in the back of his mind. He had no wish to argue and he understood what she said. His duty and the uncertainty of it still tugged at him. Still, today had had such a pleasant start. So, he kissed her again before, hand in hand they answered the bell's call to breakfast.

*

As they traveled down the Laek Gritter the many tributaries transformed it into a river. They passed many fishermen and several villages. Most had no more than two or three houses. The children looked well fed. The villagers had a good income during the salmon run in the fall.

It was about fourth shadow as they traveled down the banks of the Laek Gritter that they were hailed from the opposite bank. It was the felag of horse that had been assigned to watch the opposite shore. They had happened upon two lost pyris. They soon found a fisherman with a small boat who they persuaded, for a farthing, to transport the two pyris across the river.

Cu lain was soon enlisted to help translate for the two. While Ceri sought a place near Jae. She was leery of her former fellow porters. She had few pleasant encounters with pyris males, and she felt safe near her siwgwy (egg juggler).

Seeing Catherine standing near, Læknir Litill called her over to help examine the two. With Cu lain's help they soon had them settled enough to be examined. It started with Catherine doing much of the examining, the other læknir wanting to learn how to better rally the lorki. The examinations ended with læknir Litill pronouncing them sound. She pulled Catherine away to a cup of hot tea. While the two pyris were fed, she and Catherine discussed lorki and herbs.

Herr Vogan with the help of Vaetta and Cu lain, puzzled out the story of the two pyris. Their names were Lir and Balor. Each had been captured in their different villages at the edge of Obygo, the wilderness that offered many tribes of the pyris a semblance of shelter from the slave raiders. They spoke no daonna. Each spoke a slightly different dialect of the pyris tongue making understanding them a challenge.

Both yearned for their homes in the forest. As best they could the three tried to help them understand the new circumstance they had fallen into. They would be transported to Arnarhvall. There they would have to make some choices. They could travel to Gandvik. Transport there provided by the kind king of Alfheim. From there they would be on their own. Responsible for finding their own way home and the way to pay for it. That journey would be difficult and not without the possibility of once more finding themselves enslaved. The other choice was to join the pyris that dwelled in Alfheim. There were colonies of pyris scattered up and down the lower Elfra. The best prospect for jobs was in Risker. It was the lower port of Arnarhvall. There were many jobs there. From the unskilled porters moving cargo between the upper and lower Elfra; to the skilled, woodworking, metalworking, and many others. They were now freemen responsible for their own lives. It took Lir and Balor some time to understand this new world they had entered.

It was after they had journeyed another two shadows, and had stopped for lunch, that Balor found Cu lain and excitedly inquired. "Am I really free?"

"Yes," Cu lain assured him.

"Then I need a new name. I never had an evil eye. My eyes were crossed when I was a child and so that hateful name. May I now be named Brac, because now I'm free?" Balor asked.

Cu lain laughed, slapped Brac on the back. "Yes, Brac you are indeed free."

*

Since Catherine was busy, Jae took a moment to start composing a letter to his mother. He needed to assure her he was fine. By the time she received his letter the news of their adventure would have traveled there. Riders had already taken the news to Arnarhvall. No doubt those riders, those that believed themselves to be bards, would have stopped at a tavern or inn and shared the story in song. They would highlight the dangers before bringing the battle to its glorious conclusion. Jae hoped they got his name wrong. Crispin had started it the evening after they made it down the mountain. At least he could carry a tune. Half the riders out there couldn't sing a ballad through in the same key. Halfway through his letter, he mentioned Catherine. He hoped it sounded casual, just a bit of news about who had been kidnapped. He hoped his mother didn't read between the lines. She would start asking if she was the one, and even though he was starting to believe that was so, he wasn't ready to share that information with his mother. He well remembered when he first introduced Asleif to his parents. When his mother got him alone, she quizzed him about the lovely young lady. The lovely young lady who held her own arm wrestling any male who dared challenge her, and who was a better archer than he was. He wasn't going to repeat that, he hoped. He finished the letter and sealed it. He would send it by the rider who should be through soon. His mother should receive it within two or three five-days.

CHAPTER 29

Dawn was breaking. The camp was packing and almost ready to move. Today they would reach Utroor. Catherine found Karl sitting on the bank of Laek Gritter watching a fisher king practicing its art. The bird, hardly bigger than her hand, was sitting on a branch overhanging the river watching intently the water below. As she watched, it slipped off the branch and dove into the water. Disappearing under the water's surface for a moment before popping out of the water with a small fish in its beak. It then flew to its nest in the upper branches of a nearby oak. He was starting his day by feeding his young. A task he and his mate would be doing for the next few weeks till their young flew. Then the parent's task would be teaching them to fish, something the young almost inherently knew.

As the bird flew off to its nest Karl turned. "Good morning Catherine." He smiled. "Shall we walk together today? I haven't spent much time with you this five-day." Before he could stand, Catherine, wrapped her arms around him, and held him close. With tears, she said. "I don't believe I know how to thank you for all you have done for me."

"Friend," He replied, as he returned her hug. "I believe I have reason to thank you. I did help in your rescue, but that helped me to awaken to myself. I did not know who or what I was when I opened my eyes on that distant mountain. You helped me see myself again. More than your gift with the lorki, your presence was a balm. I don't know how to explain. You and your new friends have brought me into this age. That is for me both a blessing and a curse. If I had happened upon the dryad alone, I may not have been drawn into this age. If not, the dryad and I would have parted ways. She with her desire for Midgard and me before our experiences on the mountain seeking isolation. Isolated I may have never remembered who I am.

"Do you think Jae will want me as much as you want her?" Catherine asked.

"It appears to me, your desire for each other is growing that way. But, my friend, time is the only proof we have." Karl stood as he said this. "And there our friend comes." He waved, and Catherine turned to see Jae approaching.

"The camp is ready to move." He told them. "We should reach Utroor before dusk. May I join you today?" Catherine smiled her assent and Karl nodded his approval. Together they gathered their burdens and walked on toward Utroor.

Karl had grown to trust this group of people. True there were some who he could tell despised Cu lain, Cere, and all things pyris. They distrusted anyone who stood outside of their concept of good. Karl could tell that some distrusted him more than the pyris. They hid their prejudice as best they could. The king was watching so they put on their best behavior.

Karl envied the young couple. They walked hand and hand when they could. Sharing the morning. That stirred his hunger for the dryad, for Esmeralda. The further his journey led him from her, the more he yearned to be near her. There were times he could hear her laughter. Times he almost turned back.

Watching Jae and Catherine walking together brought shadows of memories to Karl. A touching of hands, a caress. It seemed to him that memories of Esmerelda should have more substance than they did. They seemed to sit just past his perception. This made him yearn more and more to be in her presence. The further down the Laek Gritter the further he was from her. But she and he needed to know more of the world that was before they knew what help they could give it. So, she had sent him away to discover what he could.

CHAPTER 30

From Larea Visiput's "Etytha Kendt Verden" (Study; the Known World).

Gandvik is the city-state that shares the lower Elfra with Alfheim. Its territory is separated from Alfheim on the west by the Elfra, and the north by the A' Brun. Gandvik boasts the largest fleet that sails Nordrhaf. The largest portion of this fleet is composed of karf the small fast rowing ships used to patrol the maze of Islands that make up Gandvik's Vanaheim territories.

Styra Norden walked the deck of his ship as it slowly rocked. How he loved the movement of the ship under his feet. If he could he would never walk on the still earth again. Sadly, there were things that required going ashore. Teitra Bruder was a wide beamed merchant ship, and she sailed between the ports along the dragon's belly. Here in Gandvik, she waited with him for word from an agent of his client. The other traders thought they were the purpose of this journey. Little did they suspect that they were just a cover for him being here. His real purpose lay in the raid that should have taken place over a month ago. As it was now, the messenger was over two five-days late. The traders were more than ready to head home. All but one of them had completed all the transactions they wanted. Now they longed to be bound for home, where they would discover how much profit (if any) they would gain. The trader holding them back from sailing was one of his client's agents, and his delaying tactics had worked up to this point. Styra Norden knew that he would have to sail soon, news, or no news. He would skirt by the appointed pickup point on the way back to Teitra Bruder's home port. But if no message arrived before they departed, he would expect no one to be waiting for a ride.

He had given his crew shore leave, half the crew at a time. They would bring back rumors and tales. It was possible he would learn more from the stories told in the taverns and whorehouses gathered in a day than the client's agents and men would in a week. He had experienced that before. While the other pirates were snooping around the merchants, the story of the rich merchant vessel sailing without escort reached his ears from a very drunk sailor. The sailor received double bounty that voyage. And Styr Norden gained this vessel. After a name change, it served well for trading and delivering raiders to their targets. Now her name called out "happy bride" and gave the illusion of respectability. In a couple five-days, he would choose a different name and new targets. For today, and the last couple of months, Teitra Bruder served his purposes well.

The merchants had been happy to see the band of pyris porters leave the ship. The rich patron who left with them was supposedly hunting bears. The ruse was transparent to anyone who cared to open their eyes, but the merchants were more relieved to have help paying for the trading voyage than conscience enough to care. The yetann were landed a few hours later by one of his schooners. If the raid had gone according to plan the band would rejoin them, minus the pyris. They would again carefully not be seen or cared enough about, to be reported to some port authority. Even with the prize, the odd occurrence would not interfere with their business.

His pyris mercenaries Mort and Dirt stood at the gangplank. Though they appeared to be napping, Norden knew they were ready to stop any stranger who appeared too curious.

There he was, that beautiful child. A mop of light brown hair and a pretty face. Too bad he couldn't find some way to persuade the boy aboard. Hordosen would be jealous. A smile crossed Vinda Nordan's face. With a little competition for his attention maybe he could persuade Hordosen into some more exciting games. Well, he could not afford to rouse the port authorities. A new cabin boy would have to wait. Though Hordosen was older than the styra preferred, he still served the purposes he had been acquired for. Hordosen could be used a little longer. It was possible that Styra Norden would keep his promise of giving the care of the sloop Ekkja Alf to Hordosen. Perhaps not.

Jari was staggering up the plank. He seemed somewhat in a hurry. As much in a hurry as his condition allowed. It was as if he had some news. He waved to the styra as he stumbled onto the deck. "I've some," he paused to try to balance himself to the movement of the ship and the lightness of his head. He succeeded though he swayed a little. "Styra, I knew you'd want to hear." He paused again and belched. Styra Norden waited. He knew that if Jari did not get his story out, soon another crew member, not quite so drunk but a slower pace would fill in more of what had excited Jari enough for him to return to the ship as sober as he was. "There's been a flock of pyris flooding through a settlement up near Thor's goats. They bear tails of yetann battling giants." He swayed. "Didn't we drop off some pyris on our way here?" He looked around to be sure no one but his styra could hear him. He raised his finger to his lips. And then whispered, "I didn't say that sir. Must be the grog confusing me.

"Go to your hammock Jari. You've earned a gold piece." Styra Norden told him. "Don't leave the ship or we may leave without you. And, I would hate to have to cut off your tongue for babbling to some of the traders on board. Do you catch my drift?"

Jari nodded his head. He wasn't so drunk that he didn't know to shut up and sleep his drunk off. His silence might even gain him another gold piece, the styra could be generous when he was pleased. So, he stumbled off below decks and kept what little thought he had all to himself.

Norden turned and looked out to the open sea, his lust for the boy forgotten. There was no reason to hurry. Hurry was the enemy. If he rushed away, suspension would follow. The port master might send warships after him if this news appeared to rattle him. No, best to stick with what he had already planned.

He motioned to Mort and when he approached, told him. "Go below and wake Geir. I have need of him. Then go tell Hakon to come to me. We will sail with the tide tomorrow."

Hakon appeared before Geir arrived, rubbing his eyes. Finishing the orders, he had for his first mate, Norden turned to Geir and said, "Go to Merchant Odder. He's in the Horsehead inn. Tell him to be on board before noon tomorrow. Tell him he's delayed the others long enough, if he hasn't located the mechanize, he was after yet, he won't. We sail at the tide and he will be left if he is not here. Return without delay. I may have other errands for you if the other traders don't arrive in the morning to complain about the delays we've had." With those words he turned back to the sea, trying to scry the best course of action.

The boy on the dock watched the men on the ship. He knew they were wicked men, whose well laid plans had gone askew. He was only sad he had not been the cause of their mishap. Perhaps next time he could hinder them himself. He then turned and walked away, considering whether he wanted to play a game of tag with the other street urchins.

*

The mug of mead in Folr Tugle's hand was getting warm, not that it had ever been cold, but now it was warm. It was barely drinkable when it still held the cellar's coolness. Half a mug that he could not drink. He had nursed it as long as he could like he had nursed delaying the departure of Styra Nordan's knorr (merchant ship). With the news Crow had just relayed, the good styra would be sending a man to fetch him back to the ship. He would be sailing with the next tide. If Folr remembered correctly (and he did) the next tide would be soon after the noon meal. It was a half-tide to be sure, but it would help the knorr float over the mud bank that almost blocked the port. He had heard talk that the city's council was planning to dreg the channel. They had been talking about dredging the channel since the last time Folr passed through. That was another name and several years ago.

He called the serving wench over and offered her a farthing extra if she would bring him a cold brew from the proprietor's ice room. She shook her head no, but for a katl which was two farthings more than the price, she went to fetch it. Folr couldn't understand how anyone could drink this stuff at room temperature.

Crow stood at the bar drinking what the locals called beer. He was downing his second full mug. It twisted Folr's gut just thinking about it. Crow always could blend with the locals. When they entered a town, they were soon friends with half the town. Crow in the taverns and Bait with the farmers. That was their special gift. They were able to supply Folr with tidbits of information. Together they could work up a nice quilt of information.

From what Crow had heard, the hunting party north had been disbanded. There were rumors flying about the port. There had been a yetann raid in the northeast of Alfheim and that hundreds of pyris were flooding down the mountains. From his investigation, Crow believed that one or two of the porters that had been acquired for the hunt had wandered through some villages, apparently looking for the place on the coast they had been dropped off. Their stories indicated that the yetann were dead.

Flor had sent his man to his room to pack while he and Crow waited for Bait to return. Bait had been trading to the north trying to fetch a rare spice from the mountains of Alfheim. The information Bait would gather would tell them how bad a disaster the hunt had been.

Flor felt secure on his and his assistants never being suspected. Even if the Teitre Bruder was identified as the ship that had dropped the pyris off on the coast. Styra Nordan had papers to show that it had all been innocent on their part. The pyris they had dropped off were hired hands for a summer of work in the cotton fields east in the foothills. The documents were forged, to be sure, but no one in the surrounding area would be able to tell. All the merchants traveling on the good ship had witnessed the landing. True it was early in the season, but still, it was an easy ruse to pull off. And if that failed, well Flor was just another duped merchant.

Flor called one of his local laborers over, tossed him a far-thing, and in a voice that anyone who cared to hear would, told him "Rouse the others. I'm tired of waiting. It's obvious that I've been made a fool of. The trader's promise of a supply of hengafr (a supposed aphrodisiac) was empty. Begin transferring my goods to the knorr Teitre Bruder. The ship's master will be happy to sail tomorrow. He told me I was chasing fog. And so, I was. I'll send my man Thor along with a key as soon as he is fin-ished upstairs." With that, he waved the man away. The wench appeared with his cold mug. Bending low in an effort not to spill the mead, she earned another farthing for the view. Flor considered bedding her again but decided not to. He needed to at least appear perturbed by his failure to acquire the hengafr, which in his books looked to fetch more than all his other trad-ing.

CHAPTER 31

Asvald, hid in a dark shadow trying to discern if anyone was watching the ship. The dock guards kept a close eye on the two gates to the shipping district and patrols roamed the docks but the patrol through this area had just passed. Now was the time to gain the safety that that ship would give him. He hoped. To his bad luck, he did not possess the small package he was supposed to retrieve. And that small package was the main object of this hunt. The girl would have been an added bonus for them. A desired bonus no doubt. Her heritage might change the fate of the huldra. But the artifacts in that small box, those were the treasures. His successful recovery of them would have sealed his ascent to full member of the huldra. It would have opened up opportunities for him. Well, that would not happen now. Curse his luck, he had it in his hands and was just minutes away from success. Then before he could disappear into the forest, he was surrounded by a band of scouts. Their leader, a hateful daonna, had confiscated his prize. Thankfully, his friendship with the town's elders (and the gifts that sealed that friendship) had prevented his arrest. That spiteful daonna had left a felag guarding the house where the prize had been locked. Locks had never stopped him but the alert and vigilant felagi did. Then, a contingent of the king's army appeared. They had relieved the felag of the responsibility of guarding the victim's home, but not their diligence to their leader's orders. Even with them still watching, Asvald had found what he thought was an opportunity to enter the house without the felag watching. Damn the vanir scout who caught him opening the back door. He was arrested. This time the head elder (where he was paying for lodging) intervened and so he was given strict orders not to leave the building, else he would be chained to a hitching post until transported to the court in Goa Vollar. A guard was placed under his window and a guard patrolled the perimeter. Asvald watched them from his window and judged that he would be able to escape from the window in the room opposite his. The elder's daughter was surprised when he entered her room through her door and not her window. He had to pause for some sweet nothings, that allowed the guard to pass on his rounds. With a final kiss, he had slipped out the window and made his escape.

On the roof of a dockside warehouse, hidden in the darkness, Bait watched the Teitra Bruder. This adventure was drawing to a close. This time there would not be a satisfied client and unsatisfied clients tended to not make the final payment. Hell, satisfied clients sometimes had to be persuaded to.

There was something about this unsuccessful hunt that made Bait uneasy. Their client had expended large sums of money on a complex plan, and Bait suspected that no one but the client knew the whole scheme, or exactly how many agents they had hired. And not all of them might know. The fact that the client was a they, in itself, was disturbing. They were a small elitist group of old men. Whom, Bait suspected, didn't trust one another as much as they wanted to appear to. How they wanted to appear, or not appear, that is, be invisible, really didn't matter to Bait. The information Flor had been able to gather pointed to this small group of incredibly wealthy people. Their identities were supposedly secret, but Bait suspected Flor knew who at least a few of them were.

There was some movement on the docks. Just who was this rat scurrying toward the Teitra Bruder? Once again Bait was thankful for the gift of night vision a wayward youth had gained by having chosen, by accident, the right parents. Bait watched the man approach the ship. There was just a brief moment that the man's face appeared in the light of a lantern. But it was enough for Bait to recognize the face. Flor would want to know about this. So, was this the person who should have appeared weeks ago with a particular package that needed to travel south? It appeared to Bait, that that package was not in the possession of this scurrying little mouse. Another disturbing sign of how badly the huldra's plans had unraveled. Most troubling of all was that the man might be able to identify Flor as an agent of the instigators of the hunt.

As Bait watched, the man tried to board the ship. The sailor at the top of the gangplank stopped him. They argued for a moment, then the sailor sent his companion guard below. It was not long after that, that Styra Norden appeared still wearing his nightshirt, though he had the presence of mind to pull in some pants. The man made a hand sign. Bait could not quite make out the whole sign, but it appeared to cause the styra pause. There was another brief discussion, where Bait was sure the absence of the package was mentioned. That being the price of passage on the good ship Teitra Bruder for this passenger. No package, so Styra Norden suggested that the man find another way home. There were a few moments when Bait wondered if the rat would be found the next day floating in the bay. The styra seemed to relent. He allowed the man on board his ship. A sailor escorted him below decks, to a cabin or the bilge Bait could not know. If the bilge, the man might not be alive to know. That was none of Bait's concern. Flor knowing about this development was. Judging that there were still about four shadows till dawn, Bait quietly left the vantage point and carefully wandered to the inn where, if Flor was as canny as Bait trusted, he would be sleeping alone.

Flor woke in the dark. There was a presence in his room. The only person it could be was Bait. No one else to Folr's knowledge would have been able to circumvent the traps which would have alerted him to their entering his room. Flor was especially proud of his new arrangement at the window. Though it did not appear to hamper Bait's entry. "Well, Bait." He said, "What news do you have for me this early morning?"

"I thought you might like to know of a new passenger on the Teitra Bruder. I believe he is someone you would recognize.

More importantly, He is someone who might be able to identify you. Do you remember the little rat who first approached you three years ago about this venture?" Bait became silent and waited for Flor to process this information.

It was a few moments before Flor responded. "Ah, yes. Asvald Rett was the name he gave us. It appears that our client is not as wise as I had hoped. Did he have the package from the north?"

"That was the other point I wanted you to know, He did not. The good styra still allowed him on board, which was wiser than letting him roam the streets of Gandvik, I would think. It appears to me, that Asvald was the merchant responsible for retrieving that small treasure. That he failed, is not as troubling as the fact it has taken this long to arrive. That the king's men might know that he was involved in the hunt, well I'm glad I was never going to travel on that ship." Bait finished the story.

"I believe it is time for a change of scenery for all of us. Possibly a new business for me as well. Can you let Crow know that the fish has spoiled, and we will be changing bait buckets?" Flor gave the message for them to meet at their prearranged location. "I need a shave. I believe I'll find a new cook too." He said as he stood and watched Bait exit the same window he planned to use before dawn. But first the packing and then the shave. When Flor left this room, he planned to leave it so to a casual observer, it would appear to have not been slept in.

CHAPTER 32

At Utroor

The village of Utroor was up before dawn. The fishers were already in their small boats heading out into the lake. The cacophony of the gulls almost drowned out the other noises the bustle of the village created. Jae was glad the barracks were away from the busy port. When he had kissed Catherine good night, he had hoped to sleep past dawn. But all the noise of the village woke up Drew, and when Drew was up all of them had to rise. Just as well, Jae supposed. He would have time to wash up and change what he was wearing. The shirt and pants he had worn coming down the Laek Gritter were beginning to smell.

When he got to the morning meal, he was a bit disappointed. He had grown used to Matsveir's cooking and the gruel they served here was, well his mother wouldn't approve of what Eric called it before he left, hoping to find some scraps from Matsveir. Bland would be the politer way to tell its qualities. He couldn't bring himself to try the salted fish that was also being served with some fresh greens. They just weren't breakfast food to Jae. He would miss eating at the king's table. Specifically, he would miss Matsveir's bread. He finished the bowl of gruel at that thought and took the bowl to the bucket of warm water. He rinsed it out as was expected.

He left the cook shack looking for Catherine. His baggage was already headed for the king's ship. Drew and Cu lain had left together. They may have already boarded the ship. Jae thought it more likely the two were seeing what the locals were eating this morning. Vaetta had told them that if they got the chance, they should try some of the fried fish sold near the fishing docks. But fish no matter how it was prepared did not suit Jae for breakfast. What he had this morning would do until the noon meal. Which he expected Matsveir to at least have a hand in.

Catherine and Ceri had spent the night in the cabin rented by Thane Awrick while his dirfylk was stationed there. It had been vacant since their march to Boar Akarn. He knocked on the cabin door and was surprised when Elgar opened the door. The smell that escaped from the interior made Jae's mouth water. Catherine looked up from the stove and smiled at him.

"Matsveir gifted us with some of his starter." She told him. "I've been cooking pancakes this morning. You're almost too late. There's only enough for two or three more. There's some berry preserves Elgar was kind enough to bring, you can cover them with, but the butter is gone."

Jae assured her that he would be more than happy to eat whatever was left. Crispin gave Jae his chair and poured himself another cup of tea. "The king is planning to leave by third shadow so you best hurry. Thane Awrick's valet will be here soon to pack his things for transport to Boar Akarn. We came by to rouse Catherine and Ceri only to find them up cooking. We were more than happy to eat her cooking. We've eaten what the local chef serves the scouts stationed here."

Jae grinned at that. If he had known Catherine was going to cook, he would have been here earlier. Truth told he thought he would have come to eat here if Ceri was doing the cooking.

The last scraps of food consumed he and Elgar cleaned the kitchen while Catherine and Ceri finished gathering their things. As he dried the last plate, Jae heard a wagon pull up to the door. Two town's men had been hired to gather the baggage going to the king's ship. So, he and the others helped pack what Catherine and Ceri had onto the wagon.

They watched to wagon leave for its next stop. Then Catherine took his arm while she planted a kiss on his cheek. Arm in arm they walked with the others toward where the king's ship was docked.

Karl was on the dock early; he wanted a tour of the king's

ship. The Kjoll looked like a glorified barge to him. Styra Jord Datorsen was glad to help a friend of the king, being green didn't hurt. He called a sailor over and instructed him to show Karl the ship. He apologized for not guiding the tour himself, but he needed to prepare for the king's arrival and the journey to Arnarhvall.

While waking the deck they came across Matsveir fussing over the young dryad. "She's not greened a bit" He lamented.

To please him Karl stuck his fingers into the earth around the dryad. "She needs to dry another day before you water her again. She's beginning to stir. Unless I miss my guess, a few buds will open within another week." He assured him.

*

Karl knew it was foolish. Inspecting a ship to be sure it was sound. What did he know of ships, let alone riverboats? But here he was taking up the time of a sailor. He knew it was because he was torn. His desire to be with Esmerelda pulled him. Yet he felt a need to protect these new friends. He knew he could not return to her now. He trusted she would understand him being away for a summer and winter. It felt like they had missed so much time. He had no trouble believing it had been a thousand summers since they had been together. Next spring, he could journey up the mountain. He would be with her next year. Hopefully, he had many summers, falls, and winters to be with Esmerelda.

He thanked the sailor. Men and women around him were busy loading cargo. He tried to stay out of the way. Only once or twice did his greenness distract. As he neared the gangway, Catherine and Ceri appeared, escorted by Crispin and the felag. Ceri ran up to him and wrapped her arms around his neck when he stooped to talk to her. She clung there for a moment. "Are you coming with us?" She asked.

He pulled her close. "I am." He told her. "Down to Arnarhvall and see where that will lead."

ACKNOWLEDGMENTS

There are many people who I have to thank for their help. My kids, my wife Carrie, and my other friends, who proofread, corrected, and encouraged me. Without their help, I would still be dreaming about writing a book. Special mention needs to be made of Carrie who did the red top illustration. And my granddaughter Hailey who illustrated the cover.

I should not forget my inspiration for the yetann. Our two cats. Boots, dedicated to outdoor living, and Pooka, equally dedicated to indoor living.

ABOUT THE AUTHOR

Marvin D Bare

Stories have been a part of my life forever. I have heard them, read them, and told them as long as I can remember. I've written hundreds of stories. Bits and pieces of stories. This is my first novel. It is the result of a story that refused to die. It kept unreeling in my mind. After a year of this haunting, I had no choice but to write it. What started as a simple damsel in distress story changed once I met the damsel. As I wrote this set of stories the world I imagined grew. The simple damsel in distress that the story started with changed. After rewrites, revisions, and letting it bake. I've discovered more. More of the politics of the region. More relationships between people. Now as I begin a sequel to this first book, I'm finding more complexity than I ever imagined and more loose strings that need to be explored.